To my husband, who has supported me
from day one of this endeavor.
Thank you for your editing skills
and thoughtful readthroughs.
You've made me a better writer
and a better person.
I love you.

"Speak up," My third-grade teacher told me in front of the class.

Tears welled in my eyes as humiliation sunk in. Didn't she know that if I could speak louder, I would?

I was soft-spoken and meek, and this wasn't the way to encourage me.

"The answer is CHLOROPHYLL." I mustered loudly.

"What did she say?" Some kids asked from the other side of the room.

"Miss Rowling said Chlorophyll, which is correct. Thank you, Tori. You may take your seat."

"She's so quiet," one of the girls giggled as I sat down.

Quickly, I sprang up, grabbing the hall pass and crying for ten minutes in the bathroom stall. I was worried what people would say when I came back into the classroom with red, tear-stained cheeks and puffy eyes. But when I finally made it back to class, no one noticed.

HOLD ON LOOSELY

It was happening again. Every girl in our school gathered around the petite blonde with the iron-straight hair, Clinique face, Marc Jacobs top paired with a Prada mini skirt, complete with Jimmy Choos and three diamond bracelets on her wrist. She began handing out envelopes to the chosen ten—the ten girls invited to Amber Lawrence's birthday party. Girls spent years sucking up to her just to have a chance at being in the chosen ten. The girls who got an envelope squealed with delight and the others crossed their fingers and bit their nails in anticipation. There were envelopes for Britney and Alice, for Michelle and Taylor, but never one for Tori. It was exactly the same as it was every year.

Except for one thing—I got an envelope.

The summer before my senior year smelled like wooden chess pieces, library books, and sweat.

"Watch closely, Tori." My best friend Tammi said to me as she moved her queen on the chess board.

She and my other best friend Kyle were playing chess on my bed as I watched from my desk chair in my bedroom.

"Check-mate," Tammi said as Kyle let out a sigh of defeat.

"You were lucky that time, Tammi." Kyle said with a grin.

"There is no luck in chess, Kyle. Only skill."

"And skill is what you are lacking." I said, laughing.

Kyle hurled a pillow at my face in mock anger.

"It's your turn now, Tori, let's see how much skill YOU have."

Tammi and I met in third grade and we've been best friends ever since. It all started with a lead pencil. You see, some things like lead pencils are important in elementary school. The pencil you used helped identify your status in the hierarchy of Parkside Elementary. For example, someone using a plain number two pencil was nowhere near the level of someone using a sparkly Bic mechanical pencil.

I was the new girl that year and I didn't have a writing utensil on my first day. My seat was across from Tammi's in a cluster of desks. She introduced herself to me and offered me her bright-orange lead pencil with a soft white gripper and fuzzy top. I couldn't believe a girl I just met would offer me such a luxurious item. We bonded over the pen, which then turned into discovering that we both loved to read manga and had ambitions to join the school band when we came of age.

Tammi had always been the tallest girl in our class. Therefore, kids would call her "stork" and "Godzilla." It always upset me that kids made fun of her because she was so tall and skinny. Actually, I thought Tammi was naturally pretty. She couldn't help how thin she was, but the bullies treated her like she was some freak show due her 5'11" frame. She was never chosen first for gym class teams or invited to the popular girls' sleepovers, but Tammi was extremely smart. She was in our school's "gifted" program and always earned all A's on her report card. She was the smartest person I knew, and she was set to become our class valedictorian.

You see, Tammi was the girl in the front row of the classroom, the teacher ignoring her raised hand in hopes that someone else could answer the question that we all knew Tammi was dying to share. In my opinion, boys were intimidated by her. Either that, or they were all too superficial to see beyond her stature. But Tammi never seemed to care. She knew who she was, and she wasn't going to compromise that to win any popularity contests. This was why she was my best friend.

Tammi and I met Kyle in 5th grade when we girls decided to create our own paper clothing company. Tammi and I were what you would call creative types. Also, we were bored.

It was an idea we came up with during indoor recess one day. We created patterns and designed various tops, pants, skirts, and shoes. Each item was drawn, cut, and colored on plain white paper, about 8 to 10 inches in size. We created paper dolls to wear our paper clothes, and during recess each day we would try to get people to play with our paper dolls and clothing.

Have I mentioned that we weren't popular?

Anyway, one day Kyle came up to us and told us he would buy our business for $1 if we promised to never start the business back up again. Tammi and I decided that it was a deal worth taking, so we took his dollar and gave him our merchandise. He burned it, and then became our friend. He introduced us to video games, comic books, and chess.

I had so much love for these two humans.

Tammi had brown, curly hair that she kept in a short bob. Her purple glasses made her stand out in the hallways of our school. That was one of my favorite things about her: She loved to attract attention by being unique. She and I were classic introverts, quiet and studious, only opening up to each other instead of to large groups of people. Tammi planned on going to Princeton after high school in order to fulfill her dream of becoming a scientist. And Lord knew the world needed more female scientists.

"I'm thinking about starting a book club," Tammi said as I moved my pawn forward a square.

"I would most definitely join your book club." I said to her.

"Who all would be invited?" Kyle asked.

"Well, I was thinking of inviting anyone in school who wanted to join and then see what happens. I honestly don't think many people will be interested."

"What kind of books would we be reading?"

"Well, Kyle, I was thinking about making it a Young Adult female author book club."

"Meaning I'll be the only guy participating." He said with a playful smirk.

"Seems highly probable." Tammi teased.

"I think it's a great idea, and I fully support you." I told Tammi, giving her a big smile and a thumbs-up.

I knew that Tammi could succeed at anything she put her mind to. Tammi was our research queen, always in the advanced classes at school and received high marks in every class. She was a force to be reckoned with, and I didn't think she knew how much potential she truly had in life. Sometimes, I wished I could be more like her instead of my positively ordinary self.

Kyle was also a force to be reckoned with, but in a much different way. Kyle wasn't necessarily book smart, but he had a thirst for adventure like no one else in our school. When he loved, he loved hard. And when he fell, he fell hard. His bleach-blonde hair and thick black frames gave him a reputation for being studious, but Tammi and I knew better. Kyle was 100% social butterfly, which is probably why he wanted to get into Public Relations after high school.

"Looks like I have no more skill than Kyle does," I said after Tammi took my last bishop.

I pulled my long dirty blonde hair into a ponytail and pushed my glasses up the bridge of my nose.

"Anyone want to stay for dinner? Mom's making grilled cheese tonight." I asked.

"Hell yes." Kyle and Tammi answered in unison as the three of us piled down the stairs in search of mom's cheesy goodness.

•••

It was a ten-minute walk to my local library, a walk I made every day in the summer. The library was my place of solace. She was old-faithful, a reliable source of quiet. I loved walking into the dimly lit building, taking my time moving along each aisle of the classics and YA sections.

This summer I would attempt to finish the Sweet Valley High series. I was always interested in a good throwback. The twin sisters were everything I wished I could be. Popular, pretty, and desired.

The books were an easy read, but they posed a challenge for me due to the size of the series. I had 181 books to read, and so far, I had made it through 87 of them. I had only one more month to go until school started. Last year, my summer book challenge was the Harry Potter series. It was fun to read each book and then watch the corresponding movie afterwards. I loved seeing how the books and movies differed from one another.

I liked being by myself, it gave me an opportunity to recharge from the social interactions of the day. That's why I loved summer so much; I wasn't forced to be in a classroom of people for 8 hours straight.

I returned my last two books at the counter and checked out the next two books in the series. I sat down at a small window table and basked in the natural sunlight radiating onto my yellow-faded book pages. Before I knew it, I had finished both books and it was now dinnertime. Before heading home, I picked up the next two books in the series and got in line.

While examining the covers of my new books, a tall boy cut in front of me. I gave him my death-stare, but he looked right past me. I couldn't believe how blatantly rude this kid was, but I was too afraid to say anything to him. I didn't want to cause a scene and he didn't look like someone who would concede in a confrontation. So instead of calling him out, I stewed in anger until it was my turn at the counter.

The next day, Tammi, Kyle, and I laid out in my backyard to tan. We set up our lounge chairs on the uneven grass and wore giant sunglasses, staring up into the sky or down at our phones. What else was there to do during the summer, anyway? You can only spend so much time playing chess and practicing the saxophone. Without school, the three of us were severely lacking in social connections. But we had each other, and that was enough.

"Are you ready for your very last year of band camp?" Kyle asked the two of us.

"Yeah, it's kind of sad and relieving at the same time." I answered him.

"Who knows, maybe they'll be a marching band at whatever college you choose, Tori. There's one at Princeton." Tammi said.

"I don't even know if I want to go to college." I told her.

"Tori, you have to go to college! What else would you do?" She asked.

"I don't know what I would even go for, and I don't have the money to pay for it anyway."

"Yeah, I hope to God I don't get stuck with a heaping pile of loan debt. With any luck, I'll get an amazing job so I can pay it all off. Or maybe I'll find a nice husband or wife who can support me," Kyle chimed in with a wink.

Tammi and I rolled our eyes at Kyle.

"You're lucky, Tammi. With your grades, you're sure to get a scholarship." I told her.

"You're right, Tori. But you could get one too."

Kyle and I began laughing hysterically.

"You think too highly of me." I told her.

"You need to believe in yourself more." Tammi said.

"I'll never be as smart as you, Tammi." I said.

"You don't have to be. You just have to be smart enough. And you are."

Tammi was my forever cheerleader, always pulling me along on her path to success.

"Maybe you're right," I told her, turning onto my stomach so I could tan my backside for a bit.

"How come no one mentioned that I could get a scholarship?" Kyle asked.

The three of us laughed so hard, we cried.

SMELLS LIKE TEEN SPIRIT

I couldn't believe it was our summer chess competition already. The past 3 weeks of band camp went by in blur, always a precursor to the beginning of another school year. It was a challenge to learn the songs along with the marches, but we got it done. I felt excited to perform our new show during this year's football games. Right now, though, I had to focus on chess.

The chess competition was in an hour. Tammi sat on my bed as I crimped my hair in anticipation.

"We are so gonna beat those Tyrone Titans tonight," she said while painting her nails a matte purple.

"With the amount of practice we've been doing over the summer, there's no way we can lose," I added truthfully.

I looked at my reflection in my full-length mirror, smoothing out my semi-wrinkled top. My hair was perfectly crimped and shiny. I wore a pink V-neck sweater with khakis, my white Keds, and a sparkly pink clip in my dirty blonde hair. I knew I was never going to look as good as I wanted to, so I put on a fake smile and looked away from the mirror.

"Are you finally ready to go?" Tammi asked me, pulling her glossy brown hair into two pigtails so short they looked like puff balls. *Her nails dried fast*, I thought.

"The tournament doesn't start till seven. We still have half an hour," I said.

"Well, I like to be early, you know," she smiled, "to concentrate."

I grinned. "Yeah, sure, to concentrate on Brian."

"No, he doesn't even like me anyway," Tammi said.

She pushed her thick purple frames up from her nose, disappointment on her face. I thought Tammi was beautiful, but I could see how boys wouldn't be interested at our age. They wanted perky blonde cheerleaders with minuscule vocabularies, not studious girls with glasses and opinions.

Tammi wasn't curvy like me, she was tall and lanky. Her bangs came just above her eyebrows, revealing her striking blue-grey eyes. Despite her gorgeous olive skin and short bob of brown hair, bullies would still pick on her. I hated how you could have ten attractive qualities about you, but kids would always pick one flaw to exploit until graduation. Boys didn't seem to notice her, except for Brian. He was a little too nerdy for my taste, but Tammi was in love with him.

"Alright, let's go." I told her as we turned off my bedroom light and ran down the stairs.

"Bye, guys!" I yelled to my parents as I grabbed the keys to my mom's Volvo.

"Sure you guys don't want to come?" Tammi asked.

"Maybe next time," my dad answered as he stared at the TV.

"Why even ask?" I said, looking at Tammi.

"You never know when they might change their mind," she said.

I rolled my eyes. I didn't resent my parents for not coming to any of my school-related activities. I understood how chess and band could seem a tad boring to the average person. I mean, sure, my little brother's soccer games were never missed, but I was certain my parents didn't get *conveniently* busy or sick whenever my chess competitions or band concerts came up.

It was whatever. Anyway, I supposed it was a little weird having chess competitions where people could come and watch, but our school believed that intellectual sports were just as important as athletics. Even though probably no one else on the planet thought that chess was a sport. Our competitions were supposed to promote teamwork and a sense of camaraderie. And now, a bunch of chess clubs from nearby schools began competing with us.

"Have fun, hon. Don't stay out too late," my mom called back to me.

Yeah right. As if I regularly went out partying with all my popular friends, chugging beer from a funnel, singing karaoke, and grinding to Cardi B's "Money" with an incredibly hot and wasted jock.

"Yeah, I know mom."

Tammi and I went outside and hopped into the Volvo. I started the engine and began my way to Parkside public high school, basically my home since freshmen year. Seriously, I practically lived there. With all of my chess and reading competitions, band concerts and practices, and marching band every Friday night, it was kind of hard *not* to think of the school as a second home.

"Turn that off," Tammi said to me, referring to my choice of car music.

"Tammi, this is Bach's 'Brandenburg Concerto No. 1' in F major."

"Also known as *boring*," Tammi said as she reached to turn it off.

I slapped her hand. "It stimulates the mind. Trust me, it will help us for tonight's competition. Besides, my car, my music. Now shh...'"

All of my friends detested my love for classical music. But that didn't make me love it any less. It calmed my nerves, which was important for our chess competitions. I didn't like being the center of attention, so playing chess in front of an audience was nerve-wracking for me. Anyway, they just didn't feel the music like I did. The way those chords pulled at my heart, the notes boring into me, unraveling all my emotions until I was completely breathless was a feeling like no other.

We walked into the gymnasium to find the usual set up. One round table right in center court, with two chairs on either side. The chess board sat in the center, with a chess clock right next to it. Parents and onlookers, not very many of those, sat in the bleacher section closest to the table, and members of both teams gathered on the next bleacher section over.

Tammi and I headed over to our teammates in that direction. I pulled at my top, making sure it flattered me instead of showing off my fat rolls. I wanted to look as good as possible in front of my fellow chess mates.

Tammi and I waved and smiled to our coach, who was sitting in the bleachers with our friend Carla. Everyone in the bleachers stared at us as we took our seats, and I instantly felt my cheeks flush. Sometimes, I thought maybe I was a little too self-aware.

•••

The competition had finally begun. There were five rounds and eight people on our team. I was third on our roster. We had just started round one, and Billy Morris was playing against a tall and lanky junior from the Titans. I didn't know who I'd be up against.

"Nervous?" A voice behind me asked.

I turned around. It was Joey Manson, my crush, something I hated to admit. He was totally out of my league, with his cropped blonde hair and creamy hazelnut eyes.

I liked Joey the moment I laid eyes on him in eighth-grade science class. He was boldly unassuming. A quiet guy with magnetic looks and high intelligence. He had a bad-boy confidence that sent my fantasies to places uncharted. Back then, I naively hoped he would ask me to be his girlfriend, but the pretty girls always seemed to monopolize his attention. Joey never appeared to notice plain-Jane Tori Rowling, but I still watched him from afar every day.

"Um, a little, I guess…how about you?" I asked him, nervously twirling a lock of hair around my finger.

"Not really. These guys don't look very tough," he said with a smile.

He brushed his blonde hair out of his eyes, his taut muscles exposed underneath his thin T-shirt. *Ah, that gorgeous hair!*

"So, um-" I started to say, but he had already turned away.

I turned around in my seat and saw him talking to Lauren, another girl on our team. It was no secret that Joey was a ladies' man, but I had this fantasy that if he and I started dating he wouldn't want anyone else.

I never knew what to say to Joey, let alone to any other boy. I was the girl who watched the guys in class and on the playground, but I was too nervous to interact with them. I wanted a boyfriend, but I wanted him to ask *me* out. And no one ever had. I knew I wasn't as thin or as pretty as the popular girls, so why would guys want to talk to me? Isn't a girl's worth measured by her beauty?

I felt like there were two parts of me. The person I actually was and the person I wanted to be. I was good at being the quiet band geek, but there was so much more to me than that.

I was funny, according to Kyle and Tammi, a little devious, and creative. Deep down I did want to be invited to parties and have lots of friends, but I didn't know how to be *that* girl.

I hated how insecure I was, but I didn't know how to change it. I dreamed of having a boyfriend who cherished me and who looked like Joey. But those were only fantasies. In real life, I was the chess and band geek who didn't wear makeup and had no thigh gap. High school labels were the worst. Why couldn't people see the true me?

Fear. That's the worst four-letter word, in my opinion. Such a tiny word encompassed so much of my character. Fear and I went way back. It was the sibling that always had the upper hand but didn't always get its way. But oftentimes, it did win. I never truly conquered a fear, but rather suppressed it in one moment, or let it engulf me until I became disabled the next.

Ding! Round one was over. Billy Morris was declared the winner and our team cheered. Tammi was next.

"Go get 'em, girl," I told her.

She smiled and walked over to the competition table to face her opponent. Tammi was playing against a blonde girl with bright pink braces, a pink sweater, pink glasses, pink sneakers, and sparkly pink nail polish.

Tammi beat her with ease. The girl looked as if she'd never lost a game in her life. She reached underneath her chair and pulled out a pale pink handkerchief and wiped her eyes. We all gave her a moment, and I wondered how she could be so sensitive.

When she was finished, our team burst with applause for Tammi as she got up from the table.

"You were fantastic," I told her, "Now wish me luck."

I walked up to the table and immediately froze. My opponent was Todd Fisher. Yes, I knew his name. He was the Tyrone Titans' "secret weapon." Only it wasn't a secret. He'd won awards from all different states. Chess was basically his whole life.

"I heard he's treated like a king at his school," Brian told Tammi.

"Well, their football team does suck." Tammi added.

They both laughed.

I, however, did not. *Lucky me*, I thought to myself. I got to face off against our state's number one chess player. And I was going to lose.

Todd pushed up his glasses and ran a thin, black comb through his hair. *Oh please, could he be any dorkier*, I thought. He had on a plaid dress shirt that was tucked into his jeans, which were held up way above his waistline. *He just got way dorkier.*

We both sat down at the same time. He never even looked at me. Todd Fisher never looked at his opponent until after he beat them. At least that's what the Parkside Post Gazette had said.

The game was on. I captured one of his knights, but he got both of my bishops. He took my queen and then I heard a "check mate." I guess the Gazette was right. Todd and I stood up and then he looked at me. He gave me a wry smile.

"Nice try. Better luck next time, kid." He said, as if he was superior to me. But I couldn't think of anything to say back. And to make matters worse, he gave me his trademark "fist."

"Pound it," he said, reaching out his arm.

With flaming red cheeks, I bumped fists with Todd. I was just another chess player he had defeated. And to show that I wasn't a sore loser, I had to pound his fist. *Lucky me.*

My teammates said, "It's okay, Tori, good try," as I walked back to my seat.

But I could see that I had let them down. Brian Forbes won Round Four for us and Joey won Round Five. Being the only loser on my team made me feel even worse. But at least we had made states.

Everyone around me was laughing and cheering, but I stood as still as a tombstone.

"Tori, we're going out for milkshakes, you coming?" Tammi asked me, Brian at her side.

"Nah, I'm pretty tired." I told her. "I'll see you guys tomorrow."

"Alright," Tammi said, looking confused, "...see ya."

Once I got home, I told my parents about the competition, then went upstairs, played Gershwin on my phone, and slipped into bed. *Maybe I am a sore loser*, I thought. *Or just a loser.*

•••

I loved mornings. The first hunger pangs as your eyes opened to a fresh new day. The smell of coffee brewing and the taste of a hot steaming mug of the potent liquid.

Eggs. Pancakes. Fruit. Yogurt. The best foods were breakfast foods. Bacon. Sausage gravy. Corned beef hash. A sun-dried-tomato bagel with a thick gob of cream cheese on each half. Breakfast could be enjoyed with your friends and loved ones, or alone with the newspaper.

Either way, it always put me in the best way to start my day, my stomach full of energy just waiting to be burned. It was the time of day where everything was quiet and at peace. Anything was possible in the morning. You could wipe clean the slate of yesterday and make new plans for today.

"Hey, mom, what's cooking?" I asked as I walked into the brightly lit kitchen in my grumpy cat t-shirt and cotton candy shorts.

"We're having bacon and eggs," she said as she sprinkled cheese over the skillet.

"Where's Corey?" I asked with a yawn.

"Your brother is out playing baseball with his friends."

"At 10:00 a.m. on a Saturday?"

"You know Corey, never wants to take it easy." She laughed.

"Well, he's crazy for missing out on this breakfast." I said, picking up a slice of bacon to add to my plate of cheesy eggs.

"More for us." My mom smiled.

"Jonathan!" She yelled up the stairs. "Breakfast is ready!"

"I'll be down in a minute!" My dad called down to her.

"So, what's on the agenda for today?" She asked me.

"Well, I have a science project I need to finish, so I'll work on that after breakfast. Nothing other than that. Maybe I'll read for the rest of the day."

"That sounds nice," she said. "If you change your mind on any of that, I was thinking we could do some shopping."

"Dollar Tree and JoAnn Fabrics?"

"Why, of course." We both laughed, sipping our coffee with smiles.

My parents didn't have a lot of money, but when we wanted to go on a "shopping spree" we'd always hit up the Dollar Tree and JoAnn Fabrics. Since everything was only a dollar, we could basically get anything we wanted and it didn't add up to much. My mom and I also loved making crafts together, so we always enjoyed walking the JoAnn Fabrics aisles in search of new paints or craft ideas.

"I guess I can read tomorrow," I told her, drinking the last of my coffee. "I'll finish up my science project and then we can head out."

"Sounds good, honey."

• • •

I bought a golden heart locket at the local thrift store for $7. The necklace was slightly rusted and a little hard to open, but I found it to be charming. It's stupid, but I bought it in hopes to put a picture of my boyfriend in it. The boyfriend I didn't have yet. Everyone seemed to have a significant other except for me. Thankfully, Tammi didn't have one either.

That helped some. So, for now my plan was to place the locket in my top drawer to lie in wait. I left it open, as if maybe its energy would welcome a lover into my life.

If I could have one wish come true, it would be for Joey Manson to be my boyfriend. I'd put his picture in the locket and wear it every day. But I think for now I had to set my sights a little lower. Perhaps someone from chess club or marching band would be interested in me. Mom found a couple tops at the thrift store and a book she had been wanting for a while. We each bought about ten items at the Dollar Tree and two paint by number sets at JoAnn Fabrics.

"Can we paint them tonight?" I asked my mom on the car ride home.

"Sure, honey. Do you want to stop and get a pizza for dinner?"

I looked at the Pizza Hut billboard she was staring at along the stretch of road.

"Um, YES!!" We both giggled and took the exit for Pizza Hut.

• • •

"You brought me pizza AND wings?" My dad teased.

"No, they brought ME pizza and wings." Corey said.

"I think there's enough for everyone." Mom replied, placing the boxes onto the kitchen table.

"You better not eat more than your share," I told Corey.

"I'm a growing boy, Tori. And you're not the boss of me." He playfully punched me in the shoulder. I smacked his arm back.

"Guys, cut it out." Dad scolded.

We smiled to each other as we sat down for dinner.

"Are you two ready for your first day of school on Monday?" My mom asked.

"Most definitely," Corey said. "Freshman year better be ready for Corey Rowling."

"I don't think anybody is ever ready for you." Dad joked.

I looked around our table. This was just another Saturday night for us. Nothing exciting, but so much fun. I loved my family, but sometimes I wished I could be out with the popular kids on a Saturday night. I wondered what sort of things they did.

ORDINARY DAY

It was that time again—the first day of school. A fresh start. To erase the past. Wrong! It may feel like it, but it's not. Every year we all say, "I'm going to be different this year." But no matter how much we wish to change, somehow, we always end up as the same person we've always been.

This year I wasn't going to lie to myself. I wouldn't change and I knew it. Besides, I liked who I was at school. Well, sort of.

Maybe I wasn't popular, but I had really great friends. We understood each other perfectly, and we had each other's backs. Always. Our friendship was strong. It was the one thing we all could rely on in our lives. I didn't know what I would do without them. It was the only friend group I had, and I wasn't really great at meeting new people due to my shyness.

So, there I was, in my mom's Volvo, listening to Bach's "Toccata and Fugue in D minor," heading to school. When I got there, Tammi was already waiting for me on the front steps.

"We're seniors!" She exclaimed, jumping up and down. Several people nearby stared over at us.

I looked around, embarrassed at the looks we were getting. Tammi saw my red cheeks and pulled me into a side-hug. We both giggled and started walking up the steps and into the front door of the school.

Tammi started jumping up and down again, dancing around in a circle like she was at an EDM show, trying to pull me to join in her excitement. I could feel hallway eyes on us. I hated people watching me do anything, even playing a game. That's why our chess matches were so nerve-wracking for me.

It made me nervous to even blow out my birthday candles with everyone gathered around singing. Being the center of attention was the worst thing I could think of, and I most certainly didn't feel comfortable with Tammi dancing obnoxiously beside me.

"I'm gonna get to class," I said, leaving her to the many stares beginning to form around her.

•••

If there was one good thing about high school, it was definitely the fact that every year my locker was right beside Joey's. He rarely said a word to me, unless it was about chess, but that didn't matter. As long as I was close enough to smell his cologne, I was happy. There I was, at my locker, with Joey right next to me wearing a Bob Marley T-shirt that allowed me to stare at his incredible muscles.

"Hey, bright eyes." Joey said, looking in my direction.

Did I hear that right? Joey Manson was talking to me! And calling me "bright eyes!" I gave him a shy smile.

"Um, I--"

"Hey, muscle shirt."

My face turned 11 shades of red. Of course he wasn't talking to me! He was talking to Amber Lawrence. But what was with the *adorable* nicknames?

Joey, who knew that I had thought he was talking to me, gave me an apologetic smile.

"Tori, have you heard the good news?" He asked me, clearly in pity.

"Uh, no, I don't think so."

He put his arm around the pretty blonde.

"Amber and I are a couple now."

Amber didn't even look at me, just chomped on her gum and stared at her nails. We both watched her. Joey broke the silence first.

"Okay, well, we'd better get to class."

"Uh, okay..."

Amber looked me over from head to toe, flipped her hair, and grabbed Joey's hand. I watched them walk away, humiliation sinking deep into my chest. Not only did I embarrass myself in front of Joey, I now had to watch him walk the halls with Amber Lawrence, the most popular girl in school.

Tall, blonde and curvy, Amber was awarded the golden ticket when it came to the gene pool. She was captain of the cheerleading squad and the head of her own girl squad. It figured that she would grasp her claws into Joey. Would there EVER be a chance for me and him?

...

Gym class was always the worst. It wasn't like we had to wear uniforms or anything, but still...it was the fact than an entire group of students who didn't really like me to begin with had to watch me humiliate myself in horrible group sports. And for what? Just so we could get a required amount of exercise? It was just another excuse for athletic students to show off and make the rest of us look bad.

One day I asked my gym teacher, "Why can't we opt for walking instead?" She said that group sports taught us teamwork and other important life skills. Anyway, the point was that gym class was worse than any class you could possibly take in high school. My gym teacher and I had a charming dynamic. I would stand around doing a poor job of pretending to participate, and she would yell "Rowling! At least move!" with exasperation in her voice. But I could tell she thought it was hilarious how pathetic I was for not even trying.

As I tied the string to my black yoga pants, I could feel someone watching me. I looked up and saw a petite, freckled-faced girl with her shiny red hair in a French braid wearing the most eclectic gym outfit I had ever seen. She walked toward me with an air of confidence and hands crossed in front of her chest. She had some serious resting bitch face. I couldn't tell whether she wanted to say hi or punch me.

A tight neon orange sleeveless shirt stared me in the face paired with bright green running shorts and candy apple red Nike high-tops. "Hi, I'm Alyssa. Please tell me you're way cooler than the rest of these losers."

• • •

While everyone else participated in dodgeball, Alyssa and I compared schedules.

"So, I have first lunch. What about you?" I asked her, tossing a ball at a kid in a red t-shirt with curly hair. I missed him, of course.

"Me too!" Alyssa exclaimed.

Thankful that I at least knew one person in my lunch period, I relaxed a little.

"So, your parents are both doctors?" I asked Alyssa.

"Yeah. And we're like totally rich." She laughed.

"Okay..." I said, unsure of how to respond to such a brazen answer.

"My parents have a crazy awesome house about two miles from here. But they got me my own apartment to live in so I can have my privacy."

"What?!" I exclaimed, getting hit fiercely in the stomach by a red rubber ball. We both walked over to the "Out" sidelines.

"Oh yes." Alyssa said, proudly smiling.

"That doesn't even sound real." I told her in disbelief.

"Well, it is. As long as I keep my grades up, I can stay in the apartment."

"That's incredible! So, what's it like living on your own?"

"It's amazing, honestly." Alyssa flipped her hair and beamed at me. "I have a maid come in twice a week to clean the place, and she brings me meals too."

"No way!"

"Yes way. I try to be out and about as much as possible, though, because it gets lonely living on your own."

"I bet."

"So what year are you?" She asked me.

"I'm a senior. What about you?"

"Same here! I wonder if we have any more classes together. So where do you live? What do you do for fun around here?"

"Well, I live in Richland, only about 6 miles from the school. My family is pretty boring. My dad is an accountant and my mom is a preschool teacher. I like to read and draw, and I love playing chess and my saxophone, but my parents couldn't care less about that stuff. They'd rather watch my brother's soccer and baseball games."

"Oooh, you have a brother?! What's he like? How old is he?"

"My brother's name is Corey, and he's a freshman. He plays a lot of sports, so he's not home a lot."

"Well at least you have a sibling. I'm an only child, and it can get pretty lonely. My parents try to make up for it by giving me whatever I want." Alyssa laughed.

"Oh, that sucks. Do they at least spend time with you?" I asked her.

"Not too often, but I'm okay with that."

"Yeah, same here. Well, I do hang out with my mom a lot. My parents are well-meaning, but we don't actually do much as a family except watch TV after dinner. They're more concerned with making sure I'm not out partying every night."

"And are you?" Alyssa asked.

I burst out laughing. "As if I'd be invited to any!"

She smiled. "Oh, honey, trust me, that will change."

I wasn't sure what she meant by that, but I was excited to find out. This girl seemed conceited, but nice. And she appeared to have picked me out of the crowd to be her buddy, so I was flattered. She was gorgeous, no doubt. I would've killed to have her fire engine red hair and tiny body.

We both endured the rest of gym class together and afterwards we went to lunch. Alyssa saved us seats while I got in line for my meal.

As I set my dark green tray down on the gray plastic table, Alyssa exclaimed, "Are you for serious? You're really gonna eat that?"

I looked down at my steaming meatloaf with a side of sliced carrots and burnt sugar cookie with pink and yellow sprinkles on it. "Yes, I'm going to eat this. What's wrong with it?"

Alyssa laughed. "What's wrong with it? How about the fact that it's moving?"

The meatloaf did appear to be jiggling. I laughed. "You have no room to talk...have you looked at what you brought to eat?"

We both stared at her protein bar and bottle of water.

"What? I'm watching my weight."

I couldn't imagine starving myself like that just to lose some weight, but I wasn't going to risk having an argument with this new acquaintance. I did wish to be thinner, but eating less food didn't appeal to me. At least I could always attempt to cover up my unwanted fat. So I just laughed, and she did along with me. Once school let out, I walked to my car and stuck my book bag in the trunk. As I closed it, a red-headed figure stood before me. Alyssa.

"Hey, girlfriend!" She said.

"Are you stalking me?" I teased, though I was a little creeped out.

Laughing, she said, "I was stalked once...trust me, you wouldn't know if I was stalking you, girl! Oh, the boys I've stalked. Ha ha! But seriously, we should go shopping!"

"Well, I would, but I've really got a lot of studying to do." This wasn't a total lie. I honestly had *some* studying to do tonight. Alyssa laughed.

"Are you for serious? C'mon, girl, live a little! Where's your sense of adventure?"

I stared at this pretty new girl with her Ralph Lauren top and Guess jeans, and decided that while she was a little odd, she wanted to be my friend, and maybe I *should* live a little.

"Okay," I said with mustered enthusiasm. "Let's go shopping!"

"Great!" Alyssa squealed. "We'll take my car. C'mon."

We walked over to the nicest car in the whole lot, an orange Mustang with just a tad too many floral decals on it for my taste. She turned the key and rap music blared from the speakers.

"What is this?" I yelled to her over the thunderous noise.

"You're kidding, right?" I really wasn't. "It's Travis Scott!" Alyssa said as if I should know.

"Don't you listen to anything with a piano in it?" I asked. Alyssa burst out laughing.

"Are you for serious?"

I swear this phrase was permanently embedded into her vocabulary. By the expression on my face, she knew that I was.

"Oh Tori, you have *so* much to learn."

It felt good to arrive at the mall in such a stylish car and with a popular girl. I felt people's eyes on my shopping partner, stunned by her beauty. I found myself staring back at the people passing by us, and they smiled at me. I smiled back, feeling an odd sense of pride instead of embarrassment.

I usually got my clothes at Walmart or JCPenney. The stores Alyssa liked were filled with overpriced items that only people of high status wore. Nothing in these stores screamed ME. And all of the screaming in the world wouldn't have made any item come close to my price range.

I watched Alyssa get bogged down with all her bags of purchases while I had none.

"Do you want me to carry something for you?" I asked her.

She looked relieved. "Oh yeah, that'd be great! …Wait a sec! Where are your bags? Didn't you get *anything*?"

"I just didn't see anything I liked." I told her.

Alyssa gave me a look that said she could see right through my lie.

"I'm gonna buy you something." She stated loudly as we walked into a really cool-looking clothing store.

"Alyssa, I don't want you to buy me anything," I shouted over the music.

Ignoring my declaration, Alyssa said, "Let's play dress-up."

The store had dim lighting and loud music, but I soldiered on, following Alyssa from clothing item to clothing item and trying to find the perfect outfits for us to try on. I'd never enjoyed clothes shopping, but I had to admit that Alyssa was making it laid-back and fun. With armfuls of garments weighing us down, we staggered towards the fitting rooms and began trying stuff on.

I looked at my reflection in the full-body mirror as Alyssa sang along to one of the boisterous songs on the stereo system. I turned around and stuck my butt out, doing a model pose of my ensemble. The dark-wash denim jeans hugged my curvy body in all the right places, and my bright yellow top emphasized my plump chest, flowing right down to my hips.

"I love how I look." I heard myself saying to my surprise.

"Let me see, let me see!" Alyssa exclaimed as she flung open her fitting room door.

I came out of my room and did a little twirl for her.

"I LOVE it!!"

"Really?" I asked.

"REALLY really." Alyssa answered.

"Now how does mine look?" She asked, giving me a reciprocated twirl.

"Absolutely stunning!" I said in laughter.

Alyssa clapped her hands together. "Super! Let's keep trying!"

We each took turns showing off our various outfit creations, which ended up turning into a mini dance party. But every party must end at some point. And our point just happened to be when Alyssa and I started dancing on top of the benches in our fitting rooms to an Alessia Cara single.

"I'm sorry, but you two need to leave now," said a tall, buff, blonde employee. We both stopped mid-headbang.

"Are you for serious?" Alyssa snorted.

"Yes. We don't allow this sort of behavior in our store. You may buy your things and go."

While I was completely mortified, Alyssa laughed.

"Seriously, dude? Do you know how much money I'm about to drop in your store?"

"I appreciate that, but we have our policies, miss." The worker said with an edge to his voice. Alyssa took the hint.

"Okay, okay. I'm not trying to cause any trouble here. C'mon, Tori, let's buy the stuff we want and go."

I ended up with five new outfits from that store, and then we were on to "bigger and better places," or so said my fiery red-headed companion.

The mall was closing by the time we finally made it out of the enormous building. My boring night at home with schoolwork and a book had turned into a four-hour shopping escapade. Alyssa had seriously ignored my protests and basically ended up buying me a new wardrobe. She flirted with two boys standing outside smoking, convincing them to help us carry our bags to the car. Once we got in the car and waved goodbye to the cute guys, I noticed a number written on one of my shopping bags:

Trevor 262-4486

Alyssa looked down at the handwritten note on my bag.

"OMG!" She squealed. "That guy gave you his number!"

"I'm sure it was meant for you," I said, still unable to stop a smile from forming on my face.

"Which one was Trevor?" Alyssa asked, tilting her head to the side and creasing her brow in confusion.

"I have no idea!" We both started laughing.

YOU'RE MY BEST FRIEND

The next day of school felt empowering. I took a hot shower and ran de-frizz hair serum through my curly locks just like every other day. Then I opened my closet. It was filled with an array of beautifully expensive clothing items, putting a smile on my face. There were so many choices!

I had Ralph Lauren tops, Gucci skirts, Dior heels, and Versace dresses. Jeans of various patterns and colors lined my closet, filling me with excitement and joy. I wasn't used to this, and I knew that no matter what I chose to wear that day, I couldn't go wrong. I even wore the make-up that Alyssa had bought me at Sephora, playing a YouTube video on my phone to follow so I could get the look down right.

"Tell me I'm dreaming," I said to Alyssa after Joey told me *"nice legs."*

Laughing, she said, "Girl, you're so dramatic. Thanks to me, you look hot now. Just enjoy it."

And I was thoroughly enjoying it. I had been used to covering up my body, not revealing it in the form-fitting yellow mini dress from Banana Republic I had on. I hadn't realized until that moment how clothing and makeup could transform a nerdy caterpillar into a Sephora butterfly. I felt like a damn queen.

"Whatcha doing?" Tammi asked me at my locker.

"She's been taking selfies all day." Kyle answered for me.

I turned the screen off my phone and placed it in my bag.

"Not ALL day." I smirked.

"What's up with the makeover?" Tammi asked me.

"Yeah, why do you look like Tori 2.0 today?" Kyle added.

"Are you saying that I was only a 1.0 before today?" I asked, crossing my arms.

"All I'm saying is you look…better… than usual." Kyle smiled and winked at me.

"She doesn't look better, she looks more gooped up." Tammi said.

"Gooped up?" I asked, furrowing my brow in confusion.

"Yeah, you know, you painted over a beautiful portrait with crayons or something."

"Come again?" Kyle said, ready to laugh.

Tammi sighed. "I'm trying to say that you are naturally beautiful, Tori. You don't need to cover yourself with beauty paste and wear tight clothes to get people's attention."

My cheeks flushed. "That's sweet of you to say."

The bell rang, people closing their locker doors in unison.

"But also, please stop sending me duckface snaps or I'm gonna give you my own makeover involving my fist."

Kyle howled with laughter.

"Noted." I said, turning to walk to my next class.

...

I picked up a hall pass during English so I could go to the bathroom to take a selfie in my new dress. I was in such a confident mood and I wanted it to last forever. What could be more lasting than an Instagram post? I struck my pose in the full-length bathroom mirror, making sure to angle the camera high and pushing my arm back and my hip out, like I had seen so many other girls do in photos.

After a few shots, I had my perfect picture. It gave me an hourglass shape and I looked pretty thin. *Perfect*, I thought. I uploaded it, then returned to class.

...

"Look at you, getting 50 likes on a photo you posted only 20 minutes ago." Alyssa said to me as we changed into our gym clothes.

"Yeah, I feel pretty good about it." I said, smiling.

"Well, I feel like I had something to do with the success of your photo since I bought you the clothes and makeup."

"You're absolutely right, Alyssa. You are the reason for my new look, after all."

If Alyssa wanted credit, then she could have it. I couldn't have afforded any of the new stuff without her.

"What makeup tutorial did you watch? I love how you did your lips."

"I don't even remember. I just know I tried to follow a Kylie Jenner guide."

"I absolutely ADORE Kylie!"

From that day on, Alyssa and I were inseparable. We spent every day after school either at the mall, her apartment, or the football field. It was incredible how many people sat in the bleachers to watch the football players and cheerleaders practice. As the weeks passed by, Alyssa became one of the most popular girls in our school. And I was starting to gain popularity by association.

Going to parties with Alyssa took a lot of courage for me because I was nervous in most social settings where I didn't know many of the people. I was great at meeting people one-on-one, but not in a group. The reality was that the more people there were in the group, the less I would talk. No matter how many parties she dragged me to, I never overcame the nervous feeling in the pit of my stomach beforehand. I could rationalize the fear in my head, but I couldn't make it go away. One side effect of this was not being able to eat. It sucked, but what else could I do? I still went to the parties, I just wasn't able to eat those nights. I couldn't figure out why Alyssa wanted to hang out with me. She could be best friends with absolutely anyone in school, but she chose me. I almost felt like an imposter being with her. Did people see us together and wonder what sick joke she was playing on me? I erased the thought from my mind.

• • •

Alyssa's popularity began when she volunteered to be a part of the prom committee. According to Alyssa, party-planning was "in her blood." Prom committee was made up of jocks, cheerleaders, and overachievers—the elite of our school. They held meetings every Thursday at 7 p.m., and Alyssa never missed one. So, every Thursday she spent her evening with the high school kings and queens, and they fell in love with her.

Alyssa's natural beauty, along with her up-to-date fashion, made any girl want to be her. She had a laugh that was slightly obnoxious, yet charming, and her enthusiasm was utterly contagious. She had an inspiring confidence and LOVED to flirt. Popular guys were always attracted to confident girls, which was probably why Alyssa went on so many dates throughout the weeks. She knew she had a great body, and she wasn't afraid to flaunt it. I always watched her go on dates in tight dresses and platform heels, or crop-tops and jeans you could see her thong through.

Alyssa's first few prom committee meetings consisted of heated arguments about what the prom theme should be, and Alyssa saved the day by coming up with a Vegas casino theme. For weeks I had to listen to Alyssa rattle on and on about different casino games, poker chips, possible menus, and all of the gossip that surrounded the prom committee table. Not that I should have been complaining. She was becoming part of the "in" crowd, and she wasn't leaving me behind

My first party experience was a major fail. It was at Kayla Johnson's house, a large ranch-style home in the more rural part of town. Kayla was a short brunette who was currently dating the captain of our school's soccer team. Alyssa met her during prom committee, and so she invited her to come and bring anyone she wanted. The entire prom committee was there as well as a bunch of other students I didn't recognize. Alyssa and I walked into the spacious home with dark hardwood flooring and Aztec-patterned area rugs and Kayla introduced herself to me.

"It's so nice to meet you, Tori. Alyssa's told me so much about you, I'm glad you could make it."

"Me too." I told her, my cheeks flushing.

"Well, make yourselves at home. There's beer, wine, and pizza in the kitchen. Enjoy." She said, walking back over to the living room where several girls were dancing.

"Wow," I said aloud, admiring the tasteful décor and open layout of the house. "This place is beautiful."

"You should see my parents' house." Alyssa said. "People say it's impressive, but to me it's just more space to feel lonely."

"Do you feel less lonely in your apartment?" I asked her.

"Way less lonely now that I have you coming over all the time." She laughed.

"Want to get some food?" I asked.

"If by food, you mean drinks, then yes."

As we walked into the kitchen, a huge group of people standing around the island stopped talking and turned to face us.

"Hey, Alyssa! Good to see you." A cute blonde boy said.

"Tori, I'd like you to meet the prom committee members."

I looked around at the many faces staring at me, feeling anxious and overwhelmed with the sudden attention. I completely froze in my tracks, didn't even say hi, just stared at them like a deer in the headlights. The only thing I could think to do to make it less awkward was to pull out my phone and pretend I was getting a call. I held the device to my ear and began nodding my head as if I was listening to someone on the other line. I walked out of the room so fast that I didn't see anyone's reaction to my behavior, including Alyssa. I booked it outside and inhaled the crisp fall air.

It felt calm outside the house, the bass from the music softly echoing in the night. Faint voices of casual conversations seeped through the windows, a rival to the chirping crickets' melody.

The calm was interrupted by a slamming door.

"What happened back there?!" Alyssa asked.

I stared back at her with embarrassment.

"I just...froze."

"Yeah, that was obvious."

"I'm sorry, I don't really know what happened. There were too many people, I guess."

"Social anxiety much?"

"I suppose that's what it is."

"Well, I really wanted you to meet my friends in the prom committee, but it's okay. Maybe another time."

"Thanks." I told her, wrapping my sweater around my shoulders.

"Want to get out of here?" She asked me.

"Yes please."

We went back to Alyssa's apartment and listened to the new Selena Gomez album. Alyssa pulled out two containers of Ben and Jerry's as I sat on a barstool at her kitchen island.

"Chunky Monkey or Phish Food?" She asked, setting the two pints on the granite counter-top.

"I'll take whichever one you don't want."

"Phish Food it is." Alyssa said, handing me a spoon and a pint of creaminess.

THE AUTUMN EFFECT

It didn't feel like my makeover was only 3 weeks ago, but here I was eating lunch with Tammi and Kyle in my Versace skirt and Tommy Hilfiger boots.

"Where's your new friend at?" Kyle asked me as he shoved his face with a deli sandwich dripping with mustard.

"Alyssa's over there with Amber and her crew," I answered, directing my head towards the table covered in makeup bags instead of lunch trays.

"Those girls are so vain." Tammi said.

"Yeah, but I would be vain too if I looked like them."

"Maybe. You are starting to rival them in appearance, Tori."

"Thank you, Tammi!"

"It wasn't a compliment." She said with a smirk.

"Okay, let's be nice," Kyle said.

"It's okay, Kyle. I am aware that Tammi disapproves of my new look. I can admit that Amber and her crew are bitches. But Alyssa is different."

"Maybe we can all hang out together and find out." Kyle said.

"I'd be down for that," said Tammi.

"Okay, perfect. I'll talk to Alyssa and set something up." I said with a smile.

Now I just had to figure out an activity that could bond my best friends with my new friend.

•••

"You'll never believe this!" Tammi exclaimed to me on the ride home from school.

"What? Tell me!"

"Brian asked me out."

"NO. FREAKING. WAY."

"Yes way!!!"

"This is amazing! How did it happen?"

"He pulled me aside after Spanish and asked me if I'd like to go out sometime. I said yes, and he smiled real big and said he would think of something fun for us to do together."

I looked at Tammi in her striped high knee socks and overalls, a massive smile on her face. She let out a scream of excitement, filling the small space of the car with audible joy. I wondered if I would be that happy someday.

•••

"Have you heard about the Halloween party I'm throwing?" Alyssa asked me that evening.

"You're throwing a party here?" I said, looking around at the limited space her apartment provided for social gatherings.

"No, not here, silly. At my parents' house."

"Ah, the elusive Mr. and Mrs. Perdue." I said with a smile.

"Yes, the parents who are never home." Alyssa said. "I asked them if it was okay and they were fine with it."

"Who all is invited?" I asked.

"Everyone who is anyone at school."

"So, like everyone at school?"

"Of course, not, Tori. That would be way too many people. I'm thinking the athletes, cheerleaders, prom committee, and of course all the other popular people. That includes you." She said with a wink.

"Can I bring Tammi and Kyle? I've been wanting the three of us to hang out so they can get to know you better."

"Sure, sounds great. I'll be sure to invite them. Now I know that Halloween isn't for another two weeks, but I need your help planning this thing. I want it to be perfect."

"No problem, I love planning parties." I said, smiling.

HUMBLE PIE

"Are you ready for the pizza party in Mr. Barton's class?!" Tammi asked me from an adjacent seat in the back of Sociology.

"Oh yes. I've been dreaming about it since first period." I said, rubbing my stomach.

Pizza parties happened maybe twice a year in our school. It was a way for the teachers to relax, put on a movie the class wanted to see, and just eat and socialize for forty minutes. Everyone in class chipped in five bucks, and we got all the pizza and wings we could eat.

The bell rang, and we headed straight to Mr. Barton's class to get seats in the front of the room so we could be the first ones to get our pizza and wings. We watched the rest of the class file in, and I saw a familiar face in the crowd.

"Hey, bitch." Alyssa smiled.

Tammi furrowed her eyebrows.

"Hey, Alyssa." I returned her greeting.

"Tammi, this is Alyssa." I said, gesturing to my petite friend.

"Hi." Tammi said with a smile.

"Hey, I'm Alyssa. Nice to meet you, Tammi."

Mr. Barton let us watch *Toy Story 4* as we passed around the pizza, wings, and 2-liter bottles of Pepsi.

"So, Tammi," Alyssa asked. "You have such a unique style. Where did you get your shirt?"

"Oh thanks, I got this at a thrift shop."

Alyssa pretended like she was stifling her laugh, but it was clear as day. Some students beside us started to stare.

"Is that a problem for you?" Tammi asked with her voiced raised.

"Not at all, I just asked a question." Alyssa said with a smirk.

"Ladies, please keep it down." We heard Mr. Barton say.

The class started to stare at us instead of at the movie, and I was disturbed by how rude Alyssa was being to one of my best friends. I gave her a scolding look, and Tammi an apologetic one. We watched the rest of the movie in silence. This didn't bode well for our future co-mingling hangout.

• • •

"God, I hate that guy." Kyle said, slamming his locker door shut. I looked at the person in question walking past us. It was Joey and his best friend, Brett.

Lots of people thought that Joey was gay because he had a gay best friend, but Joey made it obvious that he was only into girls. I stood mesmerized by Joey's smoldering chocolate eyes as he laughed at something Brett said. His tight dark-wash Levi's hugged him in all the right places as he strutted along in his oversized Timberland boots. He had this sexy air of confidence when he walked that drove me crazy.

"…Hello? Earth to Tori?"

"Sorry, sorry." I said, coming out of my trance.

"Did you hear what I said?" Kyle asked.

"Yes. You hate Brett."

"Yeah, I do. The guy is pond scum."

"You have every right to hate him, after all, he did steal your boyfriend."

"Yeah, stole him just for sex. He doesn't actually care about him. I'm the only one who ever truly loved James."

"Is he talking about James again?" Tammi asked, spontaneously walking beside us to class.

"Yeah, we just saw Brett about a minute ago." I answered.

"We've been over this a thousand times," said Tammi. "James was never good enough for you. Sure, he was cute and funny. But he didn't treat you right."

"Not this again." Kyle huffed.

"What do you think, Tori?" Tammi asked me.

Confrontation gave me anxiety, and I just wanted this conversation to end.

"I liked James, but he cheated. So clearly he wasn't a good guy."

"Well said, Tori." Tammi praised.

"Anyway," Kyle said, trying to steer us back to him, "I am now single and ready to mingle."

"That's fantastic!" Tammi exclaimed.

"Are you over James?" I asked in caution.

"Yes, I am completely over him. Like you said, he clearly wasn't a good guy. And I deserve better. So, point me in the direction of some cute boys or girls."

"I'm so happy for you," I said to Kyle, waving to Tammi as she turned the corner to get to her next class.

"Thanks, Tori. It's time for me to move on. I'll see you later."

"Yep, see ya." I said, turning to enter the field house.

Gym class that day was the defining moment of a new change in my life. Mrs. Beyers lined us up and had us count off by two. Of course Alyssa and I were on opposite teams. Mrs. Beyers brought out a basketball and the game began. As usual, I walked back and forth across the gym floor, following my teammates, pretending I was desperately trying to grab the large orange ball like everyone else.

After the first game ended, Mrs. Beyers blew her whistle and told us to get a drink. Alyssa and I talked about how basketball was a waste of time while we stood in the long line behind the only water fountain near the gym.

"So, you don't like basketball?"

I turned to see the incredibly attractive boy asking this question to-could it be-me?

"Um, not really," was the most creative answer I could come up with. The boy smiled.

"Well, how do you know if you don't even try?"

"I don't need to jump off a bridge to know it's gonna hurt." That was more creative. I don't know where my confidence was coming from, but I think I liked it.

"You're comparing playing basketball to jumping off a bridge?" He asked.

"Well, they both cause severe injuries in my case, so yes."

"Okay," he said, leading me back into the gym, "how about I pass you the ball this next game and we'll see if you get any bruises."

I didn't know what game he was trying to play, besides basketball that is, but he apparently had never seen me play sports before.

"Sounds tempting, but I think I'll pass."

I turned and looked around for Alyssa, but the cute boy followed.

"Okay, we'll make it interesting then," he said as he spun the ball on his finger. "Five bucks says you can't make a shot."

I raised my eyebrows in confusion. If this was supposed to be reverse psychology, it definitely wasn't going to work. "Then you'd be making five bucks."

He laughed. "You won't owe me anything. If you make a shot, I'll give you the money. If you don't, then you owe me nothing. You can't lose."

This guy was very persistent. I didn't even see why he cared so much about my gym class performance. Was he one of Mrs. Beyers' pets or something? Whatever the reason, he was clearly cute, and was actually paying attention to me. This certainly was a rare occasion, and I didn't want it to end.

"Okay, you're on."

Mrs. Beyers blew her whistle and the game started. I ran after the ball like an idiot, but not just for the five dollars. My real prize was another conversation with this toned and tanned mystery boy.

The ball was passed in the air, through legs, and bounced off a few heads. The cute boy seemed to have forgotten our bet, so I reverted to walking back and forth, a pretender again. I watched him make two 3-pointers, and one alley-oop, the names of which I had been ignorant to at the time.

His smooth brown hair shone in the light of the musty gym and I enjoyed watching him fake people out and spin around completely to avoid having the ball stolen. Then it happened. The cute boy faked a pass to James, and instead passed it to me.

I caught the ball of leather just as it had caught me—off guard. I stood there with the ball in my hands, unsure of what to do, the cute boy yelling, "Go! Go!" to me.

I began to run, but there were so many people blocking me, so I just went for the shot. It wasn't like in the movies where everything was in slow-motion as people held their breath, waiting to see what would happen. In fact, it went by so fast that I didn't even know if I had made the shot or not. From across the gym, I looked at the cute boy with the smooth brown hair. Once again, he was smiling.

On my way out of the locker room, I felt a hand slip something into my pants' pocket.

"Looks like I was right." The cute boy said to me, walking away into the crowded corridor. I stuck my hand in my pocket and pulled out a five-dollar bill.

•••

"Who were you talking to in gym today?" Alyssa asked as I set my books down on the table. The study hall monitor sent an evil glare our way. I pulled out my phone and began to text Alyssa.

> **Eric Larson**
> What did he want?
> **He wants me to play basketball in gym.**
> Why does he care?
> **Idk**
> He's cute!
> **I know! He's on the basketball team.**
> Nice. You should totally hook up.
> **Idk if he even likes me.**
> I bet he does ;)
> **Lol**

Tammi and I had marching band practice after school. We only had a few more outdoor practices until the football season started. Even though band camp was over, we still met on an empty side field with spray painted lines. We couldn't practice on the actual football field because that was where the football players practiced every day.

"So, that Alyssa girl…not a fan." Tammi told me as we got to our starting spots.

I sighed. "Okay, I can totally understand that. She was rude to you. But that's just how she is."

"And you think that's a good excuse?"

"No, but I mean she IS my friend, so I was hoping we could all get along."

"Well, I'd like that too, but first impressions mean a lot. She blew hers."

"What does that mean? You won't hang out with her?"

"Okay, people, let's start from the top. On the drum beat." Mr. Grayson instructed.

"I don't hang out with people who make fun of me." Tammi said as the drums started their cadence. Everyone on the field began their formations. We actually sounded pretty good, in my opinion. It seemed like all of our hard work at band camp over the summer was finally paying off. I loved watching the drill and the music come together in harmony.

When we finished our last song, a busload of elementary kids slowly rode by our field and all of the kids stuck their heads out of the bus windows and yelled "band geeks!"

Now, it took a lot more than that to lower a marching band member's self-esteem. But it really saddened me that such young children were already actively demonstrating their knowledge of this stereotype. When I was that age, and I watched my first band concert, I remember my fascination with the saxophone players, thinking to myself, "I want to do that."

And when I got my chance to learn in 5th grade, I did it, and it transformed my life. To me, it would be unfortunate if a child missed out on such a life-changing activity simply because they didn't want to be called a geek.

"Can you believe those little brats?" Tammi asked me.

"Yeah, I guess they're starting them early with the stereotypes." I said. "So, when are we doing another chess night? It feels like it's been a while."

"That's because you've barely played with us since the last competition." Tammi replied.

"Yeah, I just hate being the only member on the team losing."

"How about I come over tonight? I can help you with your game."

"Sure, I'll see you then."

Tammi came over around seven o'clock with her crystal dragon chess set.

"Let's get started, our next competition is only two weeks away!" Tammi said.

We broke out the board, set up the pieces, and began to play. Tammi was having so much fun, but my heart just wasn't in it. I couldn't stop thinking about Eric.

"Do you know an Eric Larson?" I asked her.

"Nope. Why?"

"Oh, just wondering. He's someone in my gym class."

"Okay..." Tammi said in confusion.

I didn't feel like sharing my gym story with her, so I just made my next move on the board.

•••

"Guess where we're going tonight?!" Alyssa asked me the next day as she shoved a hot pink flyer into my face.

"Uh...Luke Gaynor's Frickin Funtastic Festivity," I read off of the neon piece of paper.

"Yep! It's gonna be super fun!"

"Alyssa, I have a ton of studying I need to do."

"Are you for serious?"

"How do you think I get good grades?"

"Tori, you'll be fine. You're smart. And anyway, the party doesn't start until 9. So you'll have plenty of time to study."

I thought about it and decided that I deserved to have some fun for once. I'd worked my butt off for my grades since elementary school. Plus, I'd never gone to a real high school party before. And I'm not counting Kayla's party. The only ones I'd been to had just a few people with drinks, music, and movies. Of course, I knew my nerves would be on high alert for the rest of the day. But maybe it would be worth it. Yeah, I deserve this. And Alyssa had even said I'd still have time to study. I couldn't lose.

"Okay, I'll go."

"Great! I'll come over at 8 to pick out an outfit for you." And then she was gone. *Looks like I'll have to study faster tonight*, I thought to myself.

•••

When I walked into the living room to throw off my book bag, I saw Tammi and Kyle sitting on my couch.

"Surprise!" The two yelled in unison. I just stared at them with a smile on my face.

"Hey, guys. What's up?"

"We were thinking about a *Fast and Furious* marathon tonight. You in?"

I was beginning to get nervous.

"Guys, that sounds perfect. But…I have a ton of homework to do tonight." I didn't want to lie to them, but I also didn't want them to accuse me of ditching them for Alyssa.

"Just do it now." Kyle suggested.

"Yeah, we can all do ours together." Tammi added.

"That's really nice, but this is serious alone-time studying. I have two huge tests on Monday and I can't be distracted. Can we do it tomorrow?"

They both exchanged a glance. Kyle bit his lip as if he didn't entirely believe me.

"Sure, if you really have to study. We'll just do it tomorrow." Tammi said.

"Okay, great. Thanks for coming over, though. Really. I've missed hanging out with you, Kyle."

"Later, Tor." Kyle said as they walked out my door.

"Now time to study." I said aloud as I opened my books, preparing to cram for my Chemistry test.

THE (AFTER) LIFE OF THE PARTY

The room smelled like beer and stale crackers. Empty cups and articles of clothing found their way to various parts of the floor. Beer stains were on almost every piece of furniture in the closely-cluttered house. I was already nervous, and this atmosphere was making me feel like an antisocial pessimist already.

I hadn't been able to eat all day; my nerves were so bad. I didn't want this party to end like the last one had. My typical Friday night consisted of sloppy pizza, Cool Ranch Doritos, and a classic movie like *Breakfast at Tiffany's* with my mother. Maybe it was just my nerdy side kicking in, but spending the night with my mom seemed a lot more appealing than being in a house full of drunken kids trying to see how much beer they could chug while inverted in the air before throwing up on one of Luke's thousand-dollar couches.

As I made my way through the throng of people, I managed to step my foot into something sticky. I lifted my leg to reveal a mass of bubble gum and chips that appeared to have been soaked in beer. *Just lovely*, I thought to myself, scraping the gunk off my shoe with a napkin.

"Tori!" Alyssa yelled across the room, "Come over here!"

I watched her cup dangle in her hand as she giggled like she was in line for a Kardashian audition.

"There's someone I want you to meet," she hiccupped.

"This is Joey."

He pushed his thick blonde hair out of his dark brown eyes. His strong jawline and lightly tanned skin sent tingles in certain areas of my body. Tonight he was wearing a fitted button-up.

"Hi," I said.

"Hey, Tori." He greeted, his lip curled in a drunken manner.

"You two know each other?" Alyssa asked.

"Yeah," I said.

"How?"

"Um—" I started, but Joey cut me off.

"We're on the chess team together."

I couldn't believe he openly admitted to being on the chess team with me at an A-list party like this. Alyssa began to laugh, her hiccups becoming uncontrollable.

"You play chess?! That's the funniest thing I've heard all night! You're just full of surprises, aren't you, Joe-Joe?"

Alyssa put her hands on the wall next to us to steady herself.

Feeling some awkward tension, I said, "C'mon, Alyssa, let's get you some water."

I led her to a couch, then walked into the kitchen, running into...Eric. His tall, athletic presence felt intimidating to me, but in a good way. Standing next to him, I felt like a tiny fairy. I stared at his defined jawline and toned arms. He wore a black and white flannel shirt and faded blue jeans.

"Hey, what are you doing here?" He asked me.

"My friend Alyssa wanted to come, so I'm keeping her company." I said, pouring a glass of water from the fridge.

He gave me a shy smile.

"Looks like you're doing a good job."

"I'm just getting her some water. She's pretty wasted."

He looked over towards the couch.

"She doesn't look that thirsty to me."

I turned to the couch to see her full-on making out with some random dude, who I didn't think even went to our school. He looked like he was coaxing her to come upstairs.

"You've got to be kidding me" I said, irritated that my new best friend couldn't have stayed sober until I showed up. Maybe I was jealous, but the girl had a weakness for being "friendly" with boys. I turned back to Eric.

"Let me check on her real quick, and then I'll be back."

I didn't want this rando taking advantage of her when she wasn't sober.

"Hey, 'Lyss, how's it going over here?" I asked her, the rando glaring at me with annoyance.

"Oh, it's going great." She said. "This is Troy. He and I are totes going to hook up."

"Are you sure that's what you want? You only met him just now." I said, putting my arm around her.

"Oh, I know, I know, but it feels like I've known him my whole life. Troy is a gem, Tori, a true gem."

"Why don't we take a little break outside and get some fresh air first?" I cajoled.

"No, I think I'll stay right here with Troy."

She weaseled out from under my arm and moved closer to Troy.

"At least take this water. I got it for you."

"I think she's good." Troy said to me.

"Yeah, Tori, don't be such a party-pooper. I don't want your water." She said, pushing the cup back to me.

"Okay, fine. Just come find me if you need anything." I told her, walking back towards the kitchen doorway where Eric stood talking with another guy from the basketball team.

"How'd it go?" Eric asked.

"I'd say pretty lousy, since she's now straddling Troy in the next room."

"I'm sorry."

"Well, that's fine. I think I'll just drink this water." I said, tilting the cup to my lips.

"Do you want to sit down?" He asked politely.

"Sure."

We both took a seat on the now-empty couch that Alyssa had been making out on.

"I've noticed that you're actually participating in gym class."

"Yeah, I have."

"No bruises?"

I laughed. "No bruises."

"So, it turns out that basketball isn't fatal?" He asked me.

"Apparently not."

"So, I was right."

I gave him a shy smile.

"Just say it. I was right and you were wrong."

"I'm not saying that."

"But it's true!" he laughed.

"I don't have to say anything I don't want to!"

"What if I make you?"

"And how are you going to do that?" I challenged.

He started a tickle-attack, and I retaliated with my own pokes and jabs. Our laughter became so loud that we drew the attention of what felt like the entire room. Someone cleared their throat, and we stopped our tickle-fight in the silence. My face was now completely red.

"Let's go outside," Eric said, running his hand through his hair.

I followed him onto the large wrap-around porch. He grabbed my hand and pulled me further, all the way to a half-court across the street.

"Wait here," he instructed.

"Excuse me?" I said, "I'm not standing out here alone."

"Relax," he counseled. "My car is right over there."

I watched him unlock his dirty brown truck and pull out a basketball from the back seat.

As he bounced it toward me, I asked, "Do you always carry that with you?"

"Pretty much." He smiled. *Jocks.*

Holding the ball in my hands, I asked, "So what is it that you wanted us to do?"

"Well, let's see. We have one basketball, one court, and two people. Hmmm… this one's a little tricky."

"Okay, Dave Chappell, I think I've got it. You're hilarious. But who said I want to play?"

He stopped laughing. "Well, you have no choice in the matter."

"Oh don't I?"

He came up behind me and wrapped his arms around mine, our hands holding the ball as one.

"First, we'll work on your jump shot."

I could feel the warmth of his body against mine. He was right; I really *didn't* have a choice in the matter.

"Hey, Tori!" Alyssa exclaimed as she leaned against a locker.

"Hey,"

"What happened to you last night? Me and Troy looked everywhere for you."

I raised my eyebrows. "What happened to *me*? How about what happened to *you*?!"

Alyssa looked at me like I was insane. "Um, I was hooking up...what did you think I was doing?"

Surprised at her nonchalance, I said. "And you wanted to, right?"

"Of course I wanted to."

"Okay, I'm just checking because you were pretty wasted last night."

"Don't worry, mom, we were safe. I regret nothing."

I didn't know what else to say. I couldn't imagine hooking up with a random guy from a party. I wouldn't even know what to do. Was I the weird one? If so, I needed to kiss Eric before I got too far behind in life.

"Well, I'm glad."

"So back to my original question—What happened to you?"

I couldn't stop the smile from spreading on my face.

"Ohhh...did Tori get some action too?" Alyssa humored.

"I bumped into Eric, and we hung out pretty much the whole time."

"Who's Eric?"

How much *did* she have to drink last night?

"Um, gym class?... On the basketball team?"

"Right, right. He's cute."

"I know."

"So...what'd you guys do? Don't worry, you don't have to spare any details. I love to hear the dirty stuff!"

"Dirty stuff?"

Alyssa began to laugh to herself.

"Wait...you guys didn't do *anything*?"

"We played basketball, and then he drove me home."

"You didn't even kiss?"

"Well, we weren't as drunk as you and that guy you were with."

"Tori, why didn't you guys kiss?"

"He didn't try to kiss me."

"And you're completely helpless? You can't kiss him?"

I thought about it.

"I've never been kissed before."

"Are you for serious?"

I was starting to get a little annoyed with Alyssa. It's not as if I was intentionally avoiding being kissed. I just never had a guy show any romantic interest in me before.

"Yeah, what's the big deal?"

"The big deal is that you're 17 and you're like a child."

Her words bit into me like hail.

"What, I'm a child because I don't put out to every person on the planet?"

"What are you trying to say, Tori?" she asked.

I looked at her and said the words that I couldn't take back.

"I'm saying you're a SLUT!"

Alyssa was taken aback by my ferocity. It was just the reaction I had wanted from her. Of course I didn't mean it, but it did feel good to retaliate.

"Sweetheart, it's okay to be jealous of me. But calling me a slut is crossing the line."

"Jealous?!" I spat at her. "You think I'm jealous of you? Disgusted is more like it."

Alyssa just shook her head at me. "I can't talk to you when you're like this." She then turned and left.

My face was burning with anger and tears stung my eyes. *I'm not a child*, I thought with annoyance. *Who does she think she is?*

I wiped my eyes and began walking to my next class, trying to remember what class it was. *Gym*. Of course.

Thankfully, Alyssa wasn't in class. That was a major load off my mind. We did our warm-ups, ran two laps, and then Mrs. Beyers announced that we'd be playing basketball for the next three days. All the jocks cheered, while everyone else groaned. The stoners just laughed, like they did with everything. And me? Well, I was too busy staring at the team captains to react to the choice of sport for the week. One was Jake Ortega and the other was a cute boy with smooth brown hair.

Mrs. Beyers said, "Okay, Larson, you pick first."

Without hesitation, he said, "Tori Rowling."

It was easy to see the shock in everyone's faces, not to mention Mrs. Beyers'.

With flaming cheeks, I walked over to Eric.

The captains picked their teammates in the usual back-and-forth pattern, with me shooting Eric confusing glances. He didn't seem to notice.

Mrs. Beyers yelled for the game to begin.

Eric stood beside me and said, "We're gonna wipe the floor with them."

Then the whistle blew. Maybe it was the fact that Eric had picked me first for his team, or the fact that Alyssa had been so mean to me, but I actually played the game. It was like the ball had been made for me, and everyone else in the gym was getting their grubby hands all over my possession. Adrenaline pumped through my veins, and everything around me blurred into a watercolor of bodies in motion. The feeling was like none I had ever had before. I felt so...alive. I could feel the release of my anger and frustration pouring out onto the glossy gym floor. And no one in the room could stop me. Some simply sucked at basketball, but most jocks were so surprised that it was really me with the ball that they just watched in amazement.

Our team ended up winning the game, and on my way to the locker room Eric high-fived me.

"You looked good out there, Rowling," he said with a wink.

Before I could respond, he was already on his way to the boys' locker room, exchanging celebratory butt-slaps with the other guys on our team.

...

The next day of school, I was very aware of Eric's presence. I would constantly watch for him in the hallways, and even made an effort to act cool and confident around people just in case he was watching. This was next-level self-conscious for me.

I had never met anyone like him before. He was outgoing and athletic, but also kind and funny. It felt like he was interested in me, but my natural self-doubt was telling me that he was only being nice. I still wished and hoped for him. The giddiness in my stomach brought a giant grin to my face. I didn't want to get ahead of myself, but I did feel something for Eric. Maybe he was the one I could put in my golden heart locket.

While grabbing books out of my locker, Joey turned to face me.

"So, I saw you at Luke's party the other day."

My face burned with embarrassment.

"You—You were there?"

He laughed. "Yeah, I was. You talked to me, remember?"

"Oh yeah, right." *How embarrassing.*

"Well, it looked like you were busy with that Eric kid to notice anything else." He said, smirking. The remark brought my train of thought back to our tickle-fight. Blushing, I began to laugh.

"Yeah, that was a fun party."

Joey took a step forward, close enough for me to smell his Old Spice.

"You know, I'm having a party next weekend. Just a few people, if you're interested."

"Well, I'm—I'm not sure. I may have plans, but I'll let you know."

"Okay," he answered disappointedly. "But I really hope you can make it." he said, tracing his hand down my arm. *Is this really happening?* I thought. As he walked away, I got intense chills, and decided that it was imperative I attend his party.

As I walked to my next class, elation overwhelmed me. I felt like the prettiest girl in the world. Eric seemed to like me and now Joey too? Maybe I was getting ahead of myself, but I didn't care. I was on top of the world, and nothing could bring me down. I set my books on my desk, and saw Alyssa sit down next to me.

"I'm sorry, okay?" She stated immediately.

I thought about how much her friendship meant to me, and the fact that I was invited to a party that she wasn't invited to.

"It's okay."

"And you didn't mean what you said, right?" She asked earnestly. "About the whole slut thing."

"No, of course not." I honestly was only jealous of Alyssa's popularity with the guys in school. I wanted to dress like her and be as outgoing as she was. She had such an ease and social grace with people that I didn't have. My anxiety inhibited me from fully letting go and being myself with people.

Once the school day ended, and I got my books and jacket out of my locker, Alyssa appeared at my side with two blonde girls with fake tans and full face makeup. Their fake eyelashes and contoured cheeks made them look like models.

"This is Kylie and Gina," Alyssa said to me.

"Nice to meet you guys." I said, eager to be on my way.

The blondes smiled politely.

"So anyway," Alyssa began, "we're all gonna get our nails done. Wanna come?"

"I would, but I have band practice."

"Oh, come on, Tori, live a little."

"You know you want to..." One of the blondes was prodding.

It's not like I hadn't entertained the idea of blowing off band for a day in the past. I would have loved to take a day and just go straight home after school, put on the Discovery Channel and down a bag of chips with some French onion dip. But I'd never actually done it. I felt like I couldn't. I'd never skipped band before. It was the perfect way to end the school day, and practically the only time I got to see Kyle during school. *But it would be nice to take a day off*, I thought.

"All right, I'll live a little." I told them.

The blondes squealed and clapped their hands in delight. The four of us got into Alyssa's car, and Kylie turned on the radio to the Top 40. "Lover" by Taylor Swift blasted through the speakers, and I let the beat and melody take my mind away from quarter rests and fermatas as the car took me from the school.

Later that evening, as I sat on my bed staring at my candy apple red nails, the phone rang. As I said hello, Kyle's voice came through the other end.

"Where were you today? Did you go to school?"

"Yeah, I went to school today. I just skipped band."

"You skipped band?" Kyle joked. "Wow, never thought I'd see the day. Must've been serious."

I laughed. "Um, well, actually I was getting my nails done."

Kyle joined in on my laughter.

"What? Did I hear that right? Does this have anything to do with your recent male admirer?"

The question took me by surprise.

"I wasn't aware you even knew about that!"

"Trust me, everyone I've talked to has noticed. You're like a little celebrity now."

"What? You're joking," I laughed. "Who's been talking about me?"

"I don't know," he said, "A lot of people. It's mostly the girls I hear talking about how you and Eric Larson will be the next hot couple."

I couldn't believe it. *Me? The topic of conversation?*

"Wow." I said aloud, letting this news sink in.

"Yeah, well, don't let it go to your head." Kyle warned with a smile in his voice.

We made plans to hang out after school the following day, but all I could think about was how my life seemed to be finally turning around.

I spent the evening with my mom and Corey, playing *Settlers of Catan*. Corey was beating us, as usual.

"How's soccer going, sweetie?" My mom asked him.

"Pretty good so far."

"Yeah, they're getting better." I chimed in.

"Gee, thanks, Tori." Corey rolled his eyes.

"Tori, have you been watching the games?" My mom asked, knowing how much I hated sports.

"Yes, I have, actually." I told her. "Some of my new friends are into it, so I've been checking them out with them."

"I can't believe seeing your little brother play isn't reason enough to watch the games." Corey said, crinkling his nose and pretending he was pained by this fact.

"Oh, get over it." I joked.

"Well, your father and I love watching your games too. We'll definitely be at the next one." Mom said, picking up a few more cards and placing them in her deck.

"Speaking of games," I said, "how about you and dad coming to the next football game to watch me march?"

Corey erupted in laughter. "Tori, you know nobody comes to the football games to see you play your instrument."

"Of course I know that, but mom and dad could. And you could too, you know. It's only fair."

"I already go to the football games."

"And what do you do during our half-time show?"

"Get snacks, like every other normal person there."

"Exactly! Can't you all just come and watch me play? It's important to me."

"Maybe, honey. You know how I hate sitting outside for hours."

"Yeah, mom, I know." And I let it go at that. What was the point in even trying?

...

"I had my date with Brian last night." Tammi told Kyle and me on our way to class the next day.

"How did it go?" I asked.

"Did you guys kiss?" Kyle added.

"Yes, and yes." Her smile was ear to ear.

"O-M-G!" Kyle squealed.

"That's incredible! How was it?" I exclaimed.

"We went to the rock-climbing gym and then got ice cream and took a walk along the river. It was so romantic. He kissed me in the car when he dropped me off."

"That's so adorable." Kyle said with approval.

"I'm really happy for you." I said to her. "Chess club should be more interesting now." I smirked.

Tammi playfully punched my shoulder. "Let's get to class."

IT WAS A GRAVEYARD SMASH

It was the day of Alyssa's Halloween party. The school was decorated with handmade construction paper jack-o-lanterns, cobwebs, and candy-corn streamers.

"Are you guys ready for tonight?" I asked Kyle and Tammi on the front steps of the school.

"Ready as I'll ever be." Tammi said.

"I'm determined to meet someone tonight." Kyle said, his head raised with optimism.

"It's the perfect opportunity for you, since you'll be wearing a mask." Tammi joked.

Kyle slapped her arm.

"Are you bringing Brian?" I asked Tammi.

"I want to." She answered.

"So do it! It's a great opportunity for you guys to go out again." I said.

"Alright, I think I will." She said with a smile.

"Will you be bringing your male friend as well?" Kyle asked me.

I froze in my tracks and Kyle realized his blunder.

"What male friend?" Tammi asked.

"Eric Larson. The guy I asked if you knew the other night."

"Yeah, but you didn't say anything beyond that! Do you like him? How come you didn't tell me about him?"

"I honestly don't know. I guess I just don't feel as close to you anymore."

The words came out before I could stop myself.

"Yeah, and whose fault is that, Tori? I'm not the one pulling away. You need to figure out who you really are."

"I'm sorry, Tammi. I'm just trying to get some more friends and improve my social status this year."

"Totally get it. I wouldn't want to drag you back down to geek status." She said, getting up and grabbing her bookbag in haste. Kyle and I watched her walk away.

"Sorry, Tori." Kyle apologized.

"It's okay. I should've told her in the first place. She's definitely right. I'm the one whose pulling away. I know it's happening, but I feel like there's nothing I can do to stop it."

"You can stop it," Kyle advised. "You have to be honest with her. Be honest with me."

"Okay, I can do that." I said.

"Tori, did you really stay home and study the night we wanted to have a Fast and Furious marathon?"

I looked him in the eye and knew I couldn't lie anymore.

"No, I didn't. I went to a party."

"Why did you lie to us?"

"I didn't want you guys to think I was ditching you for Alyssa."

"But that's what you were doing, right?"

"Yeah, I guess I was. I guess I didn't want to have to admit it."

"It's okay, Tori. I get it. Just don't forget who your real friends are."

"Thanks, Kyle. Do you think you could talk to Tammi for me?"

"I can try, but I think you should talk to her tonight to patch things up."

"If she even comes now." I said, twirling a lock of hair around my finger.

"I'll tell you what; I'll make sure she gets there and you make sure you work it out with her."

"Deal."

...

Alyssa and I skipped 8th period to go set up for her party.

"Do you think they'll notice we're missing?" I asked her in the car ride over to her parents' house.

"I seriously doubt it. They never take role in study hall."

She pulled her Mustang into the long, glossy driveway of an ornate and palatial home. Each room on the second floor had its own balcony and there were two stairways leading up to the front door.

"This is your parents' house?!" I exclaimed in shock.

"Yep. There it is in all its glory."

"Wow, you weren't kidding about it being huge. I can't believe you'd rather live in that apartment than here."

"My apartment is my own space." She said.

"I think you'd have plenty of space here, too."

"I just don't want a palace to feel lonely in. My apartment is cozy, and I don't have to follow anyone's rules there."

"I get it." I said, sensing that she didn't want to be talking about this.

We walked up to the front door and Alyssa turned her key to open it.

"What, no maid in a house this size?" I joked.

"No one is in this house long enough to warrant maid service." Alyssa laughed.

We stepped into the lavishly-furnished great room and I looked around at all of the first-floor rooms in awe.

"Okay, enough gawking. We need to set up for this party. It's my first time hosting one at this school and it has to be perfect."

Alyssa and I hung fake bats on the ceiling, put candelabras on the tables, and we even strategically placed fake blood bags around the first floor. Our painted pumpkins and fake cobwebs were accent pieces for the doorways and mantlepieces. After we finished decorating and placing the food, we changed into our costumes. Mine was a unicorn, complete with a rainbow ponytail and a purple tutu. Alyssa was a red devil, with horns and a fitted corset. Our first guests to arrive were Tammi, Brian, and Kyle.

"This place is insane! Can I get a tour?" Kyle asked Alyssa.

As Alyssa showed Kyle around, I led Tammi and Brian into the dining room.

"Tammi, I'm really sorry about what I said earlier today. I have been pulling away from you and it *is* my fault. I'll try to be honest with you from now on. Do you forgive me?"

"Of course I forgive you," Tammi said. "You are my best friend, after all."

I pulled her into a hug.

"I love you Tammi."

"Love you too, girl." She said, returning my hug. "Brian, have you met Tori?"

"I know you from chess team, but I don't think I've officially met you." He said, shaking my hand.

As time went on, the house began to fill with kids from our class. It felt like our entire senior class was there. People came with all kinds of crazy costumes. Most girls were wearing lingerie with animal ears, but some wore character costumes like Eleven from *Stranger Things* and Jasmine from *Aladdin*. Kyle came dressed as Chucky, and Eric came as James Bond. I had to admit that it was cheesy enough to have me swooning.

"So, this is Alyssa's parents' house?" Eric asked me as I stirred our frothing green magic potion punch.

"Yeah, I never imagined it would look like this." I answered, pouring a cup of the punch from the cauldron.

"You did a great job with the set up." He said.

"Thank you, we worked really hard on it."

"Is this the infamous Eric?" Kyle asked, stopping by us to get a good look at my male friend.

"Hey, you must be Kyle." Eric greeted, extending his hand.

"The one and only."

"Well, it's nice to meet you." Eric said.

"Likewise. Tori's told me a little bit about you, but I'd like to know more." Kyle said, guiding Eric towards the food table.

I waved to Eric as he turned his head over his shoulder, looking apologetically at me. I knew better than to try to stop Kyle. Besides, I wanted to see if Alyssa needed any help in the kitchen.

On my way there, I stopped to see Joey and Amber walk through the front door. Joey had on a Laker's jersey and a sweatband around his head. Amber stood next to him in a tight little purple Laker's cheerleading uniform. She held her pom-poms in one hand, a 6 pack of alcoholic seltzer in the other.

I stared at Joey's chiseled jaw and firm biceps. The jersey accentuated his tall, athletic frame. He looked around the room, stopping his gaze at me. I immediately blushed. He gave me a mischievous smirk, then looked away. Amber followed his gaze, staring me down with dagger eyes.

I quickly continued walking towards the kitchen, but instead I found Alyssa in the hallway.

"Alyssa! Hey, do you need any help with anything?"

She turned to look at me, her face blissfully happy.

"Tori! I love you!" She enveloped me in a giant hug, her weight heavy against mine.

"I love you too." I said, confused by her sudden bravado.

"Let's get the dance floor started!" She said, licking her lips.

She grabbed me by the arm and we ran/skipped out to the living room, laughing the entire way. Her giddiness was infectious.

Alyssa cranked the volume on her parents' speaker, and we started jumping around like we were at a rave. People started flooding in to join us, the rhythm contagious. I could feel the bass in my chest as we let go of all cares on the living room floor.

"This is insane!" Eric yelled to me, he and Kyle wading through bodies to dance with Alyssa and me.

Eric put his arms around my waist, grinding his body against mine. It took me by surprise, but I liked it. I'd never been this close to someone before, especially not in this way. Time seemed to stand still as I danced with Eric, our bodies getting to know each other. I looked around at the massive crowd of people all letting themselves give in to the EDM music.

Everyone looked beautiful and confident, not a care in the world showed on their faces. Something had changed within me. Then I realized…my anxiety was gone. This was the first time I had felt like I wasn't an outsider at a social event. I didn't feel left out or judgmental; I felt like I belonged.

…

The front door slammed with a booming echo.

All of a sudden, the room was silent. Everyone stopped dancing.

"GET OUT!!!" A woman with a brown inverted bob screamed.

"WHAT THE HELL IS GOING ON HERE??"

She pulled out her cell phone from the pocket of her blazer, frantically dialing 911.

I turned to look at Alyssa, but she was gone. I cautiously walked up to the woman.

"Are you Mrs. Perdue?"

She looked at me like I was speaking another language.

"NO, I AM NOT MRS. PERDUE! Explain to me why you are all in my house."

"Well, miss, my friend Alyssa told us that this is her parents' house and she wanted to throw a party." I answered.

"Well, your little friend is a liar, because I am a realtor, and I am showing this property to sell."

"What? That can't be right."

"I really don't care what you believe, little girl. I've already called the cops and they'll be here soon to arrest you all." She said, crossing her arms over her chest in satisfaction.

This would've been the moment I yelled "Cops are coming! Everybody get out!" if I was a loud person. Instead, I told a few people and they did the yelling for me. People scattered in droves, emptying the house in minutes.

I ran out of the house, meeting Eric in the driveway.

"Do you want me to drive you home?" He asked.

"I want to wait for Alyssa." I said.

"Really? The cops will be here any minute." He warned.

Just then, I saw Alyssa come out of the house with two people behind her, covering their naked bodies with bedsheets.

"Wow," Eric said with a smirk, "guess they didn't have time to change."

"Let's get outta here!!" Alyssa screamed, her jaw quivering in excitement.

She ran to the car, and now I had a perfect view of the two people in bedsheets. One was Brett. And the other was Kyle.

"What the hell happened last night?" I asked Kyle as the waitress poured us our coffees.

Tammi, Brian, Kyle, and I were getting breakfast at Marla's Diner after our wild and crazy night.

"I may have had a lapse in judgement," he said, rubbing his head.

"A lapse in judgment? Kyle, you slept with Brett, didn't you?" I whispered.

"What?!" Tammi exclaimed in shock. Brian's eyes widened.

"I know, I know. But I just wanted to meet someone new, and I wasn't in my right frame of mind."

"You mean you were drunk?" I asked.

"No, I didn't drink at all, actually." He said, leaning in close. "I did ecstasy."

Now Tammi was livid.

"You've got to be freaking kidding me." She said, shaking her head. "What is wrong with you? You know that can mess with your brain."

"Listen, I feel embarrassed enough as it is, okay?" He pleaded.

"Where did you even get it from?" I asked him.

"From Alyssa, actually."

Now it was my turn to be outraged. This wasn't how I wanted to blend my friends.

"I can't believe it," I told him. "That explains why she was acting so weird."

"That figures!" Tammi said through forced laughter. "You wanted us to all be best buds and look what happens. Your new friend gets Kyle to do drugs. I knew we shouldn't have come to the party."

"Okay, you're seriously gonna put all this on me?" I asked her.

"It's not Alyssa's fault, she offered and I accepted. I just felt anxious about trying to meet someone, and I thought it would give me some courage."

"I can't even with you." Tammi said to Kyle, leaning in closer to Brian.

"So how was it?" I asked.

Tammi punched me in the arm.

"What? What's done is done, but you have to admit, Brett is pretty hot."

Tammi rolled her eyes and Brian put his arm around her to comfort her.

"Well, if you must know, it was amazing. But it will never happen again. I mean, he's the one who took James from me. What is wrong with me?"

"Nothing is wrong with you," I said, rubbing his arm. "Just chalk it up to one bad night and forget about him."

"Oh, trust me, I will be avoiding him from now til eternity." Kyle said, covering his face with his hands.

"Are you mad at me, Tammi?" I asked.

"Yes, I am, Tori. Kyle, I understand why you did what you did, and I know you're sorry. But you, Tori? You are losing yourself, and you don't even see it."

She took Brian by the hand and the two of them left the booth, leaving money on the table to cover their meal.

"I'm sorry, Tori. She's just taking out her anger on me at you." Kyle said.

"No, I don't think so, Kyle. I think this time she really is mad at me."

"She'll get over it." He assured me.

But she didn't get over it. I tried calling and texting her that evening, and on Sunday, but she wouldn't answer me. I had to talk to Alyssa.

"Hey, girl." I greeted as she opened the door of her apartment to let me in.

"Hey, bitch. Crazy party, right? I think people will be talking about it til the end of the year."

"Yeah, about that...did you give Kyle ecstasy?" I asked.

"Yeah, I did. We both took some in the bathroom together. He was nervous about meeting someone new and I told him I had something to help with that. He didn't have a bad trip, did he? Last I saw him, he was flying high." She smiled.

"No, he's fine. I just didn't know you partied like that." I told her.

"Not usually, but if someone brings it, I'll usually partake. Does that bother you?"

"Not really, I guess. I'm just new to all this stuff."

"No worries, maybe next time I'll share with you." She winked.

"I wouldn't count on it." I told her with a smile.

"Anyway, I wanted to ask you...that wasn't your parents' house, was it?" I asked her.

"Yeah...so about that, it's stupid, but my parents told me last-minute that I couldn't throw the party. Well, I wasn't having that, so I had to find an alternative."

"And breaking into a random house was the alternative?"

"Well, I already told everyone that my parents lived in a mansion, didn't I? I couldn't throw it at my tiny apartment, so I started looking around for new homes for sale and landed on this empty beauty. Who knew they would do a showing at night?" She laughed.

"You are crazy, you know that?" I said through laughter. "I wanted to ask you, though. You said you'll partake if someone brings it. Who brought the ecstasy?"

"Joey."

My stomach did a flip.

"He won't stop texting me," Kyle told me in frustration.

"Who, Brett?" I asked as we walked to the band room together.

"Yes, Evil Incarnate. I apparently gave him my number that night. I'll never do drugs again."

"Are you ignoring him?" I asked Kyle.

"Yes, I am. And what's worse is that now James is giving me dirty looks. He must know. I bet you money that Brett told him."

"Why would Brett do that?"

"Because he's scum of the earth, that's why." Kyle said as we assembled our instruments and took our seats.

"Maybe you should hear him out." I said.

"I'm sorry, did you just say you want me to hear him out? Absolutely not."

"Why not? Are you afraid it's gonna happen again?" I teased.

"Ha! In his dreams." Kyle laughed.

"Tammi is still ignoring me." I said, changing the subject.

"She just needs some time to cool off," Kyle said.

"How much time does she need? It's been 2 days!" I said.

"Maybe she's waiting for you to apologize."

"Apologize for what? For being friends with Alyssa? No way."

"Looks like I'll be playing referee for a while then." Kyle said, sighing.

Mr. Grayson called our band practice to order, listing the pieces we would be practicing. I was determined to keep Tammi off my mind. After all, she and Kyle weren't my only friends anymore.

• • •

Alyssa waited for me after band practice so we could ride home together. As we walked to my car, we ran into Joey and Amber.

"Hey, Tori." Joey said, his eyes crinkled and adorable.

"Hey, Joey, what's up?"

"I wanted to let you know that I had to cancel my party this weekend for the big football game, but I'll let you know when my next one is."

"Oh, yeah, no worries." I said, trying to play it cool.

Giving me a sexy smirk, he said, "I'll see you around though, right?"

"Yeah, sure." I answered.

"That's what I like to hear." He said, walking away.

Amber lagged behind him.

"You better stay in your lane, bitch."

I was so surprised that I just stared at her in fear.

"If I were you, I'd make sure your boyfriend stays in YOUR lane, princess. Because it looks to me like he wants to get in Tori's." Alyssa snapped back for me.

"Whatever, whore." Amber said, huffing as she stormed off to catch up with Joey.

Alyssa and I looked at each other with uncontrollable giggles.

"Did you see her face?" Alyssa laughed.

"She was SO pissed!" I said. "Thanks for defending me, 'Lyss."

"No problem, Tori. That's what friends are for."

We got into my car and started driving to Alyssa's apartment.

"So, let's talk about how your crush has the hots for you." Alyssa said to me.

"Joey? He doesn't! I mean, he couldn't, right?" I asked her.

"Oh, I think we're past the incredulous phase. It's obvious, honey. Joey's into you. My question is, are you interested in him?"

"No! I mean, yes, but he has a girlfriend."

"Yeah, a big, blonde skank." Alyssa rolled her eyes.

"No matter what I feel for him, I wouldn't act on it. He's with Amber, and I respect that."

"So, what about Eric? Are you interested in him?" Alyssa asked.

"Geez, 'Lyss, what's with the interrogation?"

"Can't your best friend ask you personal questions?"

"Okay, yes, I am interested in Eric. But he hasn't asked me out. No boy has ever asked me out."

"Well, this year that will change, Tori. I mean, look at you. You transformed from a shy little band geek into a sexy social butterfly."

"I'm still a band geek, and I wouldn't call me social." I laughed.

"Okay, so we're working on the social part." Alyssa said. "But you have changed, Tori. For the better. And two hot guys are into you. So, who's it going to be?"

I took a moment to think about it.

"Honestly, the first one who asks me out."

...

"I talked to Brett." Kyle said to me at lunch the next day.

"Really? What did he say?" I asked.

"He said that he really likes me and he wants to take me on a date."

"Are you going to go out with him?"

"No. But I at least heard him out." He said with satisfaction.

"Well, I'm glad you talked to him. And now hopefully he'll stop texting you." I said.

"Yeah, we'll see. Are you going to the chess tournament tonight?" He asked.

"No, I don't really feel like it." I said.

"Is it because of Tammi?"

"Kind of. I'd rather not witness her ignoring me in person. But honestly, I'd rather hang out with Alyssa anyway."

"Oh, I see how it is." He teased. "You sick of us nerds?"

"Kyle, I could never get sick of you."

"Well, do you want to hang out before I have to leave for the tournament?" He asked me.

"Sure, sounds good." I said. "What do you want to do?"

"Video games?"

"Alright, but only for you." I laughed.

"Doesn't anyone know the answer?" My AP English teacher asked the class. I knew the answer, but I didn't raise my hand. It gave me anxiety to say my answer aloud, so I avoided it at all costs.

When I raised my hand, people would look at me. If I answered the question, they would be judging what I said and how I said it. If I didn't give the correct answer, embarrassment would flood my cheeks and people would think I was stupid. From my perspective, the more I put myself out there, the greater chance for failure I had. And I was right. People thought I was smart because I was the quiet girl with glasses. It had been that way since elementary school. Why ruin a good thing anyway?

"The answer is 'justice,' but some of you already knew that," the teacher said looking at me. I sunk a little lower in my seat, feeling the embarrassment of her subtly calling me out.

"We're now going to pair up for our original story projects. Tori, you and Amber will be partners." My heart stopped as the teacher continued listing off the pairs.

Of course she would pair us, being the vicious woman that she was.

"How much can I pay you to just do the project for us?" Amber asked me as she pushed her desk next to mine.

"Listen, I don't want to work with you either. But let's just make the most of it, okay?" I said to her with forced confidence.

"Why don't you come over to my house tonight?" Amber asked me.

I was trying to read her face to determine if this was a trick or not.

"Um, sure. What time?"

"Seven." Amber answered, flipping her blonde hair in the air.

• • •

Thanksgiving was right around the corner, and I couldn't wait. Since Alyssa's parents said they wouldn't be coming home til Christmas, my parents said that she could join us for Thanksgiving.

"I can't believe your parents said yes." Alyssa grinned, while standing at my locker.

"They're cool like that sometimes." I told her, spinning my combination lock.

"It's been a while since I've actually celebrated a holiday. Unless you count solo TV binging."

"This will be fun for both of us." I said, giving her a side hug.

"Yes, it will be! Okay, I've gotta run, but we're hanging out after school today, right?" Alyssa asked me.

"Yeah, I'll swing by your place after band." I told her as she walked away.

"Hey," Eric greeted me as I pulled my last book out of my locker.

"Hi, Eric. How are you?"

"I've been good. Just busy with basketball practice. You should come to a game sometime." He suggested, giving me a big smile.

My body heating up with infatuation, I grabbed my locker door to steady myself.

"I would love to come to a game. When is the next one?" I asked him.

"Our next home game is in about two weeks. I'll remind you closer to the time, yeah?" He winked at me.

"Sure, sounds good." I said, elation filling my chest.

"Alright, good seeing you, Tori." He said, sauntering off down the hallway.

I felt like I was floating on a cloud, thinking about the way he had looked at me. *Is this what love feels like?* I thought.

...

"I have to go to Amber's house soon," I told Alyssa as we finished our *Hello Fresh* meal in front of the TV.

"Ugh, I can't believe you have to work with her." Alyssa groaned.

"Yeah, me either. I just hope she doesn't try to kill me while I'm there." I semi-joked.

"I'm just a call or text away," Alyssa said to me as I put on my jacket and grabbed my car key.

"Alright, see ya." I waved to her on my way out the door.

Amber's house was just as gorgeous, if not more so, as the rental home that Alyssa threw her Halloween party in. The floors were glossed in hardwood and a crystal chandelier hung on the great room ceiling.

"I love your house." I told her as we walked through the foyer.

"Thanks," Amber replied, leading me upstairs.

We ascended the large, spiral staircase to Amber's bedroom. Everything in her room was a different shade of purple, from her walls to her bed set. She had a glittering canopy over her bed and satin pillows propped up against the bed frame. My eyes scanned the room, taking it all in. They landed on a massive *Pusheen* collection.

"How many of those do you have?" I asked her, pointing to the built-in shelf containing hundreds of versions of the adorably overweight cat.

"Exactly 225. I keep track." She giggled.

"This is so cool. I love *Pusheen*." I told her.

She walked over to the shelf and began picking each one up to show me.

"I've got Donut *Pusheen*, Piano *Pusheen*, Unicorn *Pusheen*, here he is eating a piece of pizza, Sushi *Pusheen*, now he's reading a book with nerdy glasses..." on and on she went.

It felt nice to have her forget about her hatred of me for a moment.

"Well, we'd better get working." Amber said, placing her stuffed cats back onto the shelf.

"I've got a lot of ideas," I told her.

"Good, because I don't," she laughed.

Amber and I weren't the greatest team, but we managed to get the job done. Our original story was about a witch who desired love and tried to conjure up a love potion. She gave it to the man she desired, but instead of him falling in love with her, he tried to murder her. So, she gave it to another man, but the same thing happened.

She tried two more times until she finally realized that she accidentally made a murder potion and now she spent the entire story coming up with clever ways to run from this handsome mob of killer men. I basically wrote the whole thing, but Amber would chime in with her opinions and ideas as I read aloud the lines that I wrote.

On my way home from Amber's house, I got a text from Tammi.

Hey

Hey, I texted back.

How have things been?

Good. I just left Amber Lawrence's house.

She and I had to write a story together for English class.

Blah. I'm sorry about that. I know how much she hates you.

Yeah, it wasn't too bad.

She was actually nice to me if you can believe that. lol

Wow, that is hard to believe. I'm done being mad
at you, OK? I want my best friend back.

I miss you too. When can we hang out?

Let's hang out tomorrow after school.

Sounds good.

I was shocked Tammi had reached out to me. I really felt she was going to stay mad at me forever. I didn't want to take her friendship for granted anymore.

"Hey, sis." Corey greeted me at our front door.

"Hey, Corey." I said, messing up his hair.

"Staying at home for once?" He joked.

"I'm not always out." I said to him.

My mom came up to me and gave me a hug.

"You're always staying over at Alyssa's house these days, sweetie. I wish you'd hang out with me again. Like we used to."

"I just have more friends these days, mom." I told her.

"I know, and I'm happy for you. I just don't want you to forget about your dear old mom, that's all."

"We'll hang out soon, mom.Maybe see a movie this weekend?"

"I'd like that."

"Then it's a date. Goodnight mom." I said, walking up the stairs to my bedroom.

• • •

We read our story aloud to the class the next day, and it honestly felt like Amber and I were friends. We shared smiles at the front of the classroom, both hoping that we could get an A. Our teacher gave us a B+ due to some grammatical errors, but we both discussed that we were happy with our grade and proud of our work. But once that bell rang, it was as if Amber and I had never been a team at all. She refused to make eye contact with me in the hallway and she tried to get Joey to ignore me as they passed by my locker.

"She's just a bitch." Alyssa told me while we touched up our makeup in the bathroom.

"I know. But I really thought we had a breakthrough at her house."

"If it weren't for Joey maybe you would stand a chance with her, but that boy has a wandering eye, and it's lining up with you. Amber's gotta be territorial with that one."

"I'm not even interested in Joey." I told her.

"You sure about that? I thought you said if he asked you out, you'd say yes."

"That is true, but I've been thinking about it and he's not exactly boyfriend material."

"Ain't that the truth." Alyssa stated. "So, you're looking for just a hookup?"

"No, I'm not. I think I'm over him."

"Well, if that's true, then good for you."

I hated the way she said that, but deep down she knew me better than I cared to admit.

• • •

"I may have hooked up with Nadia last night." Kyle told Tammi and me before band.

"Wait, really? You hooked up with a girl?" Tammi asked.

"Sweetie, you know I play for all teams. And besides, I needed a palate cleanser after that disgusting excuse of a human being."

"How was she?" I asked him with a playful grin.

"A pansexual never tells, my dear."

Nadia was a gorgeous brunette foreign exchange student. She never seemed to give anyone the time of day, but apparently Kyle had broken through the barrier.

"So, are you two gonna be a thing now?" Tammi asked.

"I just said 'palate cleanser,' so no." He crossed his arms. "We agreed this would be hookups only."

"Maybe I'd have a better chance at love if I played for all teams." I stated.

"I don't think you could handle it, Tori." Kyle said. "It's harder than it looks."

"Besides, you are doing pretty well on your own, Tor. How's Eric doing, by the way?" Tammi asked me.

"He's great. We only talk a little bit each day, but I really like him. How about you and Brian?"

"Well, I want to ask him to the Snowball dance, so I'd say it's going well." She replied.

"I forgot all about that." Kyle said, shaking his head.

"Why, are you gonna ask Nadia?" I joked.

"No way. But I do think that if Tammi goes with Brian, then the two of us should go together."

"Why? We've never gone before. Why start now?" I asked him.

"Because we're seniors this year, that's why. I don't want to regret not going to social events. They can be life-changing."

"Ha, yeah right. As in life-changing scarring me."

"C'mon, Tori…please?" He begged.

"I'll think about it."

•••

"So what are you doing for Thanksgiving this year?" Tammi asked me when we met after school.

"Actually, Alyssa is coming over to have dinner with my family. Her family won't be around."

"Don't you think that's kinda weird that her parents won't even be home for Thanksgiving?" Tammi asked me.

"Her parents let her live in her own apartment, so I'd say her life is pretty weird." I replied.

"Yeah, but something's not adding up with her. I mean, why did she throw a party in someone else's house?"

"I already told you, Tammi, her parents wouldn't let her throw one at their house so she had to look elsewhere."

"Yeah, I know. I just think it's odd that instead of defying her parents who aren't home, she breaks into a house instead." Tammi said.

"I've stopped trying to figure out Alyssa's logic." I laughed.

"Want to go to the arcade?" Tammi asked me.

"Of course!"

We drove to the arcade in the strip mall near my house, a black and white building with neon signs in every window.

"You know how I said that Brian and I are doing good?" Tammi asked me.

"Yeah?"

"Well, there is one thing though," she whispered. "I think it bothers him that I'm so tall."

"Well, you are 3 inches taller than him, I guess." I said, trying to understand.

"Yeah, but so what?"

"Does it bother you that he is shorter than you?" I asked her.

"No, it doesn't."

"Are you comfortable confronting him about it?"

"Not really. I'd have to work up the nerve. It's not bad, but sometimes when we are holding hands in the hallway, it looks like he is blushing from embarrassment." She said.

"I'm sure he's just blushing from his infatuation with you." I told her.

"Maybe…" Tammi said, looking at the ground as we walked into the building.

Tammi and I played a few hours of games, then we got dinner at the Italian place next door.

"I had fun tonight, Tori. We'll have to make sure we hang out more often." Tammi said to me on the car ride home.

"Me too. And definitely." I told her, stopping the car to drop her off at her house.

I watched her walk up to her front door, and I smiled. It felt good to have my friend back.

•••

All of my classes went by in a blur, and now it was finally my favorite holiday of the year. I just hoped I passed all of my tests.

"Happy Thanksgiving!" My mom said to me as I walked into our kitchen.

"Happy Thanksgiving, mom." I reciprocated.

"Want to help me make the stuffing?"

I looked into the living room to see what the boys were up to.

"We're watching the Macy's day parade," my dad said as a marching band went by on the TV.

"Sure, I'll help with the stuffing." I told mom.

Alyssa came over right as we pulled the turkey out of the oven.

"Perfect timing," I told her as I held the front door open for her.

"I always arrive when all the work's done." She joked.

"Alyssa! It's so nice to have you here," my mom greeted her.

"Welcome," my dad shook her hand.

"It's nice to meet you." Alyssa replied.

We gathered around the dining room table and said grace. My parents toasted with their glasses of wine and we stuffed ourselves per the great American tradition.

After dinner, the five of us sat around the living room and watched the football games. I helped my mom clean up in the kitchen.

"I like your friend, Tori." Mom said to me as I dried the dishes next to her.

"Yeah, she's pretty cool." I smiled.

"Well, I know she has her own apartment and all, but she's welcome here anytime."

"Thanks, mom."

After we ate our second helping of pie, Alyssa stood up and grabbed her purse.

"I'd better get going, but thank you so much for having me. It was a lot of fun." Alyssa said to my family.

"We loved having you." My mom said.

"Don't be a stranger, now." Dad chimed in, walking her out the door.

"See you tomorrow!" I said, waving to her as she got into her car.

"It's nice to see you have some attractive friends." Corey said.

"I'm gonna kill you, Corey." I said, chasing after him.

FAKE HAPPY

"Alyssa's birthday is next week." I told Kylie and Gina at lunch.

"I LOVE birthdays!" Gina squealed.

"I want to do something special for her." I told them.

"Let's throw a party!" Kylie said, as if this was an original idea.

"Yea, but what kind of a party?" I asked her.

"Like a themed party."

"Hmm...let's do a luau!" I said with excitement.

"Great idea!" Kylie said, pulling out a notebook from her purse.

We brainstormed for the rest of our lunch period, but we hadn't agreed on anything yet.

"Let's meet at my house after school." I told them.

"Perfect!" they answered in unison.

...

"We made up, right?" Tammi asked me after band practice on Thursday.

"Yeah..." I said in confusion.

"Just checking, because we haven't hung out all week." She said to me.

"Yea, sorry. Kylie, Gina, and I are planning Alyssa's birthday party next week."

"Sounds fun. I hope I'm invited." She said with a smile.

"Of course you are!" I told her. "It's going to be a luau at my house."

"I'll be sure to wear my grass skirt."

"I'll text you more info when we have it." I told Tammi.

"Okay. I'll let Kyle know too so he can plan his outfit accordingly."

"How's chess going? I feel like I'm not even on the team anymore." I asked.

"Well, we're doing okay. But I doubt we'll make it to finals. I know you're busy and all, but don't forget about us little people, okay?"

"You have nothing to worry about. I've learned my lesson." I said.

And I really thought I had learned my lesson. But as it turns out, I was about to ruin everything.

...

"Okay, we just have to go over the guest list." Amber said at our table during study hall. I hadn't spoken to Amber since we worked on that story project together, but Kylie and Gina had roped her into our party-planning group.

After all, she was the queen bee of the school.

"I've got it right here," Gina said, handing Amber a piece of notebook paper with 20 names written on it.

"20 people? Tori, can you even fit that many people in your house? No offense." Amber said.

"None taken. Actually, 10 would fit comfortably. Any more than 15 would be too much. We'd be crammed in like sardines." I answered.

"Great. Let's slim down this list." Amber said.

We ranked the names by how close they were to Alyssa, which meant that my friends had to go.

"We have to cut Kyle and Tammi." Amber said. "Sorry, Tori."

"No, I can't. I already told them that they were invited. They picked out outfits and everything."

"They'll understand, Tori. They're not even Alyssa's friends anyway."

"I think we can make it work." I told her. "I don't want to cut them."

"Listen, sweetie. I know you are best buds, but you are in the popular crowd now, and you have to make sacrifices. Honestly, I wouldn't want them at the party anyway. We have an image to maintain."

"Seriously? There's no way you can be that mean." I said to her.

Kylie and Gina stared at me as if I had challenged a dragon to battle.

"Okay, here's what's going to happen. You either disinvite your little friends or YOU will be disinvited." Amber said.

"But the party is at my house! And I'm the one in charge."

"Not anymore. I'll take this party from you and I'll change the venue. My house is nicer anyway."

"Fine," I told her, not wanting to argue anymore. "I'll disinvite them."

"Good girl." said Amber.

I felt like an evil person. I tried to stand up to Amber, but she threatened to take the party away from me. And I had worked so hard on it, I didn't want it to be all for nothing. But how could I tell my best friends that they couldn't come to Alyssa's party? They'd never speak to me again. Amber said I had to make sacrifices to be popular, but why? This wasn't what I had wanted at all.

●●●

Tammi and Kyle stared at me in confusion in the entrance of the school.

"But the party's at your house, right?" Kyle asked.

"Yes."

"But we can't come to your house?" Tammi asked.

"No, not this time. Alyssa has a lot of friends, and there won't be enough room."

"You're saying you can't make room for us? Tori, just tell us the truth." Tammi prodded, her anger rising.

"Amber said I have to disinvite you guys or she's taking the party away from me and I'll be disinvited."

It felt good to said it out loud to them.

"Seriously? She hates us that much?" Kyle asked.

"She just wants it to be exclusive." I said.

"Well it sounds like she's already taken the party from you." Tammi said.

"So, you're choosing the party over us?" Kyle asked.

"Well, when you put it like that..." I trailed off, feeling terrible.

"It's fine." Tammi said. "You made your choice, Tori. I hope it was the right one."

Before I could say anything back, the two of them had ran out the door. I suddenly felt sick to my stomach.

•••

After a long week of Tammi and Kyle avoiding me, knowing it was Friday felt like a relief. Alyssa was turning 18 that day, but she seemed sad for some reason.

"Are you okay?" I asked her as we walked to gym class.

"Yeah, I'm fine." She answered, looking down at the blue tiled floor.

"It's your birthday, you should be over the moon," I told her.

"I am. It just feels weird to be an adult."

"Are you excited for your party tonight? My mom is decorating the house as we speak." I told her.

"That's great. Thanks for being such a great friend, Tori."

•••

All of Alyssa's friends from school were already at the house before we arrived.

My living room was decorated like a giant tiki hut, complete with pineapple string lights and a banner that read **HAPPY BIRTHDAY, ALYSSA!**

Alyssa beamed as she took in the sight.

"I love it," she told my mom. "Thank you so much."

"Of course, sweetie. Since your parents can't be here, we wanted to help."

"Let's get you a drink." I told her, steering her to the kitchen.

"We have three different mocktails...pink sangria, lemon pie, and cherry limeade." I said, pointing at each pitcher.

"I'll try the pink." Alyssa said, pouring the pitcher of sangria into a cup. She pulled a mini bottle of vodka out of her purse and spiked it.

"Do you always carry that in your purse?" I asked her.

"Cheers," she said with a mischievous smile, tipping her cup towards me as if she was toasting.

It was her party, I guess she could get drunk if she wanted to. Either way, I had to make sure I kept an eye on her. I didn't want anyone taking advantage of her tonight.

"Great party." Eric said to me as he placed a gift and card on the gift table.

"Thank you." I said to him, watching Alyssa dance in the living room with some of her popular friends.

"It was a group effort." Amber said, sidling up next to Eric.

"Sure." I smiled.

Amber rested her hand on Eric's shoulder.

"Where's Joey tonight?" Eric asked Amber, pulling away from her touch.

"This isn't really his kind of party." She said.

"Want to dance?" I asked Eric.

"I thought you'd never ask." He said, taking my hand in his.

We waved goodbye to Amber as we joined the living room conga line.

Everyone at the party was having a blast. Kids were talking to my parents, people were laughing and eating, and the dancing was on fire. It felt incredible to be dancing with Eric again after the last party. But my elation was interrupted when I saw Alyssa sneaking towards the kitchen door with her coat on.

"I'll be right back," I told Eric, running to catch up with her.

I caught her just outside the back of the house.

"Are you leaving?" I asked her.

"Just for a bit," she said.

"What? Where are you going?"

"To meet this guy on Tinder. He's super hot."

"You have Tinder?" I asked.

"I'm 18 now, remember? This is my birthday gift to myself."

Her smile was triumphant and sad.

"We haven't even sang to you," I pleaded. "You haven't made a wish and blown out your candles. I thought you liked your party..."

"I do like the party. But I've made my own wish for tonight, and I need it to come true."

A blue sedan pulled up to the driveway.

"This is him," she said, walking towards the car. "Thanks for the party, Tori. I'll see you later."

I watched her get into the tinted-windowed car with a complete stranger, feeling paralyzed. Eric stood beside me.

"Alyssa's leaving her own party?" He asked.

"Yep. Tinder date." I answered.

He put his arm around me. "I'm sorry, Tori," he said.

"It's okay. I just need to tell my parents before they bring out the cake."

We walked back into the house to the tune of 13 people singing "Happy Birthday."

We were too late.

My mom held the candle-lit cake as people completed the song, eyes searching for the birthday girl.

"Alyssa left." I said to the group.

"What? Is everything okay?" Mom asked.

"Yes, she just had a date. She forgot to tell us." I said.

Confusion showed on everyone's faces, and they started murmuring amongst themselves. My mom and dad went into the kitchen to load up the dishwasher while I sliced up the cake for everyone to eat. For the rest of the evening, people sat around chatting. Everyone began leaving sporadically until it was only Kylie, Gina, my parents, and myself. Kylie and Gina helped us clean up, and then they went home.

"See you on Monday!" Kylie said to me.

"Sit with us at lunch," Gina said with a wink.

"Sounds great." I said to them, closing the door.

"That was very rude of Alyssa to leave her party like that." Mom said to me as I sat down on the couch.

"I know, mom."

"We did all that work for her, and she clearly didn't appreciate it," she huffed.

"I totally agree with you," I said to her.

"You need to reexamine your friends, Tori, because I don't want that girl rubbing off on you."

It wasn't fair that my mom was taking out her anger at Alyssa on me, but I didn't feel like fighting. I just wanted to go to bed.

I hugged my parents goodnight, then I climbed the stairs to my bedroom. As I bent to turn out my bedside lamp, I saw Alyssa's purse on the floor.

I hope she doesn't need this, I thought.

I opened it and pulled out her small bottle of vodka, wondering why she would carry that around with her. I placed the vodka back inside the purse, noticing a small zipper compartment. I opened it to find a stack of credit cards.

How could she have credit cards already? I wondered.

I looked at the names on the cards, thinking maybe they were her parents'. But each card had a different name on it.

SARAH ROSE
AMELIA HAWTHORNE
CLAIRE RODRIGUEZ
DEANNA COPPERFIELD

Fear prickled my skin as I turned the cards over and over again in my hands. Visa, Mastercard, Capitol One, Discover…all with these random names…

What was going on?

I had to talk to Alyssa.

PARDON ME

I sat with Amber, Kylie, Gina, and Alyssa at lunch on Monday. As I ate my French bread pizza, I looked over at Kyle and Tammi's table. They were sitting with some of the chess team people and a few band kids. I made eye contact with Kyle and he smiled.

Well, that's a start, I thought.

"Wow, that's quite an outfit…" Amber said, pointing to an overweight girl in a pair of overalls.

"What are you doing, Amber?" Gina asked, giggling uncontrollably.

I stared in horror as Amber took a video of the overall girl walking to her table.

"I'm posting this on TikTok. I'll call it 'The newborn elephant.'"

"You are awful," Kylie laughed.

"I know." Amber said with a smug smile.

"Hey, that's mean." I said to her.

Amber gave me her death glare as our table went silent.

"Go sit with her then," Amber said to me. "If you're not one of us, then you belong over there with the newborn elephant."

My cheeks flushed and I sat still while all the girls stared at me. It felt like a minute had gone by before Amber broke the silence.

"That's what I thought," she said, giving me a look that warned me never to challenge her again.

• • •

"How was your Tinder date?" I asked Alyssa during gym class. We were playing tennis, so it was easy for us to pair up and chat while casually playing the game.

"It was just a hookup, but it was nice. He was a cool guy," she said, serving the ball to me.

"That's good," I said, "Oh, I almost forgot. You left your purse at my house."

"Well, that's a relief. I noticed it was gone that night, but I forgot to text you. I was hoping it was there. Thanks, Tori."

"Yeah, I'll give it to you tonight. But I wanted to ask you…I found a stack of credit cards in your purse with random names on them?"

Alyssa froze for a moment. "You went through my bag?" She asked.

"The vodka bottle fell out, so I put it back in and that's when I looked inside." I answered.

"Well, I'll forgive you for snooping. I mean, I probably would've done the same thing. But those aren't random names, Tori. Those are my parents' employees' cards. My parents put their payroll on the card and then they use the card like a credit card. They're in my purse because they got mailed to my parents' house by mistake, so now I have to deliver them to the employees. It's annoying, really."

"Okay," I said to her, trying to determine the validity of her story. But how much did I even know about payroll and credit cards? And if she wasn't being honest with me, then what was the alternative answer? Was I trying to accuse my best friend of some type of fraud? I shook the thought from my head.

• • •

Alyssa, Kylie, Gina, and I went to watch my brother's soccer game that evening. All three of us had enough snacks and drinks in front of us to feed ten people. As the girls gossiped about members of our class, I pulled out my phone to text Kyle.

> **Hey, how's it going?**
> I hooked up with Brett again :(
> **NO WAY!!**
> I am an idiot.
> **It's ok to be attracted to him**.
> I need more self-control.
> **No lie Brett IS a hottie ;)**
> LOL

ONE DANCE

"Do you have your tickets to the snowball dance?" Gina asked me as I placed my phone back into my bag.

"Not yet. I was waiting to see if someone would ask me to go with them."

"No one's asked you?" Kylie inquired.

"No." I answered, hanging my head.

"I bet you Eric will ask you." Alyssa said with a smile.

Kylie and Gina agreed with her, their positive remarks reverberating off one another.

"Thanks, guys." I told them.

I just hoped they were right.

...

"I dumped Brian." Tammi told Kyle and me in the hallway the next day.

This news must've transcended whatever fight we were currently in. Tears welled in her eyes.

"What?! Why?" Kyle asked.

"I confronted him about how he seemed uncomfortable around me in public, and he admitted that he didn't like that I was taller than him."

It looked like she was more upset that she had to dump him than that he wasn't her boyfriend anymore. I knew my best friend wouldn't play the victim.

"Well, I think you made the right decision," I told her. "You are a fierce woman who doesn't need a weak man to drag her down."

"So, you think Brian is weak?" Kyle asked me.

"I think any man who is intimidated by Tammi's height is weak."

"Thanks, Tori." Tammi said to me.

I gave her a hug.

"Do you want to watch movies tonight and eat ice cream?"

"You know me too well." She laughed.

"I'll see both of you tonight then." I said, waving goodbye as I walked to my last class of the day.

Everything was beginning to feel right again after a night of consoling Tammi. Kyle and I listened to her talk and cry, with movies on in the background. It seemed that I had been forgiven once again, and I knew this was what true friendship was all about. I didn't need a date to the snowball dance. I'd never had one before, why should this year be any different?

"Hey, Tori." Eric greeted me at my lunch table the next day.

"Hi, Eric. Sorry about Alyssa's birthday party. I know it was a real bummer."

"No, it wasn't. I mean, it sucked that Alyssa bailed on her own party, but I had a lot of fun with you." He smiled.

My cheeks flushed.

"Well, good. I had fun too."

"I actually came over here to ask you something, Tori."

My heart started beating faster, butterflies erupting in my stomach. "Yes?"

"Do you want to go to Snowball with me?"

His face was so innocent, kind, and gorgeous. How could I say no?

"I would love to go to Snowball with you," I told him, "but my friend Tammi just broke up with her boyfriend and I kind of wanted to go with her to the dance so she's not left out."

I couldn't believe I was turning down the first boy to ask me to a dance. I hoped he didn't think I was lying or uninterested in him.

"That's okay, Tori, I get it. You should be there for your friend. No worries."

"Thanks so much for understanding, Eric. Save me a dance?"

"Of course." He wrapped me in a hug. "See you later."

• • •

"Did he ask you?" Alyssa asked me later that day. "I saw you two at lunch together."

"No, he didn't." I lied.

"No way! I can't believe that. Let me talk to him."

"Please don't, Alyssa. It's okay. Tammi just broke up with Brian, so I wanted to go with her to keep her company."

"Sounds like a lame excuse to me, but whatever. I'm going with Jeff Townsend."

Jeff was on the football team and always had a different girl on his arm each week. He was also one of the most attractive boys in our senior class, so he and Alyssa would make an excellent couple.

"That's great, 'Lyss. You two will look great together."

"Thank you, Tori. I've been trying to ask him out all week, and I finally got my hands on him. He is such a sweet guy!"

"I'm sure he is. You better introduce him to me at the dance."

"Are you going to run away if I do?" She asked with sarcasm.

"Hey, now. That's a low blow. Don't make fun of my anxiety." I teased.

I was the first person to make fun of my anxiety. At least I owned up to it.

"Sorry, sorry. Man, I wish you were going with Eric. Then we could all sit together."

"Meaning you don't want to sit with Tammi." I said.

"Tori, I will obviously be at Amber's table, and it's full already."

"Oh, I know. Don't worry, I wasn't actually going to try to sit with you guys."

"Well, maybe I'll see you there. Bye, Tori." Alyssa said, leaving me at my locker to catch up with Gina in the hallway.

RETURN TO SENDER

It was finally the night of the Snowball dance. It was cold and dreary outside, but soon we would be in a sweaty gym filled with boys and girls in formal wear listening to a budget DJ play "the hits."

"C'mon, Tori. You need to work on your attitude." Kyle said to me as he zipped up the back of my dress.

"I don't know why I thought I wanted to go to this." I said.

"Classic introvert move." He laughed.

"Tori, you know we're the same. I was all hype too, but now I keep worrying that I'm going to see Brian there. Maybe we should just stay in and watch movies." Tammi told me.

Before I could agree with her, Kyle stopped me.

"Oh no, no, no. This is not happening. We are not killing the mood," he said, steering me to my purse and my coat. "We are getting excited for a super fun night with so much potential. Plus, we already bought the tickets."

Tammi and I tag-teamed punching Kyle in jest.

...

Upon entering the gymnasium, the three of us were immersed in the snowy winter display of hundreds of hanging snowflakes, white tablecloths, and gold-colored place settings. Classical music played from the speaker system, filling me with excitement and surprise.

"You must be loving this." Kyle said to me as I nodded to the beat of the music.

"You have no idea." I said, grinning.

"I knew I shouldn't have come." Tammi said, crossing her arms.

Kyle and I looked in the direction of her gaze, landing on Brian with a short blonde girl.

"Son of a bitch moved on already?" Tammi said aloud, her eyes beginning to water.

I always hated seeing Tammi cry. She was such a strong person, sometimes I forgot that she had weaknesses too.

"Trust me, this isn't him moving on, Tammi. This is him trying to pretend he's okay." I told her.

"Let's get some punch." Kyle said as Tammi dabbed her eyes with a tissue.

On our way to the punch table, we passed by Amber's table. She and Joey were making out while everyone else at the table looked bored, staring down at their phones.

"Fancy seeing you here," Eric said, sidling up next to me by the punch bowl.

"Hey, you." I smiled.

"Hey, man, how's it going?" Kyle asked Eric.

"I'm great. Just showing up for the free food and hopefully get a dance with Tori."

"You really are quite charming. I can see what Tori sees in you." Kyle said with a wink.

"I'm going to go find our table." Tammi said, turning away.

"I'd better go follow her." I told the boys. "Eric, I'll catch up with you later."

When we got to our table, I sat down beside Tammi.

"How are you doing?" I asked her.

"I've been better. I just really hate seeing him with another girl."

"I know." I told her. "But he doesn't deserve you, Tammi. Any guy who doesn't worship the ground you walk on is unworthy."

"You mean like Eric?" She asked me.

"What? He doesn't worship the ground I walk on. We aren't even a couple."

"Not yet, anyway. And if he wants you to save him a dance, why didn't he ask you to the dance?" Tammi asked.

"He did ask me."

"So why aren't you here together then? Did you say no?"

"Yes, I did say no, but only because I wanted to keep you company."

"Really? I can't believe that! Tori, how could you say no to him?! He's like perfect!" She exclaimed.

"Tammi, you are more important to me than a guy. We've been friends for way too long for me to ditch you for a date."

"Wow, well that was really sweet of you, Tori. But totally unnecessary. Besides, Kyle would've been my date."

"I know, but somehow it wouldn't have felt right being here without you guys. After all, we did agree to go to this thing together."

"Did I miss something?" Kyle asked, sitting down next to Tammi.

"Only the fact that Tori turned down Eric Larson as a date to be with me tonight."

"Wow, look at you, turning down hot guys." Kyle teased.

"Oh, look, our salads are here." I said, trying to change the subject.

The server set our chilled salads down in front of us, with two other couples taking their seats at our table. Kyle tried to make small-talk with them, but Tammi and I whispered amongst ourselves. There was no need to have awkward conversations with people we had no intention of ever seeing again. Once the meal ended, the DJ began playing "Yummy" by Justin Beiber and people started making their way onto the dance floor. Tammi and I stayed at our table, watching everyone else wind their bodies in motion to the music at the center of the gym. Tammi obviously didn't feel like dancing, and neither did I.

"May I steal you for a dance?" Eric asked me, standing in front of me at my chair with his hand out.

I looked at Tammi.

"Go ahead. She's all yours." She said.

"I'll be back." I told her.

Eric and I danced for two songs, the muscle memory of our bodies giving in to the pulsating beats reverberating through the gym. I could feel the bass in my chest as Eric slid his hands around my waist, gently pulling me closer to him. He held me against him as we swayed to the music, making me feel like nothing bad could ever touch me again.

As I walked back to Tammi, I saw Brian talking to her at our table.

"I know, but I made a mistake, Tammi. I want you back."

"I haven't shrunk in inches, so I'm not sure what's changed for you." Tammi said with her hands on her hips.

"I was wrong, okay? Yeah, I felt insecure about our height difference and I thought I couldn't handle it. But that was stupid."

"What about your date?" Tammi asked him.

"She's a nice girl, but she's not you. I told her about you and how I wanted you back. She understood. I want the girl who intimidates me and challenges my beliefs and insecurities."

"Okay," Tammi said with a smile, "we can try this again. But you can't just leave your date."

"Don't worry, I got it." I told Brian before he could speak.

"Thanks, Tori." He answered.

A slow song started, and the two of them began to dance as if they were the only ones in the crowded gymnasium. I spotted the short girl, meeting her at the snack table.

"Hey, I'm Tori. Brian told me what happened. Are you okay?"

"Yeah, I am. I honestly just went with Brian because he was the only guy that asked me. I just want to dance and have a good time." She said.

"Well, that's easy." I told her.

I waved Kyle over and he slowly made his way to us.

"Can we join you on the dance floor?" I asked him.

"Why, of course. Let's go!" He said, grabbing both of our hands and leading us into the throng of dancing bodies.

It really was the perfect evening. The three of us danced freely, and Eric, Tammi and Brian eventually joined us in a circle. There were no couples, just a group of individuals dancing their hearts out. We showed off our goofy dance moves with Amber looking over and rolling her eyes at us. But I didn't feel self-conscious this time; Instead, I felt protected by friendship.

"Hey, bitch." Alyssa ran over to me as they began announcing the Snowball king and queen.

"Hey, Alyssa. Where's your date?"

"Oh, he got sick and had to go home. Drank too much of his flask, I guess."

"That's too bad. How was it at Amber's table?" I asked her.

"Very boring. Those people are too wrapped up in their socials to actually experience anything real. I should've just sat at your table." Alyssa said, hugging me.

"So, what are you going to do now?" I asked her.

"I'll probably just go home and Netflix and chill." She said.

"By yourself? 'Lyss, do you know what that means?"

"Of course I do. Have you never 'chilled' with yourself?" She said, eyebrows raised.

We both started cracking up.

"There's something I have to tell you guys." Kyle announced at our lunch table on Monday. "I danced with Brett at the snowball dance."

"What?! No way." I squealed.

"Did you guys hook up again?" Tammi asked him.

"No, we didn't. James saw us dancing and ran off. Brett chased after him... so I'm not really sure what's going on right now."

"Are you mad that Brett ran after him?" I asked.

"Not really." Kyle said. "I'm just annoyed. I mean, if he wants to be with me then why would he go console his ex? I don't know, this is all too dramatic for me. I felt like giving in to my desires and it blew up in my face. Maybe I'm better off staying away from Brett."

"I'm all for protecting your heart, but if you really like him, then you need to give him the benefit of the doubt. Don't just assume the worst. Talk to him and find out what happened." Tammi advised.

"Thanks, Tammi. Glad to have my wise friend back to her old self."

"Glad to be back." Tammi said, grinning.

"Group hug!" I exclaimed, wrapping my arms around the two of them.

...

It felt weird to be back in band after so many weeks of skipping practices. The week before, Mr. Grayson called me into his office to talk to me about my commitment to the band. I apologized and told him that I'd be sure to come to more practices from now on. Band had always felt like the one activity where I was an active participant, instead of a social bystander. But my heart didn't seem to be in it.

Every time Mr. Grayson stopped to work on sections that I didn't have a part in, my mind kept wondering what Alyssa and the girls were doing. What conversations was I missing out on? What inside jokes would I not be a part of?

I still talked to Kyle during our down time, but I couldn't shake the feeling that I was above all this now—playing music that wasn't challenging with the same people day after day, year after year. I took my saxophone apart, placing the pieces into my instrument case. The people around me watched with confusion, but thankfully Mr. Grayson didn't notice.

"Where are you going?" Kyle asked in a whisper.

"I have to go." I told him quietly. "We can still hang out tonight, though."

Kyle had a worried look on his face, and I had a sinking feeling in the pit of my stomach. But I pushed past it. I had made my decision.

And before he could say anything, I picked up my book bag and left the band room. Once in the hallway, I pulled out my cell phone and FaceTimed Alyssa.

As soon as Alyssa's face appeared on my phone, she said, "Girl, get your ass down to my apartment, pronto!"

"Will do," I answered back with a smile.

• • •

It was only 4:00 p.m., but Alyssa, Kylie, and Gina all had glasses filled to the brim with wine.

"Pour this woman a drink!" Alyssa told Gina.

Gina turned to me and said, "We have Moscato, Riesling, and Merlot."

Since I'd never had wine before, I really had no clue which one to pick. "You choose," I told her.

Gina squealed. "Oh, goody! You're gonna have Moscato, Just. Like. Me." She laughed, pouring from the bottle with the pink liquid.

"You'll have to drink fast to catch up with us," Kylie told me.

"Oh, I'm not looking to catch up."

Alyssa finished off her white wine, and then asked, "So how was band?"

"Boring," I told her. "So I left early."

"Wow, look at you go, miss rebel." Alyssa joked.

I smiled and said, "I couldn't have you girls causing trouble without me."

The blondes laughed hysterically as I chugged my first glass of Moscato. It felt so good to just up and leave something scheduled and be released into complete and utter freedom. The whole evening, I felt as if I was someone else, not just Tori Rowling - good student, band geek, loyal friend.

We played lawn games for hours in Alyssa's spacious yard and snacked on veggies with dip and pita chips with hummus, Kylie's contributions. The wine loosened me up, and I began thinking about how much fun I used to have in chess and in band. I really did enjoy being part of a team who truly cared about the activity and each other.

But popular girls weren't in chess and band. They enjoyed drinking after school, attending parties to socialize, and focused on appearances. I felt like an imposter, not truly believing that I was one of them. Even now I still couldn't get past the labels I'd carried my whole life.

"Is it worth it?" I asked Alyssa while we sat on a bench as Kylie and Gina went inside to grab more wine.

"Is what worth it?"

"Is being popular all it's cracked up to be? I just don't want to lose the person I was before you found me."

Alyssa laughed. "Tori, no one's making you do anything you don't want to do. If you don't want to hang out with us, then you can go back to band. This was your choice. It's always been your choice. If you want to know my opinion," she said, taking a sip from her wine glass, "I think you like being popular more than you care to admit. Look how much fun we're having, Tori. I doubt you'd be having this much fun at one of your chess meetings."

"Why does it have to be one or the other, though?"

"It's just the way it is, Tori. Nobody thinks you're cool if you're in band or if you play chess. Stick with me, and you'll be having the best senior year ever."

I thought about it, and maybe she was right. After all, it was getting easier and easier for me to skip practices and cancel plans with Tammi and Kyle. Maybe this was truly what I wanted.

Three glasses of wine later, Kylie and Gina were dancing around the crackling flames of the fire pit, Alyssa was singing "Old Town Road," and I was spinning in circles looking up at the stars above me. Just as Alyssa began the line "You can't tell me nothin'," a car door slammed. Four guys got out of the truck and walked toward us, one of them looking very familiar to me.

"Boys!" Alyssa screamed into the evening air, as the blonde guy picked her up in his arms. Two more of the guys made their way to our little bar of wine and campfire food, and the fourth boy walked up to me.

"Hey, Tori." Eric said shyly.

My heart jumped, butterflies spreading their wings in my stomach.

"Hi, Eric."

I could still feel his hands on me that night of Luke Gaynor's party, guiding me through the proper way to shoot a basketball. And here he was alone with me.

"So, what's up?

"Oh, not much," I said, searching my brain for something to say.

"Want a drink?" was all I could think of.

"No thanks," he replied. "But I will take a hot sausage."

"Well then, you're in luck," I said with gathered bravery, "because sausages are my specialty."

As soon as the words left my mouth, I knew the error in my word choice. I put a hand over my mouth in embarrassment, eyes wide. Eric burst out in laughter.

"Oh, they are?"

I started to laugh along with him.

"That's not what I meant!" I was laughing so hard my eyes were watering.

"I just didn't know you were like that, Tori." He said with a smirk.

"Well, now you can just do your own sausage." I told him as our laughter subsided.

With the smirk still on his face, Eric replied, "What, you don't think you can handle my sausage?" He cracked up again.

"Okay, I'm done." I said through laughter, walking over to a wooden bench by the fire. Eric followed behind and sat down with me.

"I'm sorry, Tori," he said in his laughter, putting his arm around me.

My skin tingled. I looked at him, trying not to smile, but it was impossible. I leaned into his embrace, my head against his chest.

He stroked my arm as we watched the fire burning brightly in the night. He asked me questions about my life: my interests, hobbies, and family. I found out that he was originally from Wisconsin, he loved hip-hop, and he was very close with his dad.

We sat there together talking about our lives, watching our friends as if they were background noise. I could see Alyssa passed out on the couch through the living room window. Two of the guys were talking and eating by the fire and Jamal was chasing Kylie and Gina around the yard, their shrieks echoing through the night air.

Once it hit 11:00, Kylie and Gina were passed out, and the boys wanted to leave. I couldn't believe it was that late. We had school tomorrow.

"I'd better go too." I said aloud, stretching my arms above my head. The boys were already getting into the truck.

"Hurry up, Eric, or we're leaving without you," One of them yelled across the yard.

"I'll be there in a sec." Eric yelled back.

We looked at each other in silence. After maybe five seconds, I broke it.

"Well, it was nice talking to you," I said lamely.

Just as I turned to walk away, Eric took my hand.

"Tori," he said, "Would you want to go out with me sometime?"

I couldn't believe it.

"Yes." I sputtered.

He smiled. "Okay, then." Then he walked away, into the truck with his buddies.

I watched them drive out of the stone walkway and let a smile creep onto my face. The smile didn't leave as I lay in bed that entire night.

...

The next day of school seemed so ordinary to me. I found myself daydreaming in most of my classes. I felt as though I was floating down the hallways, simply going through the motions. Tammi woke me up from my dreamlike state.

"What did you do to Kyle?" She asked me on our way to Trig.

"What are you talking about?" I asked in confusion.

"He said you guys had plans last night, but you ditched him."

My jaw dropped. I had forgotten Kyle.

"Oh, crap..."

"Yeah, he's been down all day."

"I can't believe I forgot our plans."

"What happened? He said you left band early?"

"I went to hang at Alyssa's house, but I lost track of time."

"What were you guys doing?"

I tried to stop the smile from spreading onto my face.

"Well, actually," I began telling her all about Eric and me.

"Wow," she said as I finished my story. "He finally asked you out."

She smiled. "So, when is the big date?"

That was the question I'd been thinking about all day.

...

At lunchtime I sat across from Alyssa, as usual, eating a chicken patty sandwich. Kylie and Gina joined us, talking about how much fun they had had the night before. As I opened my chocolate pudding cup and laughed at Gina's impression of Kylie's shrieking, a boy came up to our table and handed me a chocolate milk carton with a note attached to its side.

"This is from the man over at that table," he told me, pointing to Eric two tables over from us.

He smiled and waved. As the girls teased me with chants of "Tori and Eric sitting in a tree..." I opened the note. It read:

Mini golf and ice cream at Gilligan's 7:00 tomorrow night?
( )Yes   ( )No

"That is so adorable and old-fashioned!" Alyssa exclaimed.

I smiled to myself and made my check mark, giving the note back to the boy. He walked away to Eric.

"So...?" Gina prodded.

"We're going out tomorrow night." I said cheerfully.

I looked over at Eric as he opened the note. He looked up and winked at me. All four of us giggled and discussed my outfit options as we finished our lunches.

When I got to band at the end of the day, I expected Kyle to act coldly towards me. But he was as cheerful as I'd ever seen him, acting like I hadn't blown him off last night. As he went on and on about our upcoming chess tournament, I had to cut him off.

"Kyle, I'm really sorry that I forgot to call you last night."

"Oh, it's not a big deal," he said.

"Yes, it is," I told him. "We had plans and I should've let you know if I wasn't coming anymore. I honestly was still planning on it, but I just lost track of time at Alyssa's. Not that that's an excuse."

"It's okay," he said.

"So what are you doing tonight?" I asked.

"Me and Tammi are gonna play some chess to prep for the big tournament. Do you wanna come?"

"That sounds perfect."

• • •

Even though the girls were a little upset that I had other plans, it was nice having a chess night with Kyle and Tammi. We discussed strategies and laughed at each other's stories about past competitors.

"Well, there's no way I'm getting beat by Brian Forbes again." Kyle said.

"I don't think I've practiced enough to beat him." I stated with a sigh.

"Well, we've got to step up our game if we want to make it to the finals." Tammi said.

"What place are we in?" I asked, feeling a little out of the loop.

"We're currently in third, meaning someone from our team has to beat Henry Odem in order for us to make it to the finals."

"Who do you think can do it?" I asked, knowing it certainly wasn't me.

Kyle said, "Well, I've been playing with Joey every day for two weeks now, and he's getting to be a pretty strong player."

"Really?" I asked in surprise.

"Yeah, I think he might actually be able to beat Henry."

I couldn't picture Kyle and Joey hanging out, even if it was just playing chess.

"What do you guys talk about?" I asked him out of curiosity.

His expression was one of skepticism.

"Um, well, chess mostly."

"That's it?"

"And some guy stuff too. You know, girls and stuff. Certainly NOT Brett, if that's why you're asking. Why do you care?"

"Tori's always had a crush on Joey." Tammi said in a childlike manner.

"No I don't, Tammi. Not anymore, anyway." I said, doing my best to keep a straight face.

"Tori, you are a horrible liar."

We both burst out laughing. Kyle just looked at us like we were a bunch of boy-crazy girls.

"Speaking of Brett, did you talk to him about what happened with James?" I asked.

"Yes, I did. When James saw us together, Brett ran after him and told him that he is interested in me. He asked James if he was okay with that. James said he guessed he has to be. So Brett asked me out again and I said yes."

"And WHEN were you going to tell us this?" Tammi asked him.

"I was gonna lead up to it tonight, actually."

"Not sure I believe you, but okay." Tammi teased.

"I just didn't want to make a big deal out of it in case it doesn't work out," he said.

"I get that, for sure." I sympathized. "So when is the date?"

"We're going to a movie this Friday." He grinned.

"We want immediate details." Tammi said.

"Oh, don't worry. I'll FaceTime you as soon as it's over."

...

When I arrived home that afternoon, my dad and mom were making dinner in the kitchen.

"What's going on in here?"I asked.

"Your father is helping me cook." Mom said.

"I'm learning how to make beef wellington." He said proudly.

Mom loved teaching people how to cook, and my dad was usually the one she wanted to teach.He was a good sport about it, the two of them giggling like school children as they sliced bread and chopped veggies, pouring olive oil into the skillet and watching the beef slowly cook on the stove. She enjoyed teaching me to cook as well. It was something about the act of making a meal together that made us feel closer to each other. It brought both of us joy to prepare a meal and share it with loved ones. I didn't get to cook with her as much as I wanted to, but I was glad that dad helped her every so often. I couldn't wait to taste the beef wellington.

I finished my homework just as Corey came home from soccer practice.

"What's up, sis?"

"Not too much, Corey. How was practice?"

"Not bad, not bad. Oh, your friend Alyssa was at practice today."

"Really? She came to your practice?" I asked, with an odd feeling in my stomach. Alyssa hadn't mentioned this to me.

"Yeah, she did. She just sat on the sidelines and watched us, then she came up to me afterwards and started talking to me."

"Well, she's too old for you, so don't get any ideas."

"Hey, I can't stop the ladies from coming on to me. And I'm pretty sure she was flirting with me."

"No way. She wouldn't hit on a Freshman. And she knows you're my brother."

"Okay, well, believe what you want. Just thought you should know. I'm gonna grab a shower."

As Corey ran up the stairs, I sat on the couch trying to determine whether I wanted to talk to Alyssa about this or not. I mean, why would she go to my brother's practice just to watch him play? It seemed kind of weird to me, but maybe that's because I didn't like sports.

It wasn't too long after Corey's shower that dinner was done. The smell of beef and onion in a warm flaky pastry brought us all to the dinner table, our stomachs growling in unison.

"Man, this looks amazing, Mom." Corey said, placing one round pastry onto his plate.

"Your father is also responsible for this meal as well." She told him, smiling at my dad.

"Wow, Dad, look at you go." Corey said.

"This is incredible." I said, swallowing a bite of the heavenly dish.

"Thank you both," my dad said.

"Jonathan, looks like you should help me out in the kitchen more often."

"Oh, I barely did a thing, it was all you, honey."

Sometimes I was grossed out by my parents, but most times I just wished that I would find someone who made me as happy as the two of them were.

I decided to confront Alyssa at lunch the next day.

"Did you go to my brother's practice yesterday?"

"Yes." Alyssa replied, putting mascara on at her locker mirror.

"Why?"

"Because I happen to like soccer, in case you haven't noticed. And I like to watch the guys." She winked.

"Does one of those guys happen to be my brother?"

"Well, I mean, he is an attractive guy. But he's too young for me."

"And he's my brother."

"Yes, and he's your brother. So, he's totally off-limits. Did he say something about last night? I just made small talk. I was trying to be friendly."

"Yes, I know you're friendly, Alyssa. I just want to make sure you weren't hitting on my little brother."

"Tori, do you honestly think I just hit on any guy that moves? I'm starting to think you don't think very much of my character."

"Alyssa, you're my best friend. We've gone over this before. I love you, and I think very highly of you. This has nothing to do with you and guys. This has to do with me being a protective big sister."

"I totally get it, Tori. You have nothing to worry about, trust me. I was bored and I thought watching soccer practice would kill some time. Then I saw your brother and thought I'd say hi."

"Okay, good."

I felt so close to Alyssa, but the more time I spent with her, the less I trusted her. I just couldn't shake the feeling that she was hiding something from me.

…

Marching band practice went perfectly that day. Everything felt so right. I had all of my sheet music memorized and almost every step I took was in sync with the music. I felt powerful, and I hadn't felt that way in a while. I was torn between band and my new friends. I had originally thought that I could do both: hang out with Alyssa, the girls AND go to both marching band and concert band rehearsals, and still attend chess practice and competitions.

But with all of the time they spent together after school every day, I would be missing out on all of it to go to practices. And I didn't want to miss out.

Even though I had pretty much stopped going to concert band, I still went to every marching band practice because it was such a huge part of my life. It was a piece of my identity, and I didn't know who I was without it.

Other kids had their sports and their clubs, but they were nothing compared to marching band. It felt amazing to be a part of something much larger than myself, a group of misfits who loved working hard and performing every Friday night under the stadium lights. The football players were of course the reason for the games, but we were the underdogs. We were nobodies until we stepped onto that Astroturf and delivered our show.

When I held my sax and marched in rhythm to the music, I felt unstoppable. I wasn't the shy girl anymore. Performing in a large group gave me the safety I needed to put myself out there. No one in the audience was ever staring at only me. They were staring at our group. It was our ten minutes of fame. It was powerful and glorious. That's the feeling I wished I could possess in all areas of my life.

•••

"It looks horrible," I said to Alyssa.

She looked me over in my lavender blouse and tan pencil skirt.

"Well, it's not your best look. Why don't you try to *not* dress like a nun?" She said without a hint of humor.

I sighed. "All right, you do it. This is too stressful."

A cry of delight came from Alyssa's mouth. "Oh, goody! You will look so hot," she said, searching roughly through my closet. Ten minutes later I was in a black corset tank top, black mini skirt, and black platform heels.

"No."

Alyssa whined. "Come ON, Tori. You know this makes you look super-hot."

"Not in a million years."

"Tori…just wear it," she pleaded.

"I look like I should have a pimp."

"Well then I don't know what you want from me." Alyssa said, hands up in surrender.

"I want," I said, steering her back to my closet, "you to pick out a tasteful and cute outfit. Something fun and modest. More Taylor Swift and less Miley Cyrus."

"Okay…" she said with determination, concentrating hard on the items in my closet.

The final ensemble was perfect. A sleeveless, high-collared button-down purple blouse with vertical ruffles running parallel down the front, with dark denim skinny jeans and silver ballet flats. I added a sparkly headband and sliver dangly earrings.

"Ta da!" Alyssa dramatically exclaimed as she touched up my blush.

"I look beautiful." I said aloud.

"You look classy," Alyssa added, "which is a look I've never done before. I think I did a great job," she said beaming with pride.

"You did marvelous!" I uttered playfully in my best French accent.

We both giggled and began talking to each other in our fake French voices. The doorbell rang, and my insides instantly blended into a slushie.

"That must be Eric!" Alyssa sing-songed.

I hadn't been able to eat all day, knowing about our date tonight. I took deep breaths to calm my nerves.

He was here.

"Tori!" My mother called from the kitchen. "You have a gentleman caller!"

"I'm coming!" I yelled back to her.

"Have fun!" Alyssa called to me as I descended the stairs. When I got downstairs, Eric was at the kitchen table with my parents.

"Hello, everyone…" I said, glaring at mom and dad.

I did *not* want them interacting with Eric. There was no telling what embarrassing stuff they could have told him. I felt like I had to puke, my nerves were so bad. This was not helping the situation. My dad gave me a nod.

"Whelp, Tori's here, so we'll let you go."

Eric stood up and shook my dad's hand.

"It was nice meeting you both, officially."

We walked out the door toward Eric's truck, and my mom waved as we drove away.

• • •

My putter clinked against the little red ball, and I watched it gather speed over two bumps, gliding into the hole at the end of the green.

"Yes!" I jumped up and down, doing my victory dance.

"How is that even possible?" Eric asked in his amazement at my hole-in-one.

"Well, some of us just have skill." I told him with a smile.

"You weren't this good at the beginning."

"Ever hear of 'warming up'?"

He laughed.

"Okay, hot-shot, watch this next one."

We were on hole 8, and the rest of the game went on like this. At the end of the game we tallied our scores, and I beat him by 10 points.

"I don't get it," Eric said aloud, "I usually win at mini golf."

"Maybe you've met your match." I joked.

His smile sobered. "Maybe I have."

We got ice cream afterwards and talked about our classes and our families. I made sure I didn't bring up the chess tournament. I didn't need to jeopardize the success of the date.

It was 10:00 on a Friday night, and I was sitting on a bench eating chocolate ice cream with an adorable boy. I had finally found true happiness.

Elation overwhelmed me as I walked down the hall with Tammi and Kyle. My first date with Eric had been a success. Was this love? I'd never been in love before, so of course I had no idea what it felt like. All I knew is that I wanted to see Eric again, and soon.

"How was the date?" Kyle asked.

"Incredible. We played mini golf and went for ice cream afterwards." I said.

"That sounds really nice. I'm happy for you, Tori." Kyle said.

"Me too," Tammi echoed.

"Thanks, guys." I said, smiling at the both of them.

"How was your date with Brett?" I asked Kyle.

"It was great, actually." He replied. "We are going to start dating and see how things go."

The smile on his face was contagious.

"I'm so happy for you, Kyle." I told him.

"I never thought I'd see the day when all three of us had boyfriends." Tammi said.

"Hey, look, it's the jolly green giant!" Chad Brunswick, one of the football players yelled, pointing to Tammi.

"Fuck off, meat head." Tammi said right to his face, flipping him off.

"Why is someone like you with the stork lady over here?" Chad asked me, making kissing noises and rubbing his chest. He motioned me towards him.

"Come walk with me."

My heart started racing, and the three of us practically sprinted down the hallway to get rid of him.

"What a PIG." Tammi said, exasperated.

"This was NOT what I meant when I said I needed more cardio in my life," Kyle said with a big sigh, hunched over with his hands on his knees.

"Are you okay?" Tammi asked me.

"Yeah, I'm fine. What about you? I wish they would stop calling you those names."

"It's senior year, Tori. Why stop now? This is the last time they can make fun of me until I leave this town and get on a new level."

"Then they'll never be able to touch you again." Kyle said to her, grinning.

I put my arm around her.

"Never again, Tammi. Never again."

• • •

It wasn't until lunch that I saw Eric again.

I walked into the cafeteria with Alyssa, Kylie, and Gina, and I saw him wave to me from his table full of jocks.

"Well, well, well, looks like someone had a great date." Alyssa said.

"It was amazing," I told them as we got into the lunch line.

"Now let's see if he asks you out again." Alyssa said.

"You should go over to his table." Gina added.

"Um, I don't think so."

Just the thought of talking to him in front of all those popular guys was enough to make me nauseous.

"Are you scared?" Alyssa asked.

"Umm..yes?"

Then we all started laughing.

Once we got our food and sat at a table, Eric came over and took a seat next to me. All the girls smiled and looked away to give us the illusion of privacy. I knew they were listening, though.

"I had fun Friday night." Eric said.

"Me too."

"Any chance you'd like to hang out tonight?"

I did have a reading competition meeting, but I wasn't going to tell him that. I didn't want to blow this.

"Yes, I'd like to hang out with you tonight."

"Great. Meet me on the sidewalk after school."

"Okay." I answered, smiling.

The girls giggled as Eric walked back to his table.

"That was fast!" Kylie exclaimed.

Everyone started making kissing noises and teasing me, and it felt so good. It was as if all of the stuff I used to care about didn't matter anymore. I had found my way into the popular crowd and I was dating an adorable basketball player.

It felt like I didn't deserve to be this happy. There was a worry in the pit of my stomach that something was going to go wrong. I wasn't sure how long this good fortune would last, so I needed to make the most of it. Because I wasn't the girl who had it all. I was the girl who stood in the background watching the other girls have it all.

•••

After school, I sat on the sidewalk waiting for Eric. He came out of the front door with two of his teammates, walking over to me.

"Hey Tori, this is Jamal and Gavin. Guys, this is Tori."

Was I actually being introduced to his friends?

"Hey, Tori. You ready to see 'Aquaman?'" Jamal asked.

So this was a group movie date?

"Sure, sounds fun."

"See, I told you she'd be down." Eric told the guys.

We all piled into Eric's truck and drove to the theatre. The movie was great, and I really enjoyed hanging out with Eric's friends. I learned quite a bit about the three of them.

For instance, Eric and Jamal were next-door neighbors and had been best friends since third grade. The two of them used to ride bikes all over town before they learned how to drive. They'd go on make-believe adventures and explore the backyard woods together, climbing trees and hanging out in the branches.

In middle school Jamal met Gavin, and then two became three. The three of them were on the basketball team, but they were also obsessed with videogames. It felt easy to be with them like this, just hanging out. Kyle was the only guy friend I had, so I wasn't used to boy-banter. It was refreshing.

"In conclusion, Tori," Jamal said to me, "Fortnight is the better game because when else can you jump out of the sky from a party bus?"

"No, no, no..." Gavin said, "What he means to say is that Red Dead is the better game because you have to actually eat to gain health just like in real life and you can pick herbs to make stuff."

"Okay, no offense you two, but I'm sticking with Spyro. That's more my style."

Eric put his arm around me. "The lady has spoken, you two. I mean, obviously Red Dead is better, but I'll play Spyro any day."

"What?! How can you not like Fortnight?!" Jamal exclaimed, starting the whole argument over again. Eric winked at me and I rolled my eyes at Jamal and Gavin.

•••

The week went on as usual. I sat through my classes with semi-interest, daydreaming about Eric. I couldn't believe he actually liked me. I mean, there were so many other girls who were prettier and smarter than me, not to mention sportier. I wasn't sure what his type was, but I was thankful to have caught his eye. Whatever the reason was, I was sure it had something to do with my new makeover Alyssa gave me months ago. After all, no guy had ever shown any interest in me until that day.

Alyssa, Kylie, Gina, and I went to Corey's soccer game on Wednesday. We went to get snacks during the second half of the game because Gina kept telling us about these "amazing pepperoni pinwheels" we just HAD to try. On our way to the concession stand, we ran into my parents.

"Well, imagine seeing you here!" Mom exclaimed with a giant grin.

"Yes, Mom, what a coincidence."

"I remember these lovely ladies." Dad said, bowing his head.

"Corey is such a great player." Alyssa said to them.

"Yes, he is. He's really come a long way since last year." Dad said.

"Well, we'd better get in line before we miss too much of Corey's game." I replied, leading the girls away.

"We'll see you at home, sweetie." Mom called as they walked back to their seats.

"Your parents seem really nice." Gina said while we were waiting in line.

"Yeah, I guess."

"My parents don't give a shit about me." Kylie said.

"Yeah, mine either," said Alyssa.

"Parents are the worst." Gina added.

There was no way I was telling them that I considered my mom to be one of my best friends, so I just agreed.

"Yeah, they really are."

•••

Even though I felt giddy-nervous when I was around Eric, I was still happy when he and his friends showed up at my locker between classes on Thursday.

"Hey, Tori." Eric greeted me.

"Hey."

My anxiety was kicking in. I had no idea what to say to him. What if he thought I was completely weird? I could ruin his interest at any moment.

"So, how's your week going?" He asked.

"Pretty good. I'm excited for the football game Friday night."

"I didn't know you were into football." He said with his brow creased.

"Oh no, I'm definitely not into football. I'm in the marching band."

As soon as I said it, I cursed myself. I couldn't believe I let that slip out. He was going to think I was a nerd…or rather, find out that I *was* a nerd.

"Wow, really? That's awesome. I wish I could play an instrument."

"Really?"

"Yeah, I mean, I can't imagine how hard it is."

I giggled.

"Then add marching a show on top of playing, and it's crazy-hard."

"I bet. Hey, why don't I come watch you perform tomorrow night?"

"Oh, I mean, you don't have to."

"No, but I want to. I've never actually watched you guys perform."

"Yeah, you're in the majority."

Eric laughed and turned to Jamal and Gavin.

"You guys wanna go to the football game tomorrow?"

I couldn't believe that Eric was coming to the game. He wasn't turned off by my nerdiness, and he actually seemed to think that it was cool. Maybe I should've told him about me being on the chess team too. That might have been an overload. But what if he was just being nice? No, I didn't want to jeopardize anything.

I think I've told him enough for now, I thought.

•••

"You ready for tonight?!" Tammi asked me as we both got into our uniforms in the band room.

"You're pumped. Yes, I'm ready," I replied.

"Of course I'm pumped! This is my favorite thing about high school, and probably the only thing I'll miss about it. Except for you and Kyle of course." She winked.

I zipped up my jacket, feeling the giant golden buttons on it and running my hands along the ornate golden ropes on the shoulders.

"Are we okay?" I asked her, remembering our last interaction.

"Yes, Tori, we're okay. As long as you stop lying to me and Kyle. I honestly don't care that you have new friends, that's fine. But that doesn't mean you get to ditch us. And I'm really happy you found Eric. Maybe you two can double date with Brian and I sometime. It's all good, girl. Just treat us right and we don't have a problem."

"Okay," I said, feeling a little hurt. I knew I deserved it, but it didn't feel good to hear her recap my ill behaviors. This was my reality check, I guess. I didn't want to become that person who ditched her best friends for the popular crowd or for a boy.

•••

It was a crisp fall night. The stadium lights shone down onto the football field, the crowd cheering with their cowbells and elevated voices. We played "Sweet Child of Mine" from our spot in the bleachers, the people around us singing along. This was what I loved about Friday night football games... our performance.

The night was all about the music. To most people, we were just the geeks in the stands playing our instruments. But to the band, Friday night was OUR night. It was a chance for the unnoticed to become stars. I wasn't very interested in watching the game, but when it came to half-time, that's when it all mattered.

"Hey, guys." Kyle said, sitting down beside Tammi and me.

"Why don't you just join marching band already? You literally sit with us at every single game." I said.

"Tori, you know how I feel about my videogames. I'm not giving them up for another band activity."

"You wouldn't have to give them up," Tammi told him. "You just wouldn't be able to play them every night."

"And that's a serious problem."

We always joked like this with Kyle because although he didn't come to our practices, he did come to every home game and sneak into a spot on our bleachers to sit next to us.

It seemed so bizarre that he played in concert band but wouldn't join marching band. Especially when he was coming to all of the games anyway. I wouldn't have even come to the games if it weren't for marching band. I'd been to every single one my entire high school career, but I couldn't tell you what a first down was.

"Is that your lover boy over there?" Kyle asked me, motioning his head towards the set of bleachers beside ours. Sure enough, Eric, Jamal, and Gavin were all waving to me.

I blushed, my face heating up like one of the "Hot Hands" we held during freezing cold games. I waved back to them, now feeling self-conscious. I wanted so badly for Eric to look at me and be impressed, but now all I felt was worry. I didn't want to mess up in front of him, after all. Now I had to worry about how I looked playing my instrument in the stands and making sure I was interacting with numerous people so he'd think I had a lot of friends. I knew I shouldn't worry, but that was not so easily done.

The game was boring, of course, but we sure did have a blast in the stands. We watched the cheerleaders dance in time to our music, feeling the energy of the crowd.

"They may have those cute little skirts, but we have character." Tammi joked as we listened to Mr. Grayson shout out our next number.

"Haha, you're hilarious." I laughed.

If I was being honest, though, I would've taken the short skirt over having character any day. I mean, what good was having character if nobody liked you? Every year I sat on those bleachers and watched the cheerleaders shake their trim butts and jump up and down with exaggerated smiles on their faces, and I wished I could trade places with one of them.

Not because I wanted to cheer, but because I wanted people to look at me the way they looked at them every Friday night and in the hallways at school. I wanted to be envied and adored.

The players ran off the field, and herds of people began leaving the bleachers in search of bathrooms and/or snacks. It was now half-time, our moment to shine. We got into formation and marched onto the field in time with the snare drum. I looked up into the bright lights to see if I could find Eric's face. Sure enough, I saw him leaning against the railing at the bottom of the bleachers. This was where all of the band moms stood too because it offered the best view of us. He waved to me, and I gave him a nod.

We executed our half-time show perfectly, truly becoming one unit on the turf. I felt powerful in the moment, a contributor to the strong and resounding sound of 67 instruments in accord. Our formations came alive with each number, 134 feet guiding our bodies back and forth across the field. I felt accomplished as we marched off the field, finding that my worry had melted away with the music.

"You were fantastic!" Eric yelled to me from the stands in front of everyone. I blushed, but not in embarrassment. I was elated.

•••

My biggest pet peeve was how the clock stopped all the time in a football game. Of course, I knew that the clock could stop in most sports games, but I didn't watch any other sports games. I wasn't there to watch football, so I couldn't wait for it to be over once half-time was done.

It felt like a never-ending game where we were held captive in the stands waiting for something interesting to happen. But that was just me, I guess.

Everyone else seemed to be fixated by the game, the way they got riled up in the stands, screaming and chanting as if this was the end all. That was the reason why football players were treated like soldiers who just came home from the war, right?

Running out of time, the other team's quarterback threw a pass in a final attempt to take the lead, but it was unsuccessful. And just like that, we won the game.

"One, two, three, four!" Mr. Grayson shouted, waving his baton in the air.

We blared out the Notre Dame fight song, and "St. Elmo's Fire" immediately afterward. We knew these pieces by heart, because we played them after every win. Our final number was "Hey Baby" by Bruce Channel. The flutes clapped and sang along while the rest of us moved our instruments in time with the beat. It was moments like these that I lived for.

We put our instruments away and stripped out of our uniforms in the band room after the game.

"Burger King?" Tammi questioned, knowing full well that she didn't even need to ask. Burger King was our spot after every football game. Her favorite item to get was the cheesy tots. If they were out, she'd leave.

"Uh, duh." I said.

Kyle was waiting for us right outside the band room, and so was Eric.

"Hey, great job, you guys." Eric said with a smile.

"We were pretty awesome out there." Tammi agreed.

"What are you up to now?" Eric asked me.

"We're going to go to Burger King. Want to come?"

"Sure."

Eric and I met Tammi and Kyle at the restaurant. We all got our usual, mine being a spicy chicken sandwich with onion rings. I loved those onion rings.

"Anything new with you guys?" Eric asked Tammi and Kyle while munching on his Whopper.

"Just trying to beat Dark Souls 3 right now." Kyle answered.

"No way! Man, that game is way too hard for me." Eric said to him.

"What games do you play?" Kyle asked with excitement.

Now it was just Tammi and me staring at each other from across the booth.

"Looks like you two are doing well. Does this mean you're no longer interested in Joey?" Tammi asked me.

"Nope, not anymore. He lost his chance, I guess." I answered her.

"Joey's attractive, but he's not a very nice person. I'm glad you are with someone who is nice." Tammi said to me.

"Yeah, that's actually what I like about him. Maybe Joey's spell over me has finally broken."

"I wouldn't be so sure of that." Tammi said, nodding to the front door.

Joey and Brett entered, getting in line to order. Joey waved to me, and I blushed at his bad-boy smirk.

Brett looked over at Kyle, but he was oblivious when talking videogames.

"Still think that spell has been lifted?" Tammi teased.

"Let's change the subject," I told her. "How's Brian doing? Are you two doing good now?"

"Yes, as a matter of fact, we are." She answered. "He really doesn't seem to care about my height anymore."

"That's awesome, Tammi. I hope he truly has gotten past it."

"What do you mean? I just said that he's gotten past it." Tammi said.

"Yes, he seems to have. But people don't change overnight. It's something I'm sure he's got to work on."

"God, Tori, what are you trying to say? That Brian is still embarrassed of me?" Tammi began yelling in the booth.

"I'm so sorry, Tammi. Please forgive me. I didn't mean to upset you."

"It's fine, Tori. I was just surprised that my so-called best friend would try to make me doubt myself."

"That's not what I meant, Tammi. I think I was just projecting my own self-doubt onto you."

"It's okay. I just need to be alone right now," she said, getting up from the booth.

"Tammi, I'm sorry—" I said, following her out to the parking lot.

"I said I want to be alone!" Tammi yelled at me, slamming her car door.

I watched her car pull away, the headlights beaming in my face. I walked back into the building, sliding into the booth beside Eric.

Both boys stopped talking and stared at me.

"You okay?" Eric asked me, placing an arm around my shoulders.

"Not really." I told him. "I don't know why Tammi is getting upset like this lately. It's like I have to walk on eggshells when I'm around her."

"The people we treat the worst are the ones we know will never leave us."

I let his words sink in, wondering if he was right about Tammi.

"Can you take me home?" I asked Eric, my feet dangling from the edge of the booth.

"Of course."

We said goodbye to Kyle and left Burger King. Eric dropped me off at my house, hugging me goodbye.

I walked past my parents, who were washing dishes in the kitchen.

"How was the game, sweetie?" Mom asked me.

"Fine." I replied, knowing if I said any more, I would cry.

"Well, you can tell us all about it in the morning. We're off to bed in a few minutes." Dad chimed in.

"I'm going to bed too. Goodnight."

As I shut my bedroom door, I pretended that the door had the power to block out the rest of the world for as long as I wanted. The problem was, I knew I had to open it in the morning and face the consequences of my choices.

BAD GUY

"I quit reading competition." I told Alyssa.

Who am I even? I thought to myself. I was letting go of the activities that made up my being, or so I had once thought. But now that I was discovering more about myself, I felt like I needed even more time to keep exploring.

I was angry. Angry at Tammi, and angry for allowing myself to get this upset over a conflict. But I needed to get past all that drama. After all, I was Tori Rowling. I was popular.

"Good," Alyssa sighed. "Now you'll have more time for fun things like shopping. Now that that's taken care of, what are we up to tonight?"

The bell rang, saving me from answering this difficult question. Tonight was Joey's party, and I wasn't going to miss it. My exclusive invite was the only reason I had on a smile that day. I also wasn't going to tell Alyssa about it because I knew she'd end up flirting with Joey the whole time. As Mr. Andrews talked about molecules and compounds, I began to formulate a plan.

While on my way to drop Alyssa off at her house, she asked again, "So… what about tonight? There aren't any parties to speak of, and there's no way I'm sitting home alone."

I smiled, a scheme popping into my head. "Well, it's not the most amazing idea, but me, Tammi, and Kyle are gonna all hang out at Tammi's house tonight. You can come if you want."

"Sure, I'll come," Alyssa said. "It beats watching TV." I pulled the car into her driveway.

"Great. So, I guess I'll see you there around 7:00."

"Sounds good." Alyssa said as she stepped out of the car.

It was a snap decision, but I thought it was a good plan. Alyssa would come to the house and find no one there, then she would just assume our little fake get-together was cancelled.

I would ignore her texts and/or calls and then apologize to her the next day. I knew it was mean, but I was prepared to deal with the consequences of my decision. Ever since I met Alyssa, I felt something change in me. I felt more confident, surer of myself. It was as though my shyness was fading away.

Pleased with myself, I backed out of the long, stone driveway, and drove the Volvo forward into the freedom of my evening.

...

I could feel the vibrations of the bass from the walkway outside of Joey's house. Jay Balvin's "Mi Gente" was playing from the massive speaker system inside the lavish living room. When I got inside, someone handed me a cup and said "5 bucks!"

I didn't understand. "What?!" I yelled in confusion over the blaring beats. "You have to pay 5 bucks for your alcohol!" The boy yelled back to me.

I handed him the cup back. "I'm good!"

He looked at me like I was a cheapskate, then walked over to a drunk blonde, and let her grind on him. Feeling uncomfortable with the cluster of bodies all around me, I walked into the kitchen. After standing like a moron for what seemed like forever, I hopped onto the kitchen counter and stared at my shoes.

Time passed by. *There are 89 dots on the bottom of each shoe.* More time passed by. Claire from my English class and Tad the linebacker were dry humping against the refrigerator. More time passed. A few of the cheerleaders whose names I didn't know were gossiping loudly as they shoved Doritos into their pouty red mouths.

I started drawing designs on my shoe. More time went by. Once Lillian the senior class president and Jayden the school "player" started making out right in front of me, I jumped down from the counter and made my way towards the door. I had had enough. Not once did I even see Joey at his own stupid party. Plus, I didn't know anyone there, and I wasn't really feeling this vibe.

This was not the kind of party I had in mind when Joey invited me. I would've liked to be with a small group of people just chatting or playing games or something. I guess I was naïve to think that this wasn't the type of party that Joey threw. I made my way through the mass of people, climbed over the coffee table, and finally reached the front door. But just as I reached out to turn the doorknob, a warm hand touched my shoulder.

"There you are," Joey said as if he had been looking for me the entire time.

"Leaving already?" He asked with a coy smile on his face.

"Yeah, not my kind of party." I said, smelling weed on him.

I thought I liked Joey, but I didn't enjoy feeling like an outsider at school AND in the real world.

His smile broadened. "Oh yeah? Are you into more private parties?"

My immediate internal response was *I thought he had a girlfriend...*

However, my verbal response was "I'm not really into huge parties. I like just a few people."

"Is a party for two okay?"

"I mean, yeah."

I honestly didn't know why I replied that way. It was an automatic response that didn't seem like me at all. All I knew was that Joey Manson had his eyes on only me at that moment, and I couldn't turn him down.

He reached for my hand and pulled me toward him. "Well, then follow me."

My body became hot, and I instantly felt nervous. *Joey was taking me upstairs!*

He led me into a room and shut the door behind him. We sat down on the bed. "This is my room," he said.

I looked around. "It's nice," I replied.

There was an awkwardness in the air. My feeling of elation had dissipated and was replaced with anxiousness. I wanted Joey's interest, and I wanted him to like me. But now that I was alone with him, I wasn't exactly sure what I wanted to happen between us.

He looked straight into my eyes, and in that moment I could feel what was about to happen next. He leaned in, and his mouth enveloped mine, overtook it, actually, and showed me things I had only dreamed about for years.

I had never been kissed before, and learned rather quickly that what they say was true, *you just know how to kiss when it happens.* All of my worrying about whether I would be able to kiss when the time came had vanished once my lips parted and began to play tug-of-war with Joey's.

After a few minutes of making out, the door slammed open.

"What the hell is going on?!"

I fixed my hair and wiped my mouth as Amber loomed in the doorway.

"Where the hell were you last night?!" Alyssa yelled.

It was now Thursday morning, and Alyssa, Kyle, and Tammi all stood before me with anger on their collective faces.

People around us stopped and stared. I opened my mouth, but nothing came out.

"Tori?" Tammi asked with severity.

"Can we talk about this later? I have to get to Bio."

"No, we're gonna talk about this now, Tor." Kyle demanded as the bell rang. Now the hall was empty.

"You told Alyssa that we were all getting together last night?"

I sighed. "Yes, I did. I know it was an awful thing to do, but it was my only option."

"What were you doing, Tori?" Tammi asked.

"Well, I kind of went to a party."

"What?! I didn't know about any parties. Whose party? I wasn't invited and you never told me about it." Alyssa said, clearly feeling betrayed.

"Joey's."

Alyssa laughed. "That's total bull. If Joey had a party, I would've been invited."

"Just tell us the truth, Tor." Kyle said.

As much as I wanted to tell them the truth about why I ditched Alyssa for the party, I couldn't. Along with my anger, my defenses were up and it was all about survival mode.

"That IS the truth! If you don't believe me, then that's your problem. I have nothing to prove to you."

Tammi said, "It doesn't even matter if there was a party or not. Tori, you lied to Alyssa. And you've been lying to us this whole semester! I don't even know who you are anymore. You never come to band, and you've quit reading competition. Not once have you asked to hang out with us, and if we've had plans, you usually blow them off. It's like you're someone else!" She stormed out of the hallway, crying.

Kyle just looked at me with disappointment. "I'm gonna go," he said.

Though I had treated those two badly, I knew Alyssa couldn't stay mad at me for long. "Listen, Lyss, I'm sorry I lied to you. I know how I can make it up to you, though. I heard that Chris is having a bash this Sunday. You want to come with?"

And this was the first time I had ever heard her utter these two words: "I'll pass."

•••

At lunchtime, I sat down at our usual table to wait for Eric. After ten minutes, I knew he wasn't going to show. Instead, two of Joey's friends sat down with me.

"Hey, what's up?" Matt Lowell asked as he shoveled a heaping spoonful of spaghetti into his mouth.

Completely confused, I answered, "No offense, but do I know you?"

Matt laughed. "Well, I guess not. I'm Matt," he said, extending his right arm to me, "and this is Derek."

Derek waved, his mouth full of pasta.

I smiled, then went back to eating my protein bar.

After minutes of silence, Matt said, "So…are you and Joey dating?"

Completely taken aback, I said, "What? No, of course not."

"Well, we heard about Amber catching you guys making out at the party last night."

The two laughed heartily.

I blushed. "We weren't making out, per se."

I don't know what possessed me to say that. It seemed as if I was suddenly wearing a new coat of self-confidence that I had never thought would fit me before.

The boys began making cat calls as Joey walked over to our table.

"Are these dudes bothering you, Tori?"

I smirked. "Not at all. We were just getting to know each other."

"Well, good," Joey said genuinely.

I couldn't believe this. Not only did Joey and I kiss in his bedroom last night, but we were eating lunch together with his friends! However, my elation quickly died as Eric glared at me from two tables away.

"Is that a friend of yours?" Derek asked as he blatantly pointed to Eric.

"Oh, that's that Eric kid," Joey said, a smile creeping onto his chiseled face. "Let's go say hi."

"Oh, I really don't think you should," I quickly interjected. But before I knew what was happening, all three guys got up and sat down next to Eric.

I stayed in my seat, watching the confrontation without any idea as to what was being said.

Eric looked mad. Joey looked confident. Matt and Derek looked pleased. Why did I suddenly feel as if they were talking about me? Out of nowhere, Eric shot up out of his seat and lunged across the table, hitting Joey square in the jaw. My mouth fell open and my eyes grew even wider as Joey hit him back, blood gushing from Eric's nose. In a matter of minutes, two teachers rushed over and separated the two.

As they left the now-silent cafeteria, Alyssa stood beside me.

"I'm assuming this was over you?"

Staring blankly into her eyes, I thought about it. *It couldn't have been over me. I mean, I'm the nerd, remember?* Alyssa's the only reason I even became a part of the "in crowd." There's no way two hot boys were fighting over me. But maybe, just maybe…

"You think you have it all, but you've lost more than you know." Alyssa said as she walked away.

Once again, this was not something the Alyssa I knew would say. *Something has changed about her*, I thought to myself.

•••

While walking to my car after school, Joey ran up beside me.

"Hey, Tori."

"What happened to you after they escorted you out of the cafeteria?" I asked.

"Oh, they sent me to the office and then they gave me three Saturday detentions."

Being the good little student that I was, this seemed outlandish to me.

"That's horrible!"

"You're so cute," he laughed. "That's not bad at all. Trust me, I've done worse."

That really didn't make me feel any better.

"Why did he punch you?" I blurted.

"Um, because he's a douche."

"No, he's not. Tell me the truth."

"Listen, we just went over there and asked him if he minded that we were hanging out with you, and he just outta nowhere started going ape shit."

"It seemed like you guys were trying to start a fight with him."

"What?! No, I wouldn't have done that. I know you guys are friends."

I didn't want to believe him, but he sounded so convincing. And he *was* Joey.

"Okay, I believe you."

"Good. Now, are you going to Chris's party this Sunday?"

"I was thinking about it." I answered honestly.

"Well, I hope I see you there." He said, hands in his pockets.

"Joey?"

"Yeah?"

"Are you and Amber still together?"

"Yeah, we are."

He didn't offer any more information, only silence.

I drove straight to Alyssa's apartment after school, prepared to win her friendship back. I knew it would be hard, but I also knew that it would be harder for me to not be friends with her. I'd gotten so accustomed to having her around, I didn't know what I would do without her by my side.

After ringing the doorbell to her upscale apartment, Alyssa opened the door with a smile on her face.

"Hey, girl, come on in!" She said while walking into the kitchen.

Very confused, I asked, "you haven't been drinking this early, have you?"

Alyssa began to giggle like a child.

"No, no, girl! I'm just happy to see you!"

"Really? Because you were pretty ticked at me earlier today."

Alyssa smiled.

"Tori, the past is the past. We've been friends for too long to let one little fight come between us like that."

I felt a little relieved, but my confusion remained. "Listen, Lyss, I came over here because I felt so horrible about the way I've been treating you. I want to make things right. You're my best friend and I don't want to lose you."

"Aww, well isn't that sweet," she said in an exaggerated tone. "Well, Tori, I appreciate that and all, but you have nothing to worry about. You're forgiven and I don't want to talk any more about it. Want something to drink?"

It felt like things were finally back to normal. Even though Tammi and Kyle still wouldn't speak to me, Alyssa assured me that they would eventually come to their senses. It was hard not to believe her when I saw her hanging out with them at the mall that Wednesday. Apparently, they had bonded the night I had ditched Alyssa and said we were all meeting at Tammi's house. Alyssa came over and asked my parents to call Tammi since she couldn't get a hold of me. The three of them spent the evening at my house watching a movie with my parents. A night I would've been thrilled to have a few months ago.

...

My mom was in the Hallmark store trying to find a gift for a coworker while I walked around aimlessly, trying not to look completely bored. I was leaning on the railing of the second floor, looking down at the people below me when I saw a familiar head of shiny, red hair.

I shouted "Alyssa!"

All three of their heads turned immediately upward towards me, then Tammi and Kyle looked straight back down again.

Alyssa shouted "Hey, girl, what's up!"

"Not much!" I yelled back.

I was about to tell her I'd ride the elevator down to meet them, but before I could she said, "I'll see you later!"

The three of them continued walking.

As I started thinking of reasons why Alyssa would brush me off like that, I got a text from her.

> Sry bout that. Tam & Kyle r still kinda upset & I didn't want them to think I was on ur side & not theirs.

So now there were sides? I couldn't believe that Tammi and Kyle were being so petty. And Alyssa couldn't stand up for me? I mean, I guess I understood she was now our go-between, but to act like she didn't see my side at all was just wrong. Not wanting to lose the only friend I had left, I instead replied:

> **Totally understand. Thanx 4 putting urself in the middle of all this 4 me. It means a lot.**

As my mom and I walked to our car, I got a reply from Alyssa.

> No prob girl. I just don't want them to b mad @ me. ur house 2night?

Alyssa never seemed to care what anyone thought about her, so I wasn't sure why all of a sudden she cared for the opinions of Tammi and Kyle.

...

After eating my mom's delicious baby back ribs, Alyssa and I ran up to my room to listen to the new Cardi B album on Spotify. While painting my big toe an insane orange, my sparkly purple Bluetooth speaker blared "Press," Lyss and I began belting out the lyrics like we were Cardi herself.

Laughing, Alyssa said "I thought you were a classical girl!"

"What can I say, Lyss? You've transformed me!" I said, laughing out loud.

Once we contained ourselves, Alyssa said, "So I need to pass this next English test and I thought you could help me after school tomorrow."

"Oh I so would, but I have band practice."

Laughing, Alyssa said, "Like that's stopped you before. I didn't even think you were still in band."

"Yeah, I know I've missed a lot of practices, but we only have two tenor saxes and my director said I have to come to the rest of the practices in order to play at the spring concert. If I don't show up to even one more practice, I'll be kicked out."

Alyssa smirked. "And you really care what he thinks? I'm sure you can skip just one more."

I gave her a wary look.

"C'mon, Tor, I never ask you for favors! And you owe me..." she said jokingly, but not jokingly.

"You really need my help?"

"Tori, you're the only one who makes it so I can actually understand it. And if I don't pass this test, I fail the course."

"Why don't we do it after I get out of band?"

"Because I'll be gone the rest of the day! Please!!?"

"Okay, fine! But I want you to explain to Mr. Grayson why I won't be there."

"Sure, no problem, whatever you want."

•••

The next day I met Alyssa at lunch. As she sat down across from me, she said "Guess what?! I aced my test! And it's all thanks to you!"

I smiled. "Well, I'm proud of you, 'Lyss. So, what did Mr. Grayson say about me missing practice?"

"Well," she began cheerily, "it just so happens that he was perfectly okay with it. He said 'school comes first.'"

"Good! Besides, I'm getting kinda tired of concert band anyway. It's a good thing we only have like 4 more practices left till the concert."

Marching band was still my life, but I knew Alyssa would make fun of me for defending any form of band.

"Yeah, and besides...band is kinda lame. Just sayin','"she said.

She didn't need to convince me, I knew no one thought band was cool. That is, except for Eric.

"Yeah, I know. And so is chess, right?"

Alyssa began to laugh. "Chess is SUPER lame."

I decided to change the subject.

"Do you think you'll go to Chris's party on Sunday?" I asked her.

"Sure, I'll go. Chris has a nice house." She replied.

"Okay, great. I want to go, but I didn't want to go alone."

"You should invite Eric. You like him, right?" She asked.

"Yes, I do. It's just…Joey and I kissed at his party, and I've had a crush on him since forever. Maybe I'm wrong, but I feel like I might have a chance with him."

Alyssa furrowed her brow.

"Isn't he with Amber?"

"Well, yeah, but…He seems like he's into me now."

"Okay, well, if you say so."

"What does that mean?" I started getting defensive.

"Nothing at all. Just be careful you don't become a side chick."

I started laughing, Alyssa joining me.

"A side chick? Trust me, Lyss, I don't see that happening."

But the more I thought about it, one question remained, what else did you call a girl who makes out with someone else's boyfriend?

•••

On my way to English, I passed by Eric in the hallway. Feeling bad that I hadn't talked to him since his fight with Joey, I turned and walked with him to wherever he was going.

"Hey," I said, twirling my thick ponytail around my finger.

"Hi."

It was the coldest "hi" I've ever gotten.

"So…that was some fight the other day."

"Tori, I can't do this, okay?"

Taken aback, I asked "Can't do what?"

But before I got my last word out, Eric had stormed away.

I started after him, and then the bell rang. My class was on the complete other side of the school.

"Screw this," I said aloud into the empty enormity of the hallway. I let out a huge sigh and walked out of the school into the sunshine of the afternoon.

When I got home, I went up to my room to cool off. I turned on the TV and started watching "Keeping up with the Kardashians." Two hours later, neither of my parents had come home, and no one had texted me. I felt like such a loner. Had everyone just forgotten about me or something?

I texted Alyssa, but she didn't answer. I looked around my room. A picture of Tammi, Kyle, and me sat in the upper right-hand corner of my mirror. Tammi had her tongue out and Kyle had his hand trying to cover up my face. I had always loved that picture because it really showed our true personalities. It wasn't fake or posed like so many others. I thought back to our late-night chess combats with each other in Kyle's basement and how we used to make pizza and watch the audio-commentaries of our favorite movies.

A smile began to sneak onto my face, but then I really looked at myself in the picture. I wasn't beautiful. In fact, my cheeks looked like a chipmunk's. I put a Rihanna playlist on and ripped the picture up into tiny pieces. I didn't want to look like that. My newfound self-confidence was just a façade to cover up my insecurities.

Fear was still the boss of my life, enveloping me in its fierce grip. My biggest fear was of being alone. Because when I was alone, I had to face the person I was becoming.

She was strong and popular on the outside, but ugly and scared on the inside. I went around my room ripping up any photo of me that made me look fat. Just because I had popular friends didn't mean that I was truly one of them. In order to be like them, I had to look like them—like a cheerleader.

Once I had cleared my room of these pictures, I looked at my phone. Still no one had texted me. The anger was building inside of me, threatening to burst right out of my chest. I looked at my chess set on my dresser, a birthday gift from Tammi when we first became friends in fifth grade. I let out a piercing scream and threw my chess board against the wall. The pieces fell to the ground like a tiny army against a solid blockade.

BAD KIND OF BUTTERFLIES

Sunday finally came, and I was hoping that Chris' party would be the cure for my current depression. Alyssa picked me up at my house, since I would be sleeping over at her apartment after the party. I was surprised my parents were cool with it.

"I'm so happy you're getting to be more social," mom told me as I double-checked the contents of my overnight bag.

"Yeah, me too."

"You're becoming more like myself when I was your age."

"I'm not joining the cheer squad, Mom."

"I wasn't saying that. I simply meant that-- Never mind, you have a good time honey," she said, placing a casserole into the oven.

My mom had been a cheerleader in high school and my dad was a football player. I certainly didn't get the nerd gene from my immediate family.

Anyway, I'm sure this was the reason my parents didn't find much interest in my extracurriculars. It figured the first time my mom actually gave me praise was when I was going to parties with the popular kids. Wasn't she concerned about underage drinking and sex, like most parents I knew? Or maybe mom understood the price a girl had to pay to become popular.

Thank God Alyssa came through the door, her hair in a high bun, giant gold hoops in her ears.

"God, your wings are flawless!" Alyssa exclaimed, examining my jet-black eyeliner.

"Thanks, I think I'm getting the hang of it." I smiled, proud that she noticed.

"Smells good, Mrs. Rowling."

"Why thank you, Alyssa. It's baked ziti with Italian meatballs."

My parents still hadn't forgiven Alyssa for ditching the birthday party we had thrown for her, but they were at least acting civil towards her for my sake.

"Wish we could have some, but there should be plenty of food at Chris' house."

"Well, you girls have fun tonight. And I hope you enjoy your sleepover as well."

"Thanks, mom."

"Yes, thanks Mrs. Rowling, we'll see you later."

Mom waved to us from the porch as we got into Alyssa's car.

"Your mom is so cool." Alyssa said, pulling out of our driveway.

"Yeah, that's one word for it."

• • •

Chris' house was incredible, it was practically a mansion. The brick façade towered over us as we walked up to the large, wooden front door.

"What do Chris' parents do anyway?" I asked as Alyssa grasped the golden door knocker, banging it against the wooden surface.

"I think they are surgeons."

Of course.

"Welcome, come on in!" Chris' girlfriend Lisa answered the door, her black hair teased and fanned around her face, highlighting her princess-cut diamond earrings.

Alyssa and I entered the palatial living room, filled with loads of classmates and even more alcohol.

"Let's get a drink," Alyssa said, leading me to the kitchen. She grabbed a wine cooler and I grabbed a soda.

"You better be putting some Jack in that Coke, missy." Alyssa scolded.

"Yeah, yeah, I hear you. But remember, your wine cooler isn't much better on the scale of alcohol percentage."

"Tori, you are so right. Let's do shots!"

As soon as she had said it, five people came into the kitchen chanting, "Shots, shots, shots!"

"That's my cue to leave," I said aloud to no one in particular.

I left Lyss and the chanters and sat down on the living room sofa. I could hear the clink of their shot glasses tapping the granite countertop, cheers resounding to, "Let's do another!"

I laid back into the sofa cushions, staring up at the high ceiling, wondering why I kept coming to these parties if I wasn't going to participate in the fun.

"Hey, you."

I opened my eyes to see a tall boy with black hair standing above me. He looked a little older, like he could be in college maybe. He had dark brown eyes and a crew cut, taut muscles peeking through his Michael Kors button-down.

"Do I know you?" I asked in confusion.

"No, I don't believe we've met before."

He extended his hand, sitting next to me on the comfy cushions.

"I'm Paul. And you are?"

"Tori."

"Nice to meet you, Tori. Did you know you have very intense eye contact?"

"Well, I guess maybe I do. I do think that eye contact is very important."

Why were we even talking about this?

"Come here."

Those two words evoked fear inside me, a power play about to happen. Why did I suddenly feel inferior? And why did I want to obey?

He stroked my thigh and pulled my hand so I would rise from the couch. Placing his hands around my waist, he began guiding me towards a hallway. Thankfully, my anger rose above my fear.

"I'm not drunk."

"What?"

"I mean, you're acting like I'm some drunk girl who's gonna let you lead her to a side room."

"What the fuck are you doing here then?"

"Excuse me?"

"Just get outta my way, you prude bitch."

I ran into the bathroom, locking the door behind me. I took a few deep breaths and went over what just happened in my head. I couldn't believe how entitled and superior he had been. He thought he could take advantage of a drunk girl, and worse, he responded in anger to rejection as if I owed him something because I was female. What a complete and utter moron.

Beyond that, he had scared me. Thank God I wasn't drunk like he thought. Anyone could guess how that scenario would've played out. One thing I did know was that I'd never forget Paul's face.

I sat at the dining room table, deciding to browse my phone instead of talk to people, since the first and only person I spoke to turned out to be a creep. I checked TikTok and Tumblr and took a few selfies for my snapchat with the new geo filters.

A few hours went by and I was getting bored, so I got up from the table to look for Alyssa. I looked in every room I could find, all except for the upstairs bedrooms with closed doors. I'd watched enough teen dramas to know that I didn't want to walk in on anybody.

After checking the bathrooms one last time, I decided that Alyssa must've ditched me. I'm sure she didn't mean to, she probably met some hot dude and left with him. It wasn't a huge deal; I'd just call an Uber to take me to her apartment. Once she was done doing whatever it was she was doing, we could still have our late-night sleepover.

I called my Uber and waited for it in the driveway, my hands in the pockets of my denim jacket. I shivered against the wind in the night air. The car pulled up, and I got in, telling the blonde driver with pigtails where I needed to go. She dropped me off at Alyssa's apartment. I thanked her and walked up to Alyssa's door.

Crap. I didn't have a key to get in. Can't believe I didn't think about that…

I felt around her doorframe, searching for the key. Alyssa seemed like the type who would hide it nearby in case she forgot it. Bingo! The key was tucked behind her peony flowerpot to the left of her doorway. I knew her so well.

I entered her place, taking in the white carpeting and pink décor. I sat on one of the white leather kitchen bar stools and laid my head on the marble countertop. *What a night,* I thought. I turned my head towards the living room, seeing Alyssa's open laptop, her poodle screen saver illuminated in the darkness.

I didn't want to snoop on my friend, yet I was curious what Alyssa Perdue kept on her laptop. I let my intrigue get the best of me, walking over to the coffee table and moving the mouse on the keyboard. As soon as I opened her browser, her email account appeared. There was email after email relating to various GoFundMe accounts, from paying for veterinarian bills to funding a semester of college.

What was this all about? I wondered.

But I couldn't ask Alyssa about this without revealing that I snooped onto her private laptop. And I wasn't about to do that. Whatever it was, I was sure it was some sort of charity thing she was doing to please her parents.

I was starting to get tired, so I brushed my teeth and got into Alyssa's bed. We always shared her bed when I slept over. I drifted off to sleep only to awaken to the front door slamming. I got up and moved to the living room to greet Alyssa.

"Hey," I said, rubbing my eyes in the light.

"Hey," Alyssa answered, turning away from me.

"Is everything okay?" I asked, placing my hand on her shoulder.

She turned towards me, and I could see tears in her eyes.

"Why did you leave the party without me?"

"I looked everywhere, but I couldn't find you, so I figured you found a hot guy to pursue, so I took an Uber here."

She didn't say anything, just walked into the bedroom and got into bed, pulling the covers over her face.

"Did something happen tonight? Do you want to talk about it?"

"I just picked the wrong guy." She said, sniffling.

"What do you mean?"

"What I mean is, he took advantage of me, Tori. We went upstairs to make out, and before I knew it, he was taking off my clothes. When I told him to slow down, he shushed me and said 'I know you want it. You don't have to be a tease.'"

She shuddered, and I gave her a fierce hug.

"I'm so sorry, 'Lyss, I should've never left!"

"He said I was asking for it with my tight dress and how flirtatious I was."

"Do you know what his name was?" I asked.

"It was Paul."

No way. Of course, he moved on to Alyssa after me. I felt sick to my stomach.

"Don't worry, we won't let him get away with it." I assured her.

"They always do." She replied, turning away from me and shutting off the light.

DIRTY LITTLE SECRET

Alyssa and I rode to school together the next day, Top 40 blaring from her speakers, neither of us saying anything. Finally, I broke the silence.

"Are you doing okay?" I asked.

She turned down the music.

"Yes, I'm fine."

"Okay, I just wanted to check in because of what happened last night."

"Oh, THAT. Don't worry, Tori, I'm over it. That Paul guy was a perv, and now it's over. I learned my lesson about going into bedrooms at parties." She giggled.

"'Lyss, I'm serious. We can report this guy to the police. I had an incident with him earlier in the night."

She laughed even harder this time.

"Tori, I seriously don't want to press charges. It's not a big deal. This stuff happens sometimes. Besides, I knew what I was doing when we started making out with the door closed. I think he just misread my signals."

She parked the car and we walked into the school.

"'Lyss, you were raped. This is not okay."

Alyssa looked around frantically when I said the R word.

"Tori, please, it was a mistake and it won't happen again. End of discussion. I don't want to talk about this ever again."

I couldn't even deal with her right now. I walked away from her, in the direction of Eric's locker.

When I approached him, he didn't even look at me.

"Eric, I honestly don't know why you're mad at me. But whatever it is, it's not fair for you to just ignore me. I mean, I thought we were friends."

He turned to face me.

"You're right, I'm sorry," was all he said.

Not expecting an apology, I had no idea what to say.

Eric said, "Do you want to hang out after school?"

"Sure, of course!" I answered much too enthusiastically.

We met outside on the steps after school, after mostly everyone had left. The sun was shining brightly in the sky, and my shadow fell across the smooth cement of the steps as I walked over to where Eric was sitting. Wisps of his hair were curling on the ends from the heat, and when he heard me approaching, he looked up at me with his ocean-blue eyes.

"Hey," he said seriously.

"Hey," I said back.

"Okay, so I need to tell you something. I was mad at you before because that day at lunch, Joey told me that you and him made out. That's why I punched him."

Amazed by his unabashed honesty, I started, "Oh, Eric that was—"

"No, listen, okay? Yeah, I know I should've asked you if it was true, but I couldn't because then you'd ask me why I care...and anyway, it was all over the school that you and him kissed. Amber even said she caught you in his room together."

I couldn't believe this. He was mad at me because he was jealous! It was right in front of me and I didn't even see it. Since Eric had been so honest with me, I felt the need to at least be a *little* honest with him.

"Eric, Joey wanted me to see his room, so we went up there and were looking at some of his stuff. Then he kissed me, and that's when Amber walked in."

The lie came out of my mouth so naturally, like second nature. To be fair, it wasn't total dishonesty. We were in his room, and he did kiss me. I just left out the part about me wanting him to. I knew Eric liked me, but to hear him say it out loud made my spirits soar.

Eric's face looked relieved.

"So...you don't like him like that?"

This was my chance to be completely honest with him. I was hot for Joey. And I was hot for him too. Was it so wrong to want the best of both worlds?

"No, of course I don't like him like that. He came on to me! And I wasn't even sure you liked me, so that's why I didn't come explain the rumor to you."

"Well, I asked you out on a date, so I think that means I like you," he smirked. "But I shouldn't have believed the rumor in the first place. I should've trusted that you were the girl I thought you were," he said apologetically.

An awkward silence set in.

"So...now what?" I asked with a smile on my face.

Returning the smile, he asked, "do you want to see a movie tomorrow night?"

•••

"I cannot believe I have a date tonight!" I squealed as Alyssa tore through what used to be a neatly organized closet.

"You do not own *one* hot item of clothing..." Alyssa said, ignoring my exclamations.

"I just can't believe I'm going on my SECOND date with Eric!"

"Okay, maybe we'll try the sexy librarian look,"

Raising my eyebrows, I yanked the black vest and gray pencil skirt out of Alyssa's hands.

"I am NOT dressing as a sexy...*anything*, okay? We're just going to watch a movie in the dark. He probably won't even notice what I wear."

Alyssa snorted.

"Trust me, honey, he'll notice. And if you walk in there looking like Billie Eilish, he'll turn right around and that will be the end of it."

Not getting her reference, I retorted, "I'm wearing jeans and a sweater."

Alyssa eyed the dark purple Forever 21 top I was holding up.

"Okay, you do what you want, but I don't see how he'll be able to feel you up in that."

I waited on my porch for Eric to pick me up, a smile on my face. I was completely elated. *He really likes me,* I thought to myself. His rusty brown pickup truck pulled into my driveway, and I ran to the passenger door, opened it, and hopped onto the seat.

"Someone's excited," Eric joked.

I could tell by his expression that he was amused and flattered by my zeal.

I smiled.

"So," he began "I was looking up show times and it looks like the contenders are either *Knives Out*, *The Turning*, or *Frozen II*"

"*The Turning*, for sure," I said with a grin.

"That's what I was hoping you'd say."

We walked into the theatre and got our snacks, then showed our tickets to the usher who told us we would be in theatre number 4. Eric held my hand as we walked into the large room with an expanse of empty seats. We sat down in the middle section, a little further back than the front row.

Halfway through the movie, the couple in front of us was making out and moaning. I was just going to ignore them, but after ten minutes, Eric couldn't take it any longer. He leaned forward and said, "Hey guys, could you be a little more respectful?"

The couple sat up, and to my surprise, I saw that it was Joey and Amber. After the recent incident that occurred between the three of us, I had just assumed that Amber would've dumped Joey. And honestly, I felt disappointed that Joey still wasn't single. I knew that was a stupid feeling to have, but it was instinctual. Joey had told me that they were still together, but I guess I had to see it to believe it.

Amber glared at us, raising her eyebrows, and Joey looked at me with his adorable smirk.

"Hey, Tori. Good to see you again."

All eyes were on me as I was completely blanking on a response.

Smiling awkwardly, I replied "Yeah, same here."

I could feel the tension between the two boys, not to mention the anger on Amber's face.

Eric leaned forward and said, "Do you guys mind being a little more quiet?"

I swear Amber looked constipated.

"You better turn your skanky ass around before I bitch slap your fat little face!" Amber yelled at me.

My eyes widened, feeling frozen in their sockets. I didn't know what to say.

"I'm sorry, Amber. I didn't mean—"

"You don't need to explain yourself to her." Eric said, cutting me off mid-sentence.

"Yeah, babe, calm down. It didn't mean anything." Joey told her, putting his hand on her shoulder.

A security guard came over to us with his flashlight glaring in our faces.

"I'm going to have to ask you four to be quiet, or you'll be forced to leave." He said in his booming voice.

"Sure man, sure," Joey said as both he and Amber turned back around, his arm wrapped around her.

"I'm very sorry, sir." Eric apologized.

I smiled at Eric and turned my attention back towards the screen, but I couldn't help but feel embarrassed by the exchange. I knew Amber was upset with me, but I also thought she'd be even more upset with Joey. I mean, he was the one who wasn't loyal to her. I couldn't believe she tried to start a fight with me in the middle of a movie theater. We watched the rest of the movie in silence.

•••

"The movie was great," I told Eric as he pulled up to my house to let me out.

"Yeah, I had a lot of fun."

"Well, I guess I'll see you around?" I asked.

"Yeah, for sure. We always have gym class. I heard we're playing dodge ball on Monday."

"Oh, great." I said, adding "Well, I'd rather dodge a ball than catch one."

Eric laughed. "Don't worry, Tori. I'll make sure we're on the same team."

"Aw, thanks. But no one can save me from the humiliation of dodge ball."

"We'll see..."

"Okay, well thanks, Eric. I had a great night."

"No problem. See ya," he said as I stepped onto the sidewalk and closed the door of his truck.

The rusty vehicle pulled away, and I walked up to my porch and slid the key into the lock, turning the doorknob, expecting my parents to be asleep. Instead, they were sitting on the couch drinking wine.

"And who were you with?" My mom inquired.

Now I felt like a typical teenager, the kind I always wished to be. Except now I understood how the typical teenager felt.

"Um, my friend Eric."

"Oh, the boy we met last week?"

I could see that I had piqued their curiosity.

"Yes, that's him." I answered, feeling the need to end this conversation.

"How did you meet this Eric?" My dad asked.

"He's in my gym class."

"Oh. Well, I'd like to sit down and get to know him." My mom added.

Ugh, I had this feeling of defensiveness and a need to get away from them. *This is what happens when you never have any guys come to the house,* I thought to myself.

"Well, if I ever hang out with him again, I'll make sure that happens." I said, beginning to walk up the stairs to the safe haven of my room.

"Okay, honey. That would be lovely." I heard my mom say as I got into my bed.

Not only was I unsure if he'd want to go on another date with me, I didn't need the added pressure of having him interact with my parents again. I sighed, trying to calm myself. *Who knows,* I thought. *With my luck, he'll never ask me out again. Problem solved.*

...

I thought it would be weird at school after having my second date with Eric, but it really wasn't. Eric saw me in the hallway on my way to homeroom in the morning, walking towards me.

"Hello, Tori." He said with a silly grin.

I was so in love with his confidence.

"Hi, Eric."

It was like one of those dopey moments where we both just wanted to stand there and stare at each other for all eternity. Thankfully, we were saved by the bell.

As its shrill ring echoed down the hall, Eric said, "Text me later, okay?"

"I will." I said as he walked away.

• • •

The large balls flew at me from all directions, like bright-colored bullets of death. Looks like I was "out," again. I took my seat on the bottom bleacher next to the other students who couldn't manage to escape the dexterity and skill of the players still in the game. I watched Eric wind his arm back and wail a soft red ball at Wilson (one of his teammates on the basketball team), hitting him in the face. Wilson doubled over, yelling out in pain, but laughing at the same time.

"Dude! You are so dead!" Wilson yelled to Eric.

Eric was cracking up, with concern on his face.

Like what is wrong with athletes, I thought.

"I'm sorry, man! You okay?" Eric asked through laughter.

"ERIC LARSON, TAKE A SEAT!" Mrs. Beyers bellowed.

Eric continued laughing as he sat down next to me. I could feel the eyes of all the girls around me burning with envy and curiosity at our pairing.

"Did you see that?" Eric asked me.

"Of course I saw it." I said. "Did you hit him like that on purpose?"

"No way. I didn't know I'd hit his face. Now I'm out of the game."

"Yeah, that's a real bummer."

He playfully punched my arm.

"Ha. Ha. Ha…very funny, Miss Rowling…But you know," he said, picking up a ball and tossing it up in the air, "it's actually a really fun game." The ball landed in his hand. "Once you have a little practice."

"Well, I don't *want* to practice."

"I'll make you practice." He said with a grin, tossing the ball to hit my side.

"Larson!" Mrs. Beyers yelled, "You can't hit people who aren't in the game!"

"But, coach, *I'm* not in the game," he playfully answered.

She sighed. "Get back out there, Larson."

He jumped up and turned to me.

"Catch ya later, Miss Rowling." And with a wink, he ran back onto the court.

My heart rate accelerated, cheeks blushing with the heat of such a public display of attraction. I knew the other students had been watching Eric and me this whole time, witnesses to the beginning of something beautiful.

When I got home from school, my parents were waiting for me at the kitchen table.

"Oh, no, what did I do?" I asked them, sitting down on one of the intricately carved oak chairs.

"Tori," my dad started, "your mother and I have noticed some changes in you these last few months."

This wasn't going to be good.

"You quit reading competition, you haven't been going to your band practices, and you've been seeing that boy."

"Eric, you mean."

"Yes, Eric. Is he the reason you've been kicked out of band?" My mom asked.

"What?! What do you mean I've been kicked out of band?"

"Mr. Grayson didn't tell you? He spoke with us today. He said that you've missed 6 practices, and he gave you your last chance. Is this true?"

Alyssa!

"Apparently it is true," I said. "I had to help Alyssa with her homework, so I had to miss practice, but she told me that she'd explain it to him for me."

"And why wouldn't you talk to him yourself? You just don't think, Tori, do you?" My dad said.

"And what happened to your time-management skills?" Mom asked.

"I guess they went out the window." I replied, getting angry. It was ridiculous that they were treating me like this. I was, after all, a good student.

"I thought you loved band and reading competition. Why would you do this?" Mom asked.

Because I was popular now.

Because I had more things to do and more people to hang out with than before.

"Because I have a lot going on right now." I said.

"Honey, that's not a good excuse. If you need help, you come to us. You don't drop out of your extra-curriculars. And you will not see that boy outside of school until we get a chance to formally meet him again. We clearly need to get to know him better. Understood?"

Ugh.

"Fine, then I won't hang out with him outside of school." I said, running up to my room.

I was upset and in a bratty mood, beginning to cry as I laid on my bed. They had no idea that this had nothing to do with Eric. But even worse, I was kicked out of band. And not just concert band, marching band too. I completely blew it.

I picked up my cell phone and dialed Alyssa.

"You didn't tell Mr. Grayson I had to skip practice to help you study, did you?"

"Um, negative."

"Well, now I'm kicked out, so thanks."

"I am so sorry, girl! It totally slipped my mind!"

"Yeah, and then you lied to me when I asked you about it."

"I know, I'm sorry. What else can I say?"

I was still upset with her, but she was now my only link to Tammi and Kyle.

"Thanks for apologizing. I need to cool off before we hang out again though."

"Why? I thought you didn't even like band anymore."

"Well, not really. But I still love marching band, and now I'm kicked out of that too! And it's my senior year, so this was it for me, you know?"

"Yeah, it's a bummer. But at least you still have me, right?" I could hear her smile through the phone.

"Yeah, I still have you."

It didn't make me feel better, though. I didn't come down for dinner that night.

• • •

"How come I can't find you on Instagram?" I asked Eric the next day while we sat together during lunch.

I was trying to avoid Alyssa, so I asked Eric if I could join him and his friends. Ironically, I was so nervous to sit with all of those guys that I couldn't even eat my lunch. But I had to muster up my courage, because I really needed to stay away from Alyssa for a while.

"I don't have an Instagram." Eric replied, as his friends laughed.

"Eric is off the grid." Jamal said through laughter.

"What does that even mean?" I asked.

"He has no social media presence whatsoever." Gavin said.

"So, I can't add you on Facebook either then?"

"Tori, I don't have a Facebook."

I couldn't believe what I was hearing.

"How did I not know this about you?" I asked him.

"It never came up. What's the big deal, anyway?"

The big deal was that we'd never be able to update our relationship status...

"It's not a big deal, I guess. It's just surprising, that's all."

"Yeah, now she won't be able to stalk you online." Gavin joked.

My cheeks flushed.

"Do people actually do that?" Eric asked.

"Um, that's what it was invented for." Gavin answered.

Wow, Eric was the first person I met who didn't have any social media accounts. I mean, I knew people who didn't use Twitter or Tumblr, but no Instagram? He just kept getting more interesting.

• • •

It only took me a week of avoiding Alyssa to forgive her for her lie. After all, she was really my only real friend at the moment. I seemed to be spending less and less time at home these days. *And who could blame me, I thought. I mean, with my best friend living in her own apartment, rent-free?*

"Man, I wish my parents could pay for an awesome apartment for me to live in." I said to Alyssa as she did sit-ups on the living room floor.

"Tori, it's not all fun and games, you know."

"Oh really? I've never seen you clean anything in here."

"Just because you don't see it, doesn't mean I don't do it," she said. "I wash dishes, vacuum, do laundry, buy groceries..." she trailed off, now sitting up.

"Wait, I thought you had a maid?" I asked.

"My parents had to let her go."

"Okay, well, I do practically all of that at my house. I could so live on my own."

"Then why don't you?" Alyssa questioned.

"Um... there's this little thing called money..."

"No, I mean, move in with me. My parents pay the rent. And you basically live here anyway."

The idea was making my head spin. Me and Alyssa living together? It would be perfect! I'd finally be independent, wouldn't have to rely on my parents for anything. Except...

"I don't have a car, though."

"No worries," Alyssa reassured me. "We'll share mine."

• • •

"You can't be serious."

My mother's face held no smile.

"I'm completely serious." I said.

"Honey, I don't understand why you would want to leave us in the first place," My dad interjected.

"We give you everything here." Mom added.

Alyssa came down the stairs carrying one of my many bags of belongings.

As all three of our heads turned to look at her, Alyssa said, "Hey, Mr. and Mrs. Rowling."

My mom put her foot down. "Tori, you are not leaving this house, and that's final."

I looked her in the eyes. "Except that I am."

I could see the almost tangible anger and hurt in my parents' faces. I knew I was being dramatic, but I had to show my parents that I didn't have to listen to them anymore. I was 17, almost an adult now. I was sick of their rules for my life. They'd probably be happier to just have Corey in the house anyway. It's not like they ever cared about anything I was doing. Maybe I was being a brat, but I followed Alyssa out to her car anyway, leaving the only home I'd ever known.

Alyssa opened the door to her—wait, I mean our—apartment. Even though everything was set exactly the same as it was yesterday, it all looked so different to me now. We dropped my bags on the bedroom floor.

"So..." I started, "Where does all my stuff go?"

Alyssa scanned the pink and black, Victoria's Secret-scented room.

"You can shove your stuff in my closet, and I'll clear off this night stand for you. And you can just put your stuff wherever you want, basically."

It sounded easy enough. Alyssa helped me hang my clothes in her rather spacious closet, and then I set up my toothbrush and other toiletries in the cozy white-walled bathroom with hot-pink rugs.

At least, that's how it started. With time, though, our separate possessions and spaces began to mesh together as if we were one person. And we basically were. She was like the sister I never had.

...

Monday came, and as I looked down at my graded paper in Chemistry class, I saw a rather surprising mark: D-.

"How can this be?" I said aloud, not realizing that the words came out of my mouth for my teacher to hear.

"I'm just as surprised as you, Tori." Mr. Corsick replied.

Turning toward my desk, Joey said, "I thought you were smart."

"I AM smart." I answered back to him.

Now I had embarrassed myself in front of Joey and my entire Chemistry class. And my horrible grade...What was I gonna do?

Fortunately, I had Eric to cheer me up. I texted him after school to see if he wanted to study together since I obviously needed it.

> I'm too cool to study.lol
> **Haha I know u r. But r u too cool to help me study?**
> What class?
> **Chem.**
> I could prob help u. I took it last semester.
> **Cool. Alyssa's apt at 6?**
> Ok. c u then :)

And just like that, I had a study date with Eric. I was simultaneously excited and nervous.

"I can't believe you live here now," Eric said as I welcomed him inside Alyssa's spacious living room. "Did something happen with your parents?"

"Nothing major," I said, "They just keep making more rules for me to follow, and they're upset that I quit reading competition and I was kicked out of band."

"You were kicked out of band?!"

"Yeah, I missed 6 practices."

"I thought you loved band." Eric said.

"I do...but things are different now. I have more things to juggle in my life."

"Like your new friends?"

How would he know that I had new friends? He only met me after I started hanging out with Alyssa.

"Tori, I've had classes with you every year of high school. And up until this year, I've only seen you hang out with Tammi and Kyle."

"You noticed me before this year?"

"Yeah, of course. It's not like we have a huge class," he laughed. "But I guess you've never noticed me before."

"Honestly, I just kind of blended all of the jocks together." I said, awaiting his reaction.

"Wow, that hurts," he joked.

So, Eric noticed me before my makeover, I thought. Maybe I wasn't as invisible as I had thought.

My eraser chafed the paper as Eric told me once again that my answer was wrong. I was beginning to feel frustrated because I wasn't getting it. I didn't understand why math had to be involved in Chemistry. Math equations were my weakness.

"No, you are getting it, Tori." Eric said to me. "You just keep second-guessing yourself on the equations. You know how to plug in the numbers, so just do it and don't second-guess your answer."

"But .0077 just looks wrong." I told him.

"Numbers can't always be whole."

"Let's just go back to elementary school where there are no variables and ALL the numbers are whole," I joked as I took a stab at the next problem.

I'd always hated math, but somehow Eric was able to explain it to me in a way I could understand. He was able to break each problem down into a formula for me to follow. It also helped that I had individual attention. Maybe that's all I had ever needed. I found it rather funny that Eric tried to act like he wasn't book-smart when in reality he was probably smarter than most of our class. I'd always been viewed as intelligent because I was quiet and wore glasses. But my good grades were truly the result of my strong efforts in my classes. I envied Eric's natural gift for learning and teaching.

• • •

The birds were chirping outside my window and I was ready to begin my day. I got out of my soft pink sheets and stepped onto my fuzzy brown carpet. Oh, wait. Nope, I was in Alyssa's room, sleeping on her bed and stepping on her fluffy pink rug. Not that her apartment wasn't nice...it just wasn't home. But I wouldn't trade my newfound freedom for a firm mattress and 800 thread-count sheets. I would stick this out until I graduated high school, at least.

After suffering through my morning classes, I walked into the cafeteria to find everyone at my table wearing a football jersey.

"What's this all about?" I asked the girls in Parkside high football jerseys.

"Are you serious?" Amber laughed.

"Tori, it's game day. The cheerleaders and/or girlfriends of the players always wear their jerseys on game day." Alyssa told me.

"Oh, right. I forgot about that." I said, nodding in understanding.

I remembered each year watching with envy as the cheerleaders wore the football players jerseys on Fridays. It was as if they were showing that they belonged to someone. Oh, how I had wished that I could belong to someone and be able to show it in such a public way.

"Where's your jersey, Tori?" Kylie asked me.

"She's saving herself for someone," Amber said to her. "But is that someone Eric Larson or MY boyfriend?"

The entire table erupted into a chorus of Ooohs and Ouches.

"Amber, I know you don't believe me, but Joey kissed me. It wouldn't have gone any further than that, I swear. I like Eric."

Amber stuck her nose in the air and turned away from me, chatting with the girl beside her.

"We believe you, Tori." Gina said to me, the other girls nodding in unison.

"Thanks, guys. That means a lot."

"Are you guys excited for Amber's birthday party? She's handing out her exclusive invitations later today," Kylie said.

"I'm not sure I'll be invited." I told them.

"Trust me, politics trump personal feelings," Alyssa whispered to me.

What an odd world I had stumbled into.

THE LUCKY ONE

It was happening again. Every girl in our school gathered around the petite blonde with the iron-straight hair, Estee Lauder face, Vanity top paired with a Prada mini skirt, complete with Jimmy Choos and about three metallic bangles. She began handing out envelopes to the chosen ten—the ten girls who would be invited to Amber Lawrence's birthday party. Girls spent years sucking up to her just to have a chance at being in the chosen ten. The girls who got an envelope squealed with delight and the others crossed their fingers and bit their nails in anticipation. There were envelopes for Britney and Alice, for Michelle and Taylor, but never one for Tori. It was exactly the same as it was every year.

Except for one thing—I got an envelope.

I gently opened my pastel pink envelope, revealing a glittery, metallic gold invitation inside. The girls who didn't get an invitation watched me open my invite with curiosity and envy. I felt their eyes boring into me as I read the careful cursive on the pretty piece of paper.

You are cordially invited to celebrate
Amber's 18th Birthday Party!

This event will be catered by
Anthony's Italian Restaurant
at the Lawrence residence.
Gifts are not expected, but are much appreciated.
Make sure you bring a pillow and sleeping bag!

Date: December 17th
Time: 6pm till morning (brunch will be provided)

This was such an incredible moment for me, getting invited to Amber's birthday party. I smiled at the girls surrounding me as I placed the invitation into my book bag.

"*You* got invited to Amber's party?" Sarah, one of Alyssa's friends asked me at lunch.

"Yep." I confirmed.

"But I thought she didn't like you." Gina piped in.

It was surprising to me as well. Maybe Alyssa was right: politics must trump personal feelings.

"Well, it appears as though I'm growing on her." I smiled.

"Wow, look at you, getting invited to do things with the cool kids." Sarah joked.

"Yeah, soon I'll be too cool to be seen with the two of you." We all started laughing as the bell rang to signal the end of our short lunch period.

When Alyssa and I got home from school, I threw my invitation on the kitchen table for her to see.

"Awesome!! I'm glad Amber came to her senses." Alyssa said.

"What do you mean?" I asked.

"Well, you know, Amber obviously doesn't like you."

"And...?" I prodded with impatience.

"I didn't want to go to her party without you, so I convinced her to invite you too."

"Why would you do that, 'Lyss? I don't want to go if she still hates my guts."

"Oh, big deal, Tori. She's a drama queen, aren't we all?" She laughed. "Trust me, she'll be glad she invited you. All I had to do was tell her that you and Eric were a thing, so she had nothing to worry about with you and Joey."

"'Lyss, Eric and I are not a thing yet, okay? I don't want him thinking that I think that." I was getting angry.

"Come on, Tori. It's not like Amber's going to say anything to him. Relax, this is good news, right?"

The chosen 10 were the girls that Amber selected to be in her girl squad. It was the highest social rank a girl could have in our school. I was moving up faster than I thought I ever could. Not that it mattered much at this point. Our senior year was already halfway over.

"Yeah, it is good news, you're right."

...

I couldn't believe it was already the day of the party. I felt as though I'd been preparing for it for months. My stomach was in knots with anticipation.

"This party is crucial for us." Alyssa instructed me as we pulled up to the Lawrence's massive stone driveway.

"Really?" I asked. "It's not like you've been saying that for weeks now."

"Oh hush, Tori. I'm just making sure you go in there with a good attitude."

"Oh, I'm ready to rock this party." I said, humoring her.

"That's what I like to hear!" Alyssa said.

We walked up to the large golden door, our pillows and sleeping bags in hand.

"Let's do this." Alyssa said as I pushed the doorbell.

...

Our colorful array of pillows and sleeping bags found its way all around the two large rooms we were occupying in the basement of the house. The catered Italian dinner was held in Amber's dining room where we all sat at their super long table that could probably seat twenty people. Tiered tapers served as accents to the crystal figurines in the center of the cherry wood table, giving the room a classy feel. Amber's sister played on the baby grand piano as we enjoyed manicotti, lasagna, garlic bread, and chicken parmesan.

Now that we were completely full, Amber had us come down to the furnished basement to play games.

"I love games!" Alyssa exclaimed.

I, however, found that no game could compare to that of chess. I only hoped that it wasn't some ridiculous high school game like truth or dare.

We all arranged ourselves into a giant circle, with Alyssa and me beside each other.

"What are we playing? Not spin the bottle, I hope." A girl named Cathy joked.

"We're gonna play my favorite game." Amber said cheerfully.

She turned to me and asked "Truth... or dare?"

FML.

"Truth." I spoke immediately.

"Okay," Amber began to think of a juicy question to ask me.

"What's the farthest you've ever gone with a guy?"

I could feel my cheeks burning as I stared around the circle of pretty girls who I knew would laugh at me if I told the truth.

"I...well, I've never had a boyfriend before."

"But I didn't ask you that. I asked you how far you've gone with a guy."

I could hear a few girls chuckle.

"I've only ever kissed a boy." I let these embarrassing words come out of my mouth reluctantly.

Everyone around the circle looked shocked. Amber scoffed. "No way! Are you serious?"

"Yes."

"Tori is very conservative." Alyssa chimed in, trying to help, I suppose.

Embarrassment washed over my face as some of the girls began laughing.

A girl with straight blonde hair turned to me.

"Guys are so stupid. Seriously, you're so lucky you've never had a boyfriend before. They're just so annoying."

The brunette beside her rolled her eyes.

"Tell me about it. Jake is starting to get all clingy. Like I really need to go through that again."

Some of the other girls started to talk about their boyfriends, agreeing with the fact that I was "so lucky."

Amber interrupted the multiple conversations that had broken out from her "truth" question by asking me another one.

"So, you've never had sex? You've really only kissed a guy?! How is that even possible?" Part of me wondered if this was Amber's way of getting back at me for making out with *her* boyfriend.

Saying that I was planning on saving myself for marriage sounded so ridiculous right now. These girls were superior to me in everything relating to guys. There was no way I was going to tell them about my values. Especially when it seemed like no one else shared those values. But did I still have these beliefs? These were things that my parents had taught me at a young age, and I believed them. But now that I was experiencing new things and discovering myself, I wasn't so sure I thought they were true anymore.

"So, you've all had sex?" I asked towards my audience of ten.

Cathy laughed. "Sweetie, this isn't the 50's. It's totally normal."

Yep, I hated any game that wasn't chess.

• • •

A few pillow fights later, we were all dancing around the basement to a wide variety of rap and pop music. As I sat down on the floor to take a break from another Katy Perry song, Alyssa joined me on the cool carpet.

"You know what this party needs, don't you?" She asked me.

"I think it's pretty great right now." I said back to her.

"We need some boys." She looked around the room.

"And where exactly are we going to get these boys?" I asked her.

"I'm texting them right now," she said.

One hour later, we heard a knock at the basement door.

"Who is it?" Amber yelled toward the top of the basement steps.

"The life of the party!" A male voice yelled back.

The boys had apparently brought the party with them. Joey led the parade though the doorway with two six-packs of Corona in his arms. Each of the six guys that descended the basement steps had a bottle of some kind of alcohol in tow.

As we watched the table fill with alcohol, Amber said, "I'm assuming my parents left already."

"Yeah, they're gone." Joey replied, popping the tab of his beer.

"Where did they go?" Cathy asked, a question I was wondering myself.

"Oh, they went to see a Broadway show for the weekend. They won't be back till Sunday night." Amber answered.

•••

"Fill me up, Joey!" Alyssa held out her red plastic cup to him.

"Me first." Amber snatched the cup out of Alyssa's hand, giggling.

"Birthday girl gets first pour," he announced to our now large group.

As Alyssa put on her pouty face, the drinks started going around the room like the ultimate party favor. Cathy passed me a cup with some sort of mixed drink inside.

"Bottoms up!" I said as we tapped our cups together.

Once the boys came, the party took on a whole new vibe. Some of the girls were grinding on the guys, and Amber was already passed out on the floor. *So much for the sleeping bags,* I thought.

After a few more cups of the mystery mixed drink, I started dancing with Cathy and some of the boys.

"Tori!" Joey called my name.

"Hi, Joey." I smiled at the tall, muscular boy standing before me.

"Tori, you are looking fine tonight."

"Thank you!" I told him, feeling a little dizzy.

"Let's go sit on the couch and talk," he drawled.

"Okay." I said, allowing him to lead me to the brown leather sofa.

"You're so pretty."

"Thanks." I replied, tucking my hair behind my ear.

"Come here," he told me, holding his arms out for a hug.

With butterflies in my stomach, I leaned into his embrace, excitement building inside of me. I thought about him leaving Amber for me, the two of us hand-in-hand walking down the crowded hallways.

Then I felt all of his weight drop onto me. One of the boys started laughing.

"Joey passed out on that girl!" He exclaimed through his guffaws.

"Can someone help me?" I said beneath Joey's body.

Two of the guys pulled him off me and laid him on the couch as I staggered to my feet. We all continued laughing to the point of tears. The only thing I remember after that was falling asleep to the spinning ceiling above me.

•••

Sunday morning, we woke to the smell of a catered brunch, the boys nowhere to be seen.

"Oh good, they left." Amber said aloud.

The food was being passed around the table, but I turned away from it. I felt like I could throw up.

"Ooh, pancakes! My hangover food!" Alyssa exclaimed as she piled the fluffy cakes onto her plate and doused them with syrup.

I'd never been drunk before, but this hangover was not worth it.

"Does anyone have any aspirin?" I asked to the table of girls.

"I'll get you some," Amber said, walking into the kitchen.

"You okay?" Alyssa asked me as she shoved a piece of bacon into her mouth.

I puked on her lap.

"Ewwwwww!!!!!" Alyssa shrieked, the entire room along with her.

I immediately ran to the bathroom to puke again. When I was finished, I cleaned myself up and came back out to the dining room. Everyone was packing up their things to leave and Alyssa was in a towel, her hair wet and dripping.

"I had to take a shower before we left." She told me.

"I'm so sorry, 'Lyss." I apologized with flushed cheeks.

"It happens, Tori, no worries."

Amber cleared her throat and addressed the room.

"Well, thank you all for coming to my party, and I'd say it was a success."

I wasn't too sure about that, but I was sure about one thing—I couldn't wait to go home.

The Monday after the party, Joey approached me in the hallway between classes.

"Hey, sorry I passed out on you," he told me. "I was so drunk that I don't even remember talking to you."

"Oh, it's okay. It happens, right?" I replied.

"Yeah. It was a crazy night." He smiled.

"It certainly was." I told him. "Between truth or dare and me throwing up on Alyssa, it's safe to say that I should never party again."

"Wait, when did you throw up on Alyssa?" Joey asked me, covering his mouth to stifle a laugh.

"The next morning. I was really hungover." I laughed.

"I was pretty hungover the next day too. Wish I could've seen her face when it happened. Glad you're feeling better, though. I'll see you later, Tori." Joey said as the bell rang.

•••

"So, tell us about the party!" Kylie and Gina asked me after lunch.

"It was fun, but not what I expected." I told them.

"Really?" Kylie asked. "It's supposed to be THE party of the year."

"Yeah," Gina added. "I heard a bunch of people bragging about how it was 'such a crazy night.'"

"Well, it was a very girly party until the boys and alcohol showed up."

Their eyes widened.

"Amber's parents let you guys drink?" Gina asked.

"They were gone for the weekend." I said.

"What boys showed up?" Kylie asked.

"Basically the entire football team and Joey," I answered, adding, "Everything was fine until Joey passed out on me. And then in the morning I threw up on Alyssa."

They both started laughing.

"What? Are you serious? Like literally?" Gina managed to ask between her hysterics.

I then told them the story of how it happened.

"Wow, well I can see how the party mood was ruined for you. That's hilarious, though." Gina added.

"I wish we would've made the cut." Kylie said. "I would've KILLED to be there."

"I'm surprised you guys weren't invited. I feel like you're close with Amber."

"Whatever, Amber's a bitch. We all know that. No one is actually her friend. It's all a popularity contest. It just would've been nice to be at the most exclusive party of the year." Gina said to us.

"Trust me, you didn't miss out on much." I said.

•••

During art class, we had to draw a portrait of our families. As I sketched Corey's mass of curly brown hair, I couldn't stop wondering what my family was up to. I hated to admit it, but I missed them.

My mom had called me twice since I moved out a few weeks ago, but I didn't answer. I had too much pride to pick up the phone. But deep down I really wanted to hear my mom's voice and tell her I was sorry. I hoped they were having fun without me, and that they missed me too. Maybe I'd move back in this summer before leaving for college, but right now I needed to be on my own.

In health class we had to do a weigh-in, which was my least favorite day of the week. I knew the nurse would tell me I needed to lose weight.

"You're on the very high end of healthy for your height. It's not a bad thing, but you should try to lose a little bit of weight to make sure you don't end up moving to the overweight column." The nurse told me.

"How was yours?" Alyssa asked me as we changed out of our gym clothes.

"It was the same as always. I'm on the high end of healthy."

"Okay, well at least you're not overweight. Thanks to my diet, I'm underweight on the chart." She said, smiling.

On my way to 5th period, Amber caught up with me in the hallway.

"Hey, Tori."

"Oh, hey, Amber."

"Listen, I've been thinking about what you said at the party, and I want to help."

"Help me with what?" I asked.

"You know, during the truth or dare game..." she said, like this was top-secret information.

"You want to help me with that? Like find me someone?"

"Yes, unless you already have someone in mind we can work with."

"Actually, I do. Eric, remember?" I told her, starting to tell her all about my relationship with Eric so far as we walked to our classes.

I didn't want to be a charity case, but if it was going to get me in even more with Amber and her squad, then I'd do it. Besides, she clearly just wanted to make sure I was off-limits to Joey. The fact that Amber was having one-on-one time with me was weird enough. I really didn't like her, but I wanted to stay popular. Amber was my ticket to the top. Besides, maybe she did have some knowledge into the mind of guys that I was lacking. It couldn't hurt to hear her out.

"Trust me, Tori, losing your virginity is like a rite of passage. Once you've done it, you're basically an adult."

"But what if you wait until marriage?" I asked.

"Trust me, no one waits that long except religious people. Are you religious?"

"No, I'm not...I just like the idea of it, that's all."

She looked at me with skepticism, so I decided to move the conversation along.

"So, if you don't mind me asking, how was *your* first time?"

"Well, it was with Joey, of course. We were making out one day, and then he started to take off my clothes... and then we just ended up doing it."

"So, you guys didn't talk about doing it beforehand?"

"No, he basically just went for it. It was pretty hot."

"Did you want to have sex?" I ask.

"Of course I did. I let him, didn't I?"

• • •

I told Tammi and Kyle Amber's story while we were watching TV at Kyle's house. I was glad that they seemed to have finally forgiven me for always bailing on them.

"Tori, you know she just had sex with him so she'd have a boyfriend, right?"

"Yeah, maybe."

"Don't look to Amber as a 'guide to life' just because she likes you. She only has a boyfriend because she puts out."

"I don't think Joey's like that." I told her.

"I know you don't *want* him to be like that." She retorted.

I was getting upset with her self-righteous attitude.

"I know Amber doesn't know everything, but you don't either."

"Well, I at least have some common sense. Why do you think we've never had boyfriends, Tori? All guys want is sex."

"You sound like my mother. And what about Brian? Is sex all that he wants?"

"Okay, ladies." Kyle refereed. "Let's calm down now. Why don't I order us a pizza and we can watch *The Walking Dead*?"

"You know I never turn down pizza," Tammi said, clearly back to her happy self.

"That sounds good," I said, "but first we have to finish our AP English homework."

That night I couldn't stop thinking about what Tammi had said. *What did she know about guys anyway? She thinks just because she's dating Brian that she now has some vast boy knowledge?* There was no way I was going to listen to anything she had to say in that department.

CRAZY KIDS

After school the following day, Amber, Alyssa, Kylie, Gina, and I were hanging out at our apartment listening to music and discussing the latest gossip.

"Did you hear about Cathy and her boyfriend?" Gina asked, making eye contact with each of us.

"Yeah, she and Stephen have decided to 'see other people.'" Amber chimed in.

"NO way!" Alyssa exclaimed, everyone gasping at the fact.

"Wow, that's insane." I said, trying to sound like I cared.

"Oh my gosh, look at the time!" Alyssa said, jumping up and putting on her coat.

"Where are you off to?" I asked.

"It's a secret," she joked.

"Yeah, we should go too." Kylie said, speaking for both Gina and herself.

All three girls said their goodbyes, trailing out the front door into the sunny afternoon. Now it was just Amber and me.

"Soo..." Amber said aloud into our awkward silence.

I just looked at her, racking my brain for something to say.

She sighed. "Okay...so how has it been going with Eric?"

"Pretty good. We talk basically every day still."

"Has he asked you out on any more dates?"

"No."

"Hmm, that's not a good sign." She judged, shaking her head.

I wanted Amber to like me, but I was pretty sure I didn't want her "help" or advice.

"We're both really busy," I said.

"Busy? Like with band and chess?" She asked.

"Actually, I haven't been to either lately."

"Well thank God for that."

"Do you want to watch *Mean Girls* and order a pizza?" I asked her, desperate to change the subject.

"That sounds freaking awesome." she replied, grabbing the remote to get *Mean Girls* on Netflix.

The rest of our evening consisted of pizza, movies, gossip, and boy-talk (no mention of Joey, for obvious reasons). And it was actually pretty fun. I learned that Amber loved scary movies, went on bicycle trips with her parents on the weekends, and hoped to be an actress someday. She even sang me a few songs from Phantom of the Opera acapella. This girl who I once thought had the depth of a paper doll was becoming a real live person before my eyes. Who knew, maybe we'd eventually become real friends. The thought made me laugh to myself.

After Amber left our apartment, I went straight to my room. Something about watching Mean Girls really got to me. The more I looked at myself in the mirror, the more flaws I found. I could never be as skinny as Alyssa or Amber; I felt inferior standing next to them. Maybe it was time I stopped wishing for a better body and actually started doing something about it. Standing in front of my mirror, I made the conscious decision to eat no more calories than I could burn. I figured I needed to lose about ten pounds. I had been comparing myself physically to Amber, Alyssa, Kylie, and Gina for a while now. Years ago, I just accepted the fact that I would never be able to look as fit as the popular girls. After all, they were the elite of our school. But now I was one of them. I knew that I had to keep up or I'd be left behind.

The next morning, I got up and made the decision to skip breakfast. My stomach grumbled, but I was determined. Before first period, Eric stopped by my locker to talk, like he did almost every day now.

"Hey, Tori." He smiled his goofy grin.

"Hey, how was practice last night?"

"Not too bad. But Coach has got to lay off the suicides."

"I know that's right!" Louis, a broad-shouldered teammate, agreed as he passed by us. Eric laughed.

"So, are we doing anything tonight?" He asked me while playing with the blue heart magnet on my locker door.

"I don't know," I said, smiling. "Are we?"

"Oh, God..." Kyle came up behind us, rolling his eyes.

"Is there no privacy anymore?" I joked out loud.

"Yeah, Kyle, we don't need your commentary on our conversations." Eric went along with my joke.

"Here's a little tip," Kyle said, closing my locker door. "If you want privacy, don't have your 'conversations' in a crowded hallway."

Before I could come up with a retort, Eric gave Kyle a noogie, then put his arm over my shoulder and walked me to class.

I looked around me. Every girl was beautiful and skinny, and even though I had previously thought I was pretty, I now knew the truth. Makeup and a new wardrobe weren't going to make me beautiful. I had to lose some weight.

I sat down for lunch the next day, and Alyssa gave me a skeptical look.

"And what is that, missy?" She asked, referring to my lunch.

I looked down at my bottle of water and protein bar, forcing a smile.

"I'm on a diet."

"Well, good, because I'm tired of being the only one," Alyssa replied.

It felt like the longest lunch period of my life. Neither of us were particularly talkative, and I had finished both the water and protein bar within five minutes. I missed my sandwich, side, and dessert. I looked across the table at various students' trays that held thick cuts of stromboli with marinara sauce and warm cheese oozing out onto the plate. I could smell the sugary cocoa of their dark chocolate brownies as they unwrapped them from the packages. My stomach started to growl, and I kept considering going up and buying a lunch. Right as I was about to give in, Alyssa took out a pack of gum from her purse, handing it to me.

"Want a piece?"

After that day, I had gum on hand everywhere I went. I kept cases of it in my room and in my purse. It was the substance that kept my mouth busy, and my stomach empty.

The next morning consisted of classes, all of which I was somehow doing poorly in. *Maybe I should study more*, I thought. I would study harder from now on. More study time, less social time. Thankfully, it was now lunch time, and I could get a break from all of this study thought.

To my surprise, Amber waved Alyssa and me over to her table.

"C'mon," Alyssa said to me, taking the lead.

We sat down with our protein bars and bottled waters, all of the super pretty girls smiling at Alyssa and looking at me with curiosity.

"You girls remember Tori," Amber said.

"Yeah, you were at Amber's party. Hi." A short blonde girl named Ariel said to me with a smile.

The small group of girls only recently knew who I was, but of course I knew all of their names and who they were dating. They were the queen bees of the school. They were the girls we all wanted to be. And now I was eating lunch with them. Well, technically eating a protein bar with them. I didn't want to screw this up.

"Hey," I said back to Ariel.

Every single pair of eyes looked at me. I needed to say something to break this awkward tension, but nothing was coming to me. *C'mon, Tori, think!*

A girl in red overalls and pigtails walked by our table.

"Wow, some people really haven't let go of the 90's yet," I said.

For a brief second, I thought no one was going to laugh. Then all the queen bees turned towards the overall-pigtailed girl and our table erupted with laughter. The girl looked over at us with embarrassment, then quickly looked away. My face flushed with guilt for hurting a girl I didn't even know. She could've been just like me for all I knew. I felt sick the rest of lunch period.

The next day after school, I skipped chess club to hang out with Amber. I pretty much knew at this point that I wasn't considered part of the team anymore.

"So," she said as we pulled into Starbucks, "Let's talk about Eric. We need to come up with a plan."

My face suddenly felt hot.

"A plan for...?"

"Tori, don't play dumb with me. A plan for you to lose your virginity to Eric."

"Um, ok. But I just really want him to be my boyfriend."

"Well, yes, of course. The two go hand in hand." Amber said.

"Ok." I replied, nodding my head in understanding.

We ordered our lattes and sat down at a table near the window.

"So, first of all, you want to look super-hot," she said, dipping her spoon into her mug.

"Which you do now. I would definitely try to keep your weight down though."

I stared at her in shock.

"Not that you're fat, I'm just warning you because I know you aren't naturally a thin girl."

Amber was the kind of girl who was enemies with her friends. She didn't seem to have any genuine friendships, and now I could see why. She didn't know that I was sensitive about my weight, but who would say a thing like that? Perhaps I had let my guard down too soon with her.

"Ok, what's next on this list...?" I said, suspicious of her motives.

"Next are his interests. I know he plays basketball. What else is he into?"

"Um...I know he likes hip-hop."

"Ok, good, we'll start with that."

"Well, I've been getting into hip-hop too, so it's perfect." I told her, beginning to get defensive.

"Well it's always good to have things in common." Amber told me, as if I didn't know that.

"You should also try to get in with his friends. It's important for his friends to like you."

"Ok, that helps." I told her as I drank the last bit of milk and espresso from my cup.

"There's a basketball game tonight," Amber said, putting a coat of BABY LIPS gloss onto her pouty lips. "And we're going."

...

Amber, Ariel, Kylie, Gina, and I walked into the wood-scented gymnasium, all eyes on us. Or at least that's how it felt to me. I was always aware of people's eyes watching me, which was why I was so self-conscious in public. I was actually kind of nervous to see Eric. I wasn't even sure if he'd see me anyway, but knowing Amber, she'd make sure I had some interaction with him. We found a spot in the bleachers, very far down to the floor for a close view of the "eye candy," as Gina and Kylie called it.

After about ten minutes of mindless chitchat and gossip, the players took the court, running onto the glossy wooden floor with energy and excitement. I watched Eric jump and run in place, shrugging his shoulders, warming up for the game.

"There's your man." Amber said aloud for the group to hear.

"Tori, I didn't know you and Eric Larson were dating." Ariel said.

"Not yet," I told her with false confidence.

Amber smiled. "That's my girl."

I had never been to a basketball game before, so I didn't really know what to expect. I thought it would be similar to a football game. Now that I was here, I observed that it was similar to basketball in gym class, except everyone on the court was really good.

The girls chattered on about whose butt looked the best in their silver and blue uniforms, but my eyes never left Eric. He moved with such grace and confidence, weaving through opponents, faking them out, and passing the ball to his teammates. The boys ran back and forth across the court again and again, in pursuit of the orange ball. They looked like dancers moving in tandem yet also against one another.

Once we hit the third quarter, our team was down by five. By now I was used to the ball whizzing right by my head every three minutes. Amber started talking about how often she and Joey had sex, so now my full attention was on her, which she took notice of. It happened so fast, all I remember was that one minute I was listening to Amber talk about giving Joey a blow job and the next my nose felt like it had been shoved to the inside of my face.

The motion on the court halted, silence surrounding the gymnasium.

"Are you okay?!" Ariel asked as the rest of the girls giggled.

"Yeah, I'm okay." I said, tears stinging my eyes.

"Is she good?" Mr. McMullen, our team's coach, yelled up to our row in the bleachers.

"Yeah, she's fine!" Amber yelled down to him.

Eric looked at me with a frown. I just rolled my eyes and smiled. And so the game continued.

"I can't believe you got hit in the face." Amber said, laughing.

"Yes, I found it particularly hilarious." I said with bitter sarcasm.

"I mean, it's not funny from your perspective, but if you could've seen your face, you would've been cracking up." Amber said through guffaws.

I wish she could see my fist punching her face.

After sitting through the rest of the game in embarrassment, it was finally time to leave.

"Tori!" A voice called towards us in the parking lot.

I turned my head in the direction of the voice and saw a tall boy in a letterman's jacket jogging towards me.

"I thought you might need this," Eric said, sounding out of breath. He dropped an ice pack into my hands.

"Aw, how cute." Amber said aloud.

"Thanks." I told Eric, taking the ice pack from him.

"Well, we're gonna get going." Amber said to Eric and me, beginning to walk toward her Mini Cooper.

"Need a ride home?" Eric asked me. Amber rolled her eyes.

"Yes, please." I answered with a smile as I placed the ice pack on my sore nose.

"How's the nose?" He asked, placing his arm around me as we walked to his car.

"It could be better." I laughed.

"Well, let's go to my house so I can take care of you."

The cheesiest grin began to spread on my face.

"I would like that a lot."

LOVER

Christmas break came and went, with January sitting in a blanket of snow. I went to my parents' house for Christmas Eve and Christmas Day, but spent most of the break with Amber, Kylie, and Gina.

I saw Alyssa mainly at our apartment, but she seemed to be otherwise engaged. For whatever reason, she was over at Tammi's house quite a bit... I thought it was weird, but found that I liked hanging out with the popular crew without her. She tended to take the spotlight in every situation, and when she wasn't there it was easier for me to engage the girls. And it was an added bonus that Tammi and Kyle had stopped complaining about me not always being around. I was glad that Alyssa could be an extra friend for them, though I couldn't understand why she wanted to hang out with them so much. They were completely different people.

The best part about this Christmas break was how I spent my New Year's Eve. Amber had a master plan to get Eric and me to sleep together. She threw a New Year's Eve Bash at her house, to which I invited Eric. She saved a room for us and everything. I knew I wasn't going to have sex with him, but I went along with Amber's plan in order to please her. It didn't mean that I had to sleep with him. But what Eric had in store for me was so much better than I could've imagined.

• • •

"You wanna get out of here?" He asked me, placing my hand in his.

"Sure, I replied, and the two of us walked out of Amber's house into the brisk January weather. We walked down the street to a nearby playground.

The snowflakes were melting on my tongue as Eric slowly wound up the merry-go-round to launch me into a spiral.

"Why are we doing this?" I asked him, looking out into the empty playground.

"Nostalgia," he replied as the world around me began to spin.

I let out a scream of excitement.

Eric hopped onto the merry-go-round and put his arm around me. The childhood contraption began to slow down.

"Do you remember the joy you felt on the playground as a kid?" He asked me.

"Yes, I do."

"Well, that's the joy I have when I'm with you." He said, pulling me onto his lap. My heart beat faster.

"Tori, will you be my girlfriend?"

It was the sweetest gesture I could ever know.

"Yes!" I exclaimed, wrapping my arms around him.

"I think I'm falling for you," he told me.

"I feel the same way, Eric."

And I meant it, too. He was the perfect person. I didn't know what I had done to deserve him. I felt guilty about kissing Joey, I should have been honest with him. I should have told him that Joey had been my crush since forever and that I still liked him too. But I didn't want to ruin this moment. I would tell him another day. We kissed underneath the snowfall, my limbs beginning to numb. But my heart was filled with warmth, and I couldn't help but feel a certain nostalgia for the playground.

•••

"Eric is your boyfriend?" Tammi asked.

"Yes." I couldn't stop smiling.

"It's about time," Kyle said, giving me a hug.

"Wow, that's great." Tammi added.

Now I wasn't the only girl who didn't have a boyfriend. Once Tammi started going out with Brian, it felt like I was socially immature. Tammi and I always talked about boys, but we never dated them. We usually kept to ourselves, admiring them from afar. Kyle was the only guy friend we had, so we didn't have a lot of experience being around boys either.

"Have you guys kissed yet?" Kyle asked me.

"Oh yes." I grinned.

"So how did he ask you out?" Tammi asked.

I told them the story as we walked to our respective classes. Winter break was magical, but I was glad to be back in school. I wanted everyone to see me with my new boyfriend.

"Aww.." they both gushed. Then I spotted Eric in the hallway.

"Bye, guys!" I said, running to catch up with *my boyfriend*.

Kyle and Tammi looked at each other and rolled their eyes.

"Hey, there." Eric greeted me, holding a basketball under his arm.

"I have something to tell you," I told him as we rounded the corner by the biology room.

"Sounds serious."

"Yes, it is."

I pulled him into an empty classroom and shut the door.

"I lied to you about Joey's party. I did want Joey to kiss me. He's been my crush since elementary school, and I wasn't thinking straight. I'm so sorry."

"Wow," he said, shaking his head, "I don't know what to say. Do you even like me, or am I just second choice to Joey?"

"No, you aren't second choice, okay? You are my first and only choice, Eric. I love you. I was so stupid."

"That's pretty messed up, Tori. But we weren't together at the time, so I can understand. I forgive you."

I couldn't believe how understanding he was. Eric really was the perfect guy.

"And I can't blame Joey for wanting you," he said, wrapping me up in a hug, "but you're all mine now."

He smelled like clean cotton and freshly cut grass, and I felt safe and secure in his arms. The bell rang to signal the start of class, but we didn't care. We were exactly where we needed to be in that moment.

•••

The more time I spent with Eric, the more he reminded me of a little boy. He had such a passion for life that most people lost as they got older. He didn't care what people thought of him. His confidence was inspiring, the way he walked down the halls with a spring in his step and how he seemed so at ease on the basketball court.

Now that I was dating an athlete, I had an image to maintain. I knew I was lucky to have Eric as my boyfriend, and I wanted to look my best for him and for our reputation as a couple. I felt like the effects of my makeover at the beginning of the year had worn off. Sure, I was popular, but no one was really talking about me anymore. I needed to lose weight, and I needed to do more than just eat a protein bar for lunch every day. I went out and bought a scale, frozen veggies, and protein powder.

Trying to eat celery was torture. It was cold and stringy…did anyone actually enjoy eating this stalk of gross? But it had negative calories, since you burned calories while eating it. So I was determined to make it my favorite snack. Normally I'd dip it in peanut butter, but there was no way I could do that anymore.

"Embrace the hunger" had become my mantra. Any time I felt the stabbing hunger pangs, I'd say this phrase over and over in my mind. The first night of my diet was the hardest. Since I usually ate a large dinner and dessert, then a snack before bed, it was almost impossible for me to manage only veggies and a protein shake. At around 9 pm, I ended up eating the rest of my box of bars. *Great,* I thought. *Not only was I a failure, but now I needed to hit the grocery store tomorrow.*

…

The day was here…our last chess tournament until the final two schools in the country would play each other. If we made it, we'd get to play on TV. Of course, that would terrify me, but I'd love to see my teammates on TV. And it would be cool to be nationally recognized. We'd never made it this far before, and we weren't going down without a fight. It was a beautiful thing, being winners. Sure, no one at school cared about us, but everyone on the team took pride in our accomplishments.

It actually wasn't that difficult to hide my involvement on the chess team from Eric. It wasn't like our team met three days a week to practice like the basketball team did. Ever since Eric and I had made our relationship official, I hadn't been concerned with chess-related things. Oh, who was I kidding? I hadn't been concerned with chess since I moved in with Alyssa.

Eric and I had started spending a lot of time together, and I wasn't complaining. The only reason I was participating in this tournament was to keep my friendship with Kyle and Tammi. I knew they would hate me even more if I just didn't show up. Even though I hadn't been to practice in a while, I was still technically a part of the team. It was a tiny group of students anyway, and they needed all the help they could get.

Parents and teachers sat in auditorium chairs waiting to see my fellow chess mates take part in our not-so-exciting sport.

I started my first game against a tall and lanky girl with a hooked nose and choppy bangs. My mind wandered during the match, and I found myself staring off into the distance as if there wasn't a person sitting in front of me trying to play chess. She cleared her throat and I came out of my trance.

"Am I boring you?" my opponent asked me, her eyebrows raised.

"Sorry." I apologized, deciding my next move. I realized that I didn't feel nervous about the small crowd watching us play because I didn't care anymore. What was the point of this anyway? It wasn't a sport, so why were we trying to act like it was?

Looking just beyond her gaze, I moved one of my pieces directly in front of her queen. Her brow furrowed in confusion as she stared at the blatantly stupid move I had just made. I stood up and heard the girl say "check mate" as I walked past the audience and out the doorway of the auditorium. And just like that, I had finished my very last chess tournament. I knew I would never play again.

A MODERN MYTH

It's all about the clothes you wear, the way you talk, the confidence you have when you walk down the hall, the way people say your name, the events you attend. This was the life. To look back on the person I used to be was so depressing. To think that I actually listened to classical music and relished a game of chess was beyond embarrassing. And my friends? Yeah, sure they were great. But like the Barbies of my childhood, they'd been outgrown.

Making out was a new concept to me. I never really understood how the merging and contracting of lips could produce any pleasure at all. But with a little practice, it was quite enjoyable. Eric was an excellent teacher.

"Let's take a selfie," I told Eric mid make-out session.

"Tori, I told you I'm not into social media."

"It's not for that. It's just for me."

He raised his eyebrows.

Sighing, I pulled out the golden heart locket from my dresser.

"I want to put it in this locket."

He smiled. "That's pretty cheesy."

"It may be cheesy," I laughed, "but it's what I want."

"Then let's take this damn selfie, then."

•••

"I don't think I can do this diet anymore." I told Alyssa at the lunch table as a girl walked by us with three-cheese lasagna and a Caesar salad.

"But you've been doing so good!" Alyssa exclaimed.

"Yeah, I have, and I'm getting no results. I've only lost 1 pound."

"I may have another solution for you..." Alyssa said quietly just before I got up to get a tray of warm, delicious food.

"And what is that, exactly?"

Alyssa opened her mouth and motioned sticking her finger down her throat.

"Haha, yeah, okay, 'Lyss."

With raised eyebrows and a smirk, she said, "No, I'm completely serious. How do you think I stay so thin?" I laughed nervously.

"There's no way you do that. You barely ever even eat." I told her.

"Yeah, but I do slip up sometimes." She said, resting her chin in her hands. "And you know how I fix it?"

She motioned to her throat again.

I looked at her with fear and concern.

"I'm just saying, it's an option if you want to speed up this weight-loss thing of yours."

She got up from the table to chat with the queen bees, and I decided against getting a tray of hot food. I felt sick to my stomach.

...

It was now Thursday night. We all went out to eat after the basketball game, and Joey and Amber came along. They seemed like they were in love, but Joey kept playing footsies with me underneath the table the entire time. We ordered so much food, it was hard to stop eating. I scarfed down burgers and fries, onion rings, cheese sticks, and deep-fried pickles. But did I stop there? I went up to the bar to order us all a round of milkshakes. Joey came with me to place the order.

"Hey, cutie." Joey said to me once we reached the counter. He slapped my butt. Before I could react, a server asked us how many shakes we wanted and what flavors. After placing the order, I looked back at our table of friends. They weren't paying any attention to Joey and me.

"Let's go to the bathroom," Joey coaxed me.

I let him take my hand and lead me to the guys' bathroom. His hands smoothed over my frame, squeezing my breasts and trying to reach down the waistband of my jeans. I pulled away.

"What's wrong?" he asked.

"I can't." Then I ran away.

What was wrong with me? I finally told Eric about my longtime crush on Joey, but I didn't have the courage to tell him about Joey's power over me. I told myself that I only had eyes for Eric, and here I was again in a bad situation with Joey. This was not what I had in mind for the evening.

Joey and I walked back to the table, Eric giving me a concerned look.

"Where are the milkshakes?" Amber asked.

I knew Joey was looking at me, but I refused to meet his gaze.

Everyone at the table looked confused.

"They should be done by now," Joey said. "I'll go grab them."

He came back with our shakes, and we consumed them with delight as we talked about our classes and the upcoming basketball and football games.

"Are you okay?" Eric asked me, his brow furrowed.

"Yes, why do you ask?" I answered.

"You just seem a little scared right now. Did something happen while you and Joey went to get shakes?

"No," I lied.

"Okay, just checking." He smiled to me.

Why did I lie to Eric? I was surprised he had perceived my fear of Joey. If he only knew the truth, he would punch Joey in front of everyone and make this right. I just wanted to go back to the way things used to be before Joey noticed me.

"Man, I feel like I could explode." Gina said after sucking down the last of her strawberry milkshake.

"Me too." I agreed, holding my stomach.

Alyssa shot me a look from across the table, looking back over towards the women's rest room. I knew she wanted me to join her in the bathroom, but the thought of throwing up my food on purpose scared me. I tried to picture myself on my knees, head hovering over the toilet. The image disgusted me, but Alyssa still jerked her head towards the bathroom.

"I'm gonna go to the bathroom. Anyone else?" Alyssa asked aloud to everyone at the table, her eyes stuck on me.

I sighed. "I'll go too." I said, forcing myself out of my seat. Thankfully no one else had to go. To me, it seemed so obvious what we were doing, but everyone appeared to be oblivious.

I didn't know why I was following her to the bathroom. I knew I didn't HAVE to go. I was my own person, not an Alyssa-follower. But I did still want her approval, and I think a part of me was afraid of saying no to her.

The bathroom smelled like grimy washcloths, but it still didn't make me want to throw up. Alyssa went into a stall, and I just stood there staring at myself in the mirror. Alyssa peeked out of her stall door.

"Tori, what are you doing?"

I just stared at her with contempt.

"Tori, I know it's your first time," she said, leading me by the shoulders to an adjacent stall, "but trust me...you'll feel a lot better once you do it. It's okay to be scared. But part of growing is facing your fears."

While I didn't believe she was entirely correct in her philosophy, I did know that I wanted to be thin. And this was the easiest way to do it.

"Here, I'll even stand here and help you." Alyssa told me.

I got down onto my knees and took a deep breath. I breathed out hard, trying to gag. Alyssa began to laugh.

"Honey, honey. No...haha!"

She covered her mouth in laughter.

"Here," she said, grabbing my hand. "Try sticking your finger down your throat."

She guided my hand to my mouth, and I pushed my finger as far as it would go until the nasty stench of toilet water released a floodgate of vomit from my throat.

"Yay, good job!" Alyssa congratulated me.

My face was flushed with the intoxicating rush of release. Of course, my hands were a different story. Chunky, pink mucous webbed and dripped like slime between my fingers. I went over to the sink and grabbed a handful of paper towels to wipe the lumpy coating from my hands. I looked at myself in the mirror, the mascara staining black rivers down my cheeks. Wiping my eyes as best as I could, I breathed a sigh of relief as Alyssa smiled at me in the reflection.

"How do you feel?" She asked genuinely.

"Um...," I said, biting my bottom lip shyly, "I actually feel really good."

Then we both started laughing out loud in giddiness.

"All right, let's get outta here." Alyssa said, leading me to the door.

"Wait, aren't you gonna..." I tilted my head towards the stalls.

"I'll do it later." she said. "People are gonna wonder what happened to us."

• • •

I felt so different after starting my new diet of purging food. When I threw up, it felt like I was releasing all of my anxiety and fears into the toilet bowl. I knew people thought it was gross, but so had I. I hadn't realized how it could be a stress reliever for me. I didn't do it every day, more like a couple times a week. But that was all I needed to start losing pounds. A couple weeks went by, and I began reaping the rewards.

"You look really good, Tori!" Kylie told me at lunch that day.

I loved how the super-skinny model could tell me I looked good. She was only saying that to be nice. I knew I could never look as good as her. I did feel pride from her compliment, though.

During my last class of the day, I looked down at my cell phone and saw that Amber had texted me.

Can you come over tonight? I need someone to talk to.

Completely surprised that I would be the one she would want to talk with, I texted her back.

Sure! What time?
ASAP.
Be there soon.

I drove straight from my last class to Amber's house. When I walked into her living room, Amber was lying on the couch, covered in used tissues. She was sobbing, tears streaking her beautiful blushed cheeks.

"What happened?!" I asked, sitting down next to her on her powder-blue couch.

"Joey said he wants to start seeing other people."

"What? Why?"

"He told me that I was really pretty, but he wants to 'play the field.' He even said that he still wants to date me, just not exclusively."

I thought about Joey sticking his hands down my pants, anger rising within me.

"I'm so sorry, Amber. Joey's a sleaze ball, and you deserve someone way better than him."

Amber looked at me with hatred in her eyes.

"Joey is NOT a sleaze ball. You're the one who tried to steal him away from me months ago. As if he would actually be with you."

"Amber, I don't want Joey. I'm dating Eric."

"I see the way you look at him, Tori. You seriously think I don't see it? Well look all you want, sweetie, because that's all you get to do."

How sad it must be to be so insecure, I thought. I was starting to think that maybe I had it more together than Amber. I guess popularity wasn't everything.

• • •

A few weeks went by and Eric was now leaving for his basketball trip to New York. This was the first time our team had ever made it to finals, and everyone was crazy excited.

"I'll miss you so much," Eric told me as we stood beside the bus filled with his teammates.

"I'll miss you too."

"I don't know how I'm gonna make it a whole week without you." Eric said.

"I know, but you can call me anytime and we can Facetime too."

"Yeah, you're right. I'll definitely be calling you. And probably texting you every day."

"You better." I replied, kissing him on the cheek.

"You ready to go, man?" One of Eric's teammates asked him, slinging his gym bag over his shoulder.

"Yeah, I'm ready."

He hugged me goodbye and we kissed on the lips, our final touch before our imminent separation.

"I love you, Tori." Eric said, starting to walk towards the bus.

"I love you too, Eric."

I watched him get on the bus and high-five some of the guys who were standing in the aisle. He picked a seat and started talking to some of his friends.

I walked back to the car and drove to my parents' house to see what my family was up to. As I entered the living room, everyone greeted me. My parents, my brother, and... Alyssa. They were watching a movie.

"Did you see Eric off?" My dad asked as he reached into a bowl of popcorn.

"Yeah, I did. What movie are you guys watching?"

"*The Parent Trap*," my brother answered.

"Can I join?"

"Of course, sweetie." My mom replied. "Here, you can sit next to Alyssa on the love seat."

"What are you doing here?" I asked Alyssa quietly.

"I came over to hang out with you, but since you weren't here, your parents invited me to watch this movie with them, and you know I love me some Lindsey Lohan."

Alyssa made room for me on the love seat and handed me the bowl of popcorn. This little family bonding time was kind of nice, but also kind of weird. Why was Alyssa at my house without me? I couldn't believe that Alyssa was actually content to sit and watch a movie with my parents. Feeling my phone vibrate, I checked my texts. It was from Gina.

> Have you heard about Joey's party this weekend?
> **No, but it sounds like fun. Are you going?**
> Yes, of course! You should come with! Joey is single now ;-)
> **Haha yeah I know he is, but I'm not interested.**
> **I'll still come with you though.**

I'M NOT YOUR BOYFRIEND, BABY

As soon as we got to Joey's house, Kylie, Gina, and I went straight to the kitchen for some drinks. Joey saw me immediately and tried to coax me upstairs. He wasn't wasting any time, it seemed.

"Joey, I have a boyfriend." I told him. "I'm not that kind of girl."

"C'mon, pretty please? Eric's not even here." He said, pulling on my arm.

"No, I'm sorry." I told him.

"I just want to talk, Tori. Please." He pleaded, resting his hand on my arm.

"Okay, but just to talk." I told him, wondering if I could trust him or not.

We walked up to his bedroom and sat on his bed, reminiscent of the first party I had gone to at his house.

"So, what did you want to talk about?" I asked him.

He gave me a giant smirk, leaning into me for a kiss. I pulled away from him, and he pulled the sleeve of my top down below my shoulder.

"What are you doing?" I asked him with confusion.

"I didn't actually want to talk, you know." He said, smiling his typical grin.

But this time I didn't find his grin sexy at all.

His huge hands caressed my breasts, and slowly worked their way down to my pants. I thought maybe he was going to try and kiss me again, but before I knew what was happening, his fingers glided inside my underwear, groping the smooth skin of my butt, and stroking the gentle area between my legs.

There was no romance in this moment. No kisses or whispering sweet nothings in my ear. Only rough hands against innocent skin.

All of a sudden there was a huge thud against the door.

"Is anybody in there?" A high-pitched cheerleader-voice asked through the thin wooden door.

As if someone had pressed an OFF button, Joey snapped his hands back to his sides, allowing me time to quickly adjust my bra and button my jeans.

Without even looking me in the eye, Joey opened the door and said, "All yours, babe."

The leggy blonde pulled her stocky boyfriend into the room as Joey and I quickly moved down the hallway. He went back downstairs and found a group of guys to talk to, leaving me all alone, frozen on the bottom step.

I couldn't believe he could do that to me and then just go about his business like nothing had happened. What had he done exactly? And how did that make me feel? I held my locket, moving it back and forth along its golden chain.

"Tori, wake up."

I could feel the sunlight piercing through the covers, calling me toward the start of a new day. Only today I wasn't ready to answer the call.

"Tori, get up!"

Now I was being shaken by my soon-to-be-dead roommate.

"What is your problem?!" I groaned.

"We have to get out of here, like now."

Rubbing my eyes, I asked in confusion "What are you talking about?"

"Listen, I haven't been paying the rent for a while now, and the landlord is REALLY pissed. He's kicking us out unless we can come up with $3,000 by today."

I shot straight up out of bed.

"You've got to be kidding me. You're joking, right?"

"No, I'm really not. And when he finds out there's no way I can pay what I owe, he'll take me to court. Please, we need to leave NOW."

"And just where the hell are we supposed to go?! What is wrong with you, Alyssa?! I thought you were rich! How did this even happen, and how could you not tell me about it?!"

Alyssa began packing my things in giant black trash bags.

"Listen, you can hate me or whatever, but right now we need to jet. We'll talk about it later."

Once we hauled all of our possessions out to her car, Alyssa pulled out onto the highway.

I could see that she was waiting for me to say something, anything, but I just stared straight ahead.

After driving for a few miles, Alyssa broke the silence.

"So...what now?"

•••

"Well, I'm just glad you were sensible enough to come home," Mom said after Alyssa and I told her about us getting kicked out of the apartment. It turned out that Alyssa had been using the rent money from her parents on clothes, makeup, and God knows what else.

Using her best innocent voice, Alyssa asked "Are you sure I'm not imposing, Mrs. Rowling? I don't want to be a bother."

"Aren't you able to move back in with your parents?" My dad asked.

"Well, I could, but they're never home. It's really lonely there."

"I'm going to have to give them a call," Dad said.

"Please, Mr. Rowling, there's no need to bother them. They probably won't pick up anyway." Alyssa pleaded.

He pulled out his cell phone, motioning for Alyssa to write down her parents' cell numbers. She wrote the numbers down and my dad started dialing.

"She hung up on me," Dad said, "and your dad's number is out of service."

"I'm not surprised by that at all." Alyssa said as my mom and dad held conference in the living room.

"Do they know about us getting kicked out of the apartment, Lyss?"

"They know. I texted them earlier. I also told them they should pay for it too in compensation for never taking care of me."

"Wow, Lyss, that's pretty harsh. And they technically did give you the money for rent, you just used it on other things. They're still your parents, ya know?"

"You have no idea what they're like, Tori. Okay? Trust me, it's better if I just stay away from them."

My parents came back into the dining room to tell us the verdict.

"I don't want to be a bother to you guys," Alyssa said. "I can try to figure something out."

"No, no, dear. You can stay with us until we can get ahold of your parents." Mom said, placing her hand on Alyssa's shoulder.

"Thanks, Mrs. Rowling. I know I'll feel right at home."

What was going on, and why were my parents agreeing for Alyssa to stay here?

• • •

"I told you it would all work out." Alyssa gloated as we sat in my room, unpacking our things.

"*You* told *me*? Alyssa, you still owe the landlord $3,000. And just because you live here now doesn't mean my parents are gonna pay it for you."

"Tori, you worry too much. Living here is gonna be great! No rent, no cooking my own meals. It'll be like we're sisters!"

I had a bad feeling about this. "Alyssa, you don't understand. Living here for free comes with having to follow the rules."

Alyssa gave me a look of confusion.

"I know, but I've never been a part of a real family. I think it will be fun to have rules to follow and chores to do. I've never had boundaries before. This will be a new experience for me."

"Oh, it will be for me too…" I said, shoving my underwear into the drawer next to Alyssa's claimed drawer.

Needless to say, my room was quite the downsize from Alyssa's apartment. Of course, this didn't stop Alyssa from taking over my closet, my drawers, and my desk. The only clean space in my room was my bed, and even that was a daily struggle to keep clear of Alyssa's things.

Alyssa was the perfect house guest outside the confines of my room. She was polite, made sure she cleaned her plate (which was a shock to my system), and did her assigned chores without complaining. She was always on time for curfew and would entertain my parents with stories of all the places she had been throughout her life. My parents seemed to enjoy her company. I was starting to feel like she was becoming a better daughter than me.

Ever since the two of us had moved into my parents' house, Alyssa and I were constantly around each other. I'd always wanted a sister, but honestly, I was getting sick of her. The only time I had away from her was between 4-6 every weekday. I knew she was involved in something during this time, but it could remain a mystery for all I cared. As long as she wasn't annoying me with perfume- and nail-polish talk, I was happy.

I wanted to spend time with Tammi and Kyle, like old times. But they seemed to be avoiding me, which sucked because Eric was away. So I spent most nights that week in my room. I felt bored and lonely. Not to mention the fact that Joey kept sending me flirty text messages that bordered on inappropriate.

I thought that what had happened that Friday night was a clear sign that Joey had no respect for me or my body. But apparently, he didn't think he had done anything wrong. This astounded me. I realized that maybe this was my penance for trying to juggle two boys at once. Let's chalk that one up to an epic fail.

I really didn't know how to process the whole Joey thing. I didn't even have time to think, time to speak. He just went for it. And I let him. I began thinking to myself, *But look at him. I'd been dreaming of being with him since forever. Is that why I didn't tell him no?*

On the positive side of things, I was no longer the inexperienced girl. I did something physical with *Joey Manson*. That had to place me higher on the high school totem pole.

But I had also cheated on Eric, though, hadn't I? I mean, I did go willingly into a room with Joey. I let him coerce me when my mouth said I only wanted to talk. I didn't know what would happen, but I certainly hadn't expected him to grope me. Either way, I knew that I had done something terrible.

My body had felt it too. As soon as Joey left me alone on those steps, I ran to the bathroom to puke, releasing the guilt and shame of that moment. All my life I spent waiting for the boyfriend I didn't have yet, and now I had him. But was I going to lose him? Isn't that what I deserved?

…

"He what?!" Alyssa exclaimed loudly in the cafeteria. Of course everyone around us turned to see what we were talking about.

With a reprimanding look, I whispered, "Well, he took me upstairs…and yeah, that's what happened."

"Wait, I don't understand. Were you guys like making out and then it progressed? He didn't just grab into the candy bag, did he?"

Sometimes Alyssa really had no tact.

"I wouldn't put it *like that*," I told her, raising my eyebrows. "But yes, he just went for it."

"He shouldn't be doing that," Alyssa said. "That's sexual assault, Tori. You should report him."

This was not the judgment I had expected from my best friend.

"You're not really one to talk, Alyssa. You never reported that one guy, remember?"

"Hey, if you didn't want my opinion, then why did you tell me about it?"

"Well," I said, looking at her somber face, "I'm telling you because I thought you'd be able to help me talk it out. I feel sick to my stomach about the whole thing."

Alyssa ran her hand through her shiny red hair. "Okay, I totally get that. And honestly, it's kinda creepy that he got right down to business. He didn't ask for your permission to touch you like that, did he?"

Alyssa's reaction was placing me on the defensive. I agreed with what she was saying, but having her say the words out loud embarrassed me. Joey Manson wasn't a bad guy. He was my high school crush. So many girls would trade places with me in a heartbeat.

"It all just happened so fast, I didn't even have time to react." I told her.

"I'm not trying to be judgmental, Tori. I just know that you're not like that, so it seems to me like Joey just used you."

"You don't know me, Alyssa. I've changed a lot since I met you. Maybe I am like that."

Alyssa frowned. "Well, I'm here for you. And if you want my opinion, I'd take the guy that respects me over the horn dog."

"Well then you must be changing too." I said, picking up my tray and leaving the table.

• • •

Since I was angry with Alyssa, I came home as late as possible that day. I hung out at the library, working on homework and browsing their latest young adult novels. When I opened the door and walked into the living room, both of my parents and Alyssa were on the couch watching *Game of Thrones* together.

"You're home late." My dad said to me, looking up from the TV.

"Yes, it's 8 o'clock. Where have you been?" Mom asked.

"I was at the library," I said, starting to walk into the kitchen for a snack.

"What a surprise." I heard Alyssa say to my parents, all three of them chuckling.

Suddenly I wasn't hungry any more. I went upstairs and fell asleep.

• • •

I woke up the next morning to Alyssa standing beside my bed, the rays of sunlight piercing down at me.

"Time to get up, sleepy-head!" She sing-songed in the most annoying way possible, pulling the sheets off of my body.

"It's Saturday..." I grunted.

"Yes, it is, Tori, and we're all going to the farmer's market today."

Another groan escaped my mouth.

"Well, suit yourself," she said, putting the covers back on top of me. "I'll let your parents know you're not coming."

I pulled the covers over my face and turned away from the sunlight.

When I woke up, I could hear my parents and Alyssa laughing and joking in the kitchen as they put groceries away. I sat staring up at my ceiling, pondering more about the Joey encounter last weekend.

Was Alyssa right? Did Joey sexually assault me? I wondered.

In one moment where I was caught off guard, I became the girl who was okay with being treated like a sexual object. The sick part was, a part of me was proud that someone would even want to touch me like that. And if I didn't stop him, did that mean that I had wanted it? After all, he was my crush. I somehow felt proud and defeated all at the same time. I felt judged by the one person I thought I could talk to about this, so now I was stuck having to go over it again and again in my mind with no resolution.

• • •

The next day at school, I stopped in the cafeteria for a quick bite before heading to Bio. I sat down next to Tammi and smiled, but she turned away.

"Hey, Tammi."

No response.

"Tammi, what's wrong?"

"Please don't talk to me."

"Wait, why?" I asked, completely taken aback by her coldness.

"I don't want to get into it," she said.

"Tammi, I can't fix the problem if I don't know what it is."

She scoffed. "Fix the problem? *You're* going to fix the problem? Tori, you ARE the problem."

Now *I* was angry.

"What do you mean, I'm the problem? I haven't done anything to you."

She looked at me with narrowed eyes.

"You're a lousy friend," she said, and turned away.

• • •

The bell rang for class to begin, and I looked around the room for another place to sit. Joey nodded his head and waved me over to him. I grabbed my backpack and sat down next to him as Mr. Gingrich told us to take out our homework assignment from Friday.

After Bio, Joey and I walked down the hall together towards our lockers. It had always been my dream to walk down the hallway with him at my side. But before we made it to that hallway, he motioned for me to follow him to an empty classroom.

"What's up?" I asked him, curious as to why he brought me into the classroom that no one uses.

"I just wanted to know how you're doing today," he said as he stood behind me, smoothing his hands down my butt.

I immediately got flush and pretended that he wasn't doing what he was clearly doing. My heart rate increased, thoughts racing a mile a minute. I couldn't believe he was doing this again. *Should I say something?* I wanted to…but I couldn't. I just—couldn't do it. He couldn't see my face, but I wasn't smiling. How could I reject my crush? The bell rang, and Joey retracted his hands from me.

"I'll see you later, Tori."

My life was spinning out of control, and I couldn't do anything to stop it. How could I let this happen? I finally had a boyfriend, and I was cheating on him with a guy who didn't even care about me. My friends didn't like me anymore, I was kicked out of band, and I somehow allowed Alyssa to usurp my role in my family.

• • •

I shoved my finger down my throat and let the warm bile reach up, climbing from the deepest part of me. I had to release this pain. I couldn't reject Joey, but I could reject the food in my body.

I couldn't handle everything, and I had to let it go. Tears stained my cheeks, and as I wiped them away, I heard someone enter the bathroom. I quickly flushed the toilet and stepped out of the stall, going straight to the sink. The girl was fixing her hair in the mirror. She looked over at me with worry.

"Are you okay?" She could see the water in my eyes, smeared mascara running down my cheek.

How could I be so sloppy?

"Yeah, I'm okay." I told her. "Boy drama, you know."

"Oh, okay." She said as I rushed out of the bathroom.

It was then that I learned how cathartic purging was. I had known it helped my anxiety, but I didn't realize how much control it gave me. I felt as if I was taking back some power that had been removed from me. I watched the vomit swirl down the toilet bowl, everything I ate being flushed away.

Alyssa had helped me find a magic loophole to keeping my weight in check. It was a bonus that it also made me feel euphoric. I knew that some people took it too far and were diagnosed with bulimia, but I had it under control.

While at my house later that day, Eric opened the door and my face lit up. He wrapped me up in a big hug and set his gym bag on the floor. He was finally back from his basketball trip, and I had missed him more than words could say. It was as though a piece of me was missing this week.

"How was your trip?" I asked him.

"We came in second place." He said, a huge grin on his face. Oh, how I missed his smile.

"Eric!" My dad greeted my 6-foot boyfriend.

"Mr. Rowling!" Eric greeted him back like he was announcing a boxer coming into the ring.

Mom just rolled her eyes and smiled. The boys started talking sports, so I tuned them out.

"What's going on here?" I asked mom. "I thought I wasn't even allowed to see Eric, and now you guys are buds?"

"Your father gave him a call before he left for his trip."

"Come again?" I asked, assuming I had misunderstood her.

"Honey, you left us and completely shut us out. You didn't think we'd do some investigating? We thought Eric was a bad influence on you, but it turns out he's actually a very nice boy."

"Well, I'm glad you can see that. Actually, mom, Alyssa hasn't been the greatest influence on me."

"Oh, I doubt that, Tori. I know she hasn't been perfect, but Alyssa is such a sweet person."

"Well, you don't know the real her," I said. "Which reminds me, why are you guys letting her stay here instead of at her parents' house? They *are* rich, you know."

"Her parents still won't take our calls. They don't seem to care about Alyssa at all, which is revolting to me. We are happy to have her until the school year is over, but after that we will need to hold her parents accountable. Enough about that. How are *you* doing, sweetie?" Mom asked me as she dried a dish with one of her yellow sunflower towels.

"Good, Mom," I said, thankful that she was trying to change the subject. I didn't want to think about Alyssa or her parents right now. I always envied Alyssa's freedom, but now I was seeing that my parents kept me in line because they loved me. I couldn't imagine having parents who didn't care about me at all.

"You look so good, honey." She said while taking a step back to examine me.

"Thanks, Mom."

While I appreciated her compliment, I didn't want her to address my weight loss. Ten pounds was my original goal, but it actually wasn't a lot of weight. I still wasn't as skinny as I wanted to be. Hopefully this was just the beginning.

• • •

"Sorry to interrupt you guys, but we really need to get some homework done," I said, as Dad was mid-sentence in discussing Duke's current stats.

"Yeah, Mr. Alvaro gave us a lot of Algebraic equations to do." Eric added politely, slinging his gym bag over his shoulder.

As we headed to my room, mom yelled, "The pizza will be ready in twenty!"

"Sweet!" Eric yelled back. We sat down on my bed and pulled our algebra books out.

"Hard practice?" I asked him.

"Not too bad, but I burned a lot of calories."

"From just playing basketball?" I asked naively.

Eric laughed hysterically.

"*Just* basketball? Tori, it's a ton of running. A ton."

I thought for a moment.

"And is that the best way to burn calories?"

"It's the fastest way for sure," he answered.

Hmmm, I thought. *Maybe I should add running to my diet.*

...

The week consisted of classes and spending time with Eric after school. Eric had basketball practice at the same time on Mondays, Wednesdays, and Fridays, so after he'd get done, we'd go to either his house or mine to have dinner and hang out.

Usually we just did our homework in one of our rooms with the radio playing softly in the background. If we were in my room, the classical station was always on; In Eric's, it was hip-hop. We'd complain about each other's taste in music, but neither of us ever tried to change the station.

I decided to start running before school every day in order to lose more weight, along with continuing to eat less. I figured I could manage this, and if I had a slip-up and ate too much, I would just throw it up.

I got up an hour before normal and put my leggings and hoodie on, earbuds in my ears playing hip-hop to motivate me, a tip from Eric. I started jogging along our suburban road, slowly passing by the identical rows of developments.

The powder blue houses looked so uniform with their freshly cut lawns and trimmed bushes outside. I took in the scenery as I panted to the beat of the music. This was not enjoyable, and my only salvation was the music in my ears.

I could understand now why Eric used hip-hop to gear him up for a big game. I tried to reach a full circle back to my house, but I was too tired. My legs were beginning to feel like jello and I was getting light-headed. I turned and walked back towards my house.

...

"So, I started running." I told Eric after school the next day.

"Wow, I'm impressed." He said. "How far did you go?"

"So far, only a mile. I need motivation…" I said, playfully tugging on his arm.

"As in, you need *me* to motivate you?"

"Only if you want to," I said all sing-songy.

"Well, you know how good I am at motivating," He said, beginning to massage my shoulders. The tingles started creeping up my lower body.

"You're not *that* good," I teased.

Eric moved his hands lower.

"Oh, I'm not?"

I was beginning to lose my words.

"Um," was all that came out as his lips worked harder and harder against mine.

...

I rushed home after school to get my homework done as soon as possible. When I got into my room, Alyssa was already sprawled out on my bed with a magazine and nail polish.

"So how was your day?" Alyssa prodded.

"Awesome," I said, smiling.

"No details?"

"No details," I answered. "Just a fun and normal day."

"Girl, when you swiping your v-card?"

"Where do you come up with this stuff?" I said, laughing.

"I can't take the credit for that," she answered seriously. "I read it from a book."

"You read?" I asked.

"I read…*Gossip Girl.*"

We both laughed.

"So, what are you doing tonight?" Alyssa asked after composing herself from all of the laughter.

"Hanging out with Eric," --- The two of us said simultaneously.

"Tori, you always hang out with him. You should hang out with us for once."

"Well, what are you guys doing?"

She thought about it for a second.

"Shopping."

"Yeah, I'll pass."

"Fine," she began as I started walking to the bathroom. "But you're missing out."

I just smiled and shut the door.

...

"Late night with Eric?" Alyssa asked me when I got through the front door of our house. She and my parents were watching TV.

"Yep."

"Well, I'm glad you kids had fun." My mom chimed in.

"How was shopping?" I asked Alyssa.

"Oh, it was nice. Kyle bought more stuff than all of us combined."

"Kyle went with you?" I asked, surprised that Kyle went along. He wasn't big on shopping. He was more into videogames at home.

"Yeah, and Tammi too. Then they taught me how to play chess."

"No way. You know how to play chess now?"

"Yeah, and she's not too bad." My dad said with a laugh.

This was so weird. Alyssa was playing chess with Kyle and Tammi and hanging out with my parents? It was like I stepped into an alternate universe or something.

"Well, I'm going to bed." I said, walking up the stairs to my room.

"Goodnight!" The three amigos said to me in unison. Yep, this was freaky.

...

Thankfully, I had Eric to comfort my restless mind.

"I had a great time last night," he told me as we sat on his couch after school.

"Me too," I smiled. "Are you free to hang out this weekend at all?"

"My only plans are gaming with Jamal and going on a run."

"Maybe we should run together sometime," I suggested.

"I like that idea a lot." He said, smiling.

We put a movie on and cuddled for the rest of the evening, and I wondered why I ever even liked Joey. Eric truly cared about me as a person. He wanted me for ME, not for my body. I needed to be officially done with Joey. He wasn't the same boy from my dreams, and now I could finally see that.

THE PATRON SAINT OF LIARS AND FAKES

When I walked into school the next week, I passed by a flyer on the wall that said FINAL CHESS TOURNAMENT OF THE YEAR! TONIGHT, 7 PM.

"You should totally come." I turned around to see Kyle standing behind me. "I mean, I know you don't really play chess anymore, but you could still come to cheer us on."

"I thought you guys hated me."

"Tammi hates who you are right now, and so do I. It sucks that you still can't see the damage you've done to our friendship. But I'll still try to be nice to you, Tori. You know I'm not one to hold grudges. I just don't have time for fake people."

"Wow, okay, well, thanks for your honesty." I told him.

"Was it worth it?" He asked.

"Was what worth it?

"Your popularity." He said.

From where I stood, I wasn't so sure anymore.

•••

I looked at my bountiful feast fit for a queen. An extra-large pepperoni pizza, a package of chocolate chip cookies, a spray can of whipped cream, a bag of potato chips, and a tub of French onion dip. I indulged to my stomach's content, but not to my heart's. I draped myself in a robe of satisfaction and began my journey to the throne room. I uplifted my sacrifice from my body, like a warm lamb ready for the slaughter.

The lamb hit the porcelain and was torn apart. With soap and water, I stood at the sink and cleansed my body from the cleansing of my ritual. But it wasn't enough. Once again, I had submitted myself to the god of gluttony.

It was a ruthless god that couldn't be satisfied. It had no control and no limits. But it was controlling me.

I decided that night that I was done with this...whatever it was that I was doing. "Bulimic" was such a clinical term, and I knew that to other people, that's what I was. But I wasn't. Calling myself bulimic was admitting defeat. On the contrary, I had won. I had control of how my body looked. I was beautiful. Well, at least better than I was before.

•••

I felt bad for missing the chess tournament, but I decided that I probably would have been jealous seeing my friends up there and not being able to participate. Even though I technically quit the team, I still could admit to really loving the game. I was just in a new phase of my life right now.

• • •

"Congrats, Alyssa," a couple of girls said to my red-headed friend the next day.

Joey came along and high-fived her. "You were awesome."

"Congrats for what?" I asked her in confusion.

"She kicked butt last night." Joey answered for her.

"You mean she kicked butt at…the chess tournament?"

I turned to Alyssa. "I didn't even know you knew *how* to play chess."

"Oh, yeah. I think your dad mentioned it to you the other day, but you must've forgotten. Hidden talent, I guess." She smiled.

"In fact," I said with gathered ferocity, "you've always made fun of me for being on the chess team."

"Well, I always thought it was dorky. I didn't want people making fun of *me* for playing."

"So why the sudden change now?"

Joey closed his locker door. "Uh-oh, girl drama. I'm out."

He left, leaving the two of us to our "drama."

"I told them to keep it a secret because I was embarrassed."

"Are you hearing yourself right now?" I began to yell. "Alyssa, I LOVE chess. I'm the last person to make fun of you! We could've been playing together this whole time. And you've made fun of me for it since I met you!"

Despite my yelling, Alyssa was completely calm.

"That's why I was afraid. Because I've made fun of you for it since day one. I knew you'd make fun of me if I turned my opinion around."

For some reason I was more upset with Kyle than with Alyssa. How could he not tell me that Alyssa was on the chess team, taking my place?

"But I wouldn't have, Alyssa. I can't believe you think so little of me."

"Sorry?" She said, acting like she was pleading for my forgiveness.

"I have to go." I said, turning away from her.

I ambushed Kyle in the hallway after lunch.

"Alyssa's on the chess team?"

"Did she finally tell you?" he asked.

"Well, she basically had to after her 'awesome' performance on Saturday."

"Well, I'm glad you know now."

"That's all you have to say?"

He sighed. "What should I say, Tori?"

"You used to tell me everything, but now you can't tell me that she took my place on the team?"

"It wasn't my secret to tell," he answered simply.

"Do you know how it feels to have your best friends hanging out behind your back?" I asked him.

"You're just mad because Alyssa kept a secret from you because *she's* your best friend. Not Tammi. Not me. So let's get that straight. And hanging out with friends behind my back? You've done that to me too many times to count. So yeah, I think I do know how you feel, Tori."

"Kyle, I said I was sorry for all that."

"Yeah, well, so am I. I have to get to class." And with that, he left.

Once again, everything was spinning out of control. I binged on leftover Chinese food that night and threw it all up while the rest of my family watched TV. THIS would be my last time purging.

As I walked back into the living room, I saw Alyssa and Corey holding hands. As soon as they saw me come in, they let go of each other.

Feeling uneasy, I said "Corey, can you come help me in the kitchen?"

"Sure," he said, asking if anybody needed anything while he was out there.

I waited until we got to the far edge of the kitchen to question him.

"Why did I see you and Alyssa holding hands just now?"

His face reddened.

"You are seeing things, Tori."

"No, I'm not," I said, grabbing his arm as he tried to pull away from me.

"I'm done here," he said, trying to wrangle free.

"If you won't be honest with me, I'm going straight to mom and dad."

"Fine," he said with a sigh. "Alyssa and I are dating. But we're keeping it a secret for now."

"Corey, if mom and dad found out, Alyssa wouldn't be able to live here anymore."

"And that's why you're not going to tell them."

It felt like another bomb shell was being dropped on me. All in the name of Alyssa. Why was this happening to me? Now she was dating my little brother? I asked her from day one if she liked him, and she assured me that he was off-limits. Clearly, she had changed her mind. I wasn't going to let her get away with this one. It was another delicate situation, though, because I didn't want my parents to kick her out. As much as I was upset with her, I couldn't do that to her. She had enough problems in her life.

. . .

I needed someone to talk to about Alyssa, so the next day I met up with Tammi and Kyle in the hallway between classes. They stopped me before I could tell them what was going on.

"We don't want to be your friends anymore." Tammi said to me.

"You too, Kyle? I thought you didn't hold grudges." I pleaded. "I'm not holding a grudge, Tori. We just…don't need you anymore. You seem to have other priorities in life. Actually, Alyssa's been a great friend to us after you ditched us." Kyle added. "She's helped us win the chess tournament and comes to band practice all the time."

So that's what she's been doing this whole time? She stole my friends, my family, and my hobbies. She told me that day in the cafeteria that I had lost more than I knew, and she was right.

"So, this is it, then? You're done with me after all of the history we share?"

"Don't get dramatic, Tori." Tammi said, her voice elevated. "We're letting you know that we're done with the wishy-washy gray space friendship we've been having this year. We need to simplify it. We're done."

I could hear the thunder outside.

"What if I refuse?"

"This isn't a breakup, we're not dating." Tammi laughed.

"We're done being treated like dirt, Tori. Don't talk to us anymore, because you lost that right when you chose everyone else over us. And stop playing the victim, because you're not."

Tears flooded my eyes, but I wouldn't let it show. I had to get out of there. Stepping outside, I welcomed the droplets pouring onto me as I walked to my car. The rhythm of the rain beating against the windows of the Volvo was such a soothing feeling.

I sat in my car for a while, letting the melodic sound of the rain lull me into a trance. I used to dream about Joey being my boyfriend, thinking it would never happen. And now he had shown affection towards me. I smiled, but it was hollow.

What was I doing? I had Eric, and he was perfect. I loved him. Joey had been my dream, but I had finally woken up. I was done letting him use me. Then I realized that I was no better than him. I had been using people too. I was using Kyle and Tammi all year. Realizing that I had used Eric hurt worst of all. This had to stop now.

I marched back into school in search of Joey.

"Well, look who it is," Amber said to me with her squad surrounding her.

"Amber, I don't have time for this." I didn't want to be here, stopped in the hallway with Amber Lawrence yelling at me. My face reddened as I saw more and more people stopping to watch this.

"Oh, you're gonna make time for this." She said, Kylie and Gina laughing beside her.

"I heard you've been 'hanging out' with Joey. Is that true, slut?"

The old me would've backed down, but the new me wasn't going to allow anyone to treat me with disrespect.

"Kind of, I guess. But he's not dating you anymore, so you don't really get to have an opinion about it, do you?" I said, anger rising within me. Amber seemed shocked by my confidence.

"Listen, I don't know who you think you are, but let's get one thing straight. You're a whore. You mean nothing to Joey. He finds girls like you every year and uses them. So don't think you're special."

"You're right, Amber. Now, MOVE." I said, pushing past her and her girl squad.

I ran further down the hall, cutting a corner, and found Joey walking into a classroom with a short brunette. I followed them, peering in the window of the empty classroom.

He put his hands on her chest and started undoing her bra from underneath her shirt. Her face looked nervous and uneasy. It was in that moment I knew I could no longer watch in silence, be a passive observer to actions against me. I finally realized why I hadn't told Joey "no" that evening in his bedroom. I was afraid. Afraid of rejection, afraid of his power, afraid of acting impolite. But I didn't owe him anything. I didn't owe ANYONE anything.

Like a tea kettle, my blood was boiling. I was sick of being passive. I'd been passive my whole life. This time I had to act.

"Get your fucking hands off of her!" I bellowed, pushing open the door, and pinning him against the wall. His eyes widened in shock; his body caught off guard by my abrupt burst of power. With all of my might, I slammed my fist into his face.

"What the FUCK!!" He yelled out in pain.

"Get out of here," I told the brunette, who stood frozen in shock. "Don't ever let him touch you like that again."

"You're a crazy bitch, you know that?" Joey said, laughing.

"I'm not sure why you're laughing, because I'm completely serious."

"You jealous? Tori, it's not like we're dating."

"Jealous? I'm not jealous, you idiot! I never wanted you to touch me like that. Ever. You thought just because I liked you that I wanted you to grope me? Wrong!"

"Oh, come on, you liked it."

"No, actually, I didn't. I should've reported you."

He seemed to stiffen when I said this.

"Don't worry, I'm not. I'm here to tell you that I'm done with you. Don't ever talk to me or look at me again. And if you touch me, I will tell someone. My whole life I thought you were perfect. Boy, was I wrong."

I left him standing in that empty classroom, a black eye starting to form on his face. He looked like he could cry.

I put the car in drive and let the road take me home. Away from all the drama, people, and noise in my life. I didn't know why I felt so sad, because I had so much. Thunder and lightning followed me home that night, and I had a feeling they wouldn't be leaving me.

I ran into the house, thankful that no one was around to watch me cry. I let the tears pour down my cheeks, and I fell to the floor in pain.

"Honey, what's wrong?" It was my mom.

"I'm...fine." I told her through sobs.

Then she wrapped her arms around me and let me cry there. It was a peaceful moment where I was able to simply exist. Once I pulled myself together, my mom pulled away.

"What's happened, Tori?"

I told her everything. Eric. Joey. Amber. Chess. Band. Then the purging.

"Oh, honey." She hugged me again, and I began to cry from the release of so many bottled-up feelings.

"Let me show you something," she said, standing up and walking over to the side table in our living room.

She opened the drawer of the cherry-wood table and pulled out a thick hardbound book with a silver pen resting on the cover. Sitting back down onto the floor with me, she opened it up to reveal the contents inside. It was clearly handmade, with its crinkled pages and hand-sewn binding. It was beautiful.

"This is my journal." She told me, smoothing her hand over the words on the page. "My best friend in high school made this for me. She took an old book and made a journal out of it. She collaged photos of us on the cover too," she said, showing me the photos of them as kids wrapped all around the book.

"I've been writing in this thing since she gave it to me," she said, smiling. "It helps me get my feelings out so that I can figure out how I feel. Even if I just write one sentence, it helps. Then I can go back later and reflect on what the moments in my life mean. And now that I've got over 30 years of experiences written down, I'm able to see how I've developed emotionally over the years."

"I didn't even know you had this," I said, smoothing my hand over the painted cover with old pictures of my mom and her friend on it.

"I journal every night just before I go to bed," my mom said, walking back over to the table. She pulled out a different book and brought it to me.

"I want you to have this," she said, handing me the book.

"I met with that friend a few years back, and she showed me how to make the journals. I was making this one for when my current one fills up, but now I know that it was meant for you to have."

Tears stung my eyes again. "Mom, I can't take your journal. You made this."

"Oh, I can just make another one. This one is yours. I could tell you were distancing yourself from your father and me, but I didn't want to force you to talk about it. And I had no idea that any of this was going on. But know that I am always here for you, whether it's for advice or just for listening. I love you unconditionally, sweetie, no matter what. And when you can't talk, just write. It's helped me, and I know it will help you too."

"Thanks, mom." I told her, giving her a hug.

"I'm going to make you an appointment with a therapist as well. Don't worry, Tori, you aren't alone in this."

She made us hot chocolate, and we stayed on that living room floor for another hour, just talking about my choices from the past couple months. I couldn't remember the last time I talked to my mom like this, and I knew that my pride was the reason for it.

"Mom, can I ask you something?"

"Of course."

I drew in a deep breath, summoning all the courage I had in me.

"Why don't you ever come to my band shows and chess competitions? You always show up for Corey, but never for me."

She looked down at the ground and shook her head.

"I'm sorry, sweetie. I think we have been favoring your brother over you. It's not something we meant to do, but you are right. I promise we will support you from now on. You have my word." She said, hugging me.

I'm not sure exactly when it had all changed. I know for certain that it didn't happen overnight, or within a month, for that matter. But that's how it always goes, doesn't it? Factors beyond our control gradually change the shape of who we are without us even realizing it. The original beauty of our innocence starts slowly chipping away as we grow older. Time is our only enemy, taunting our patience like schoolchildren on the playground.

I hugged my new journal to my chest and thought about everything I had told my mom. I was hurt and confused about Alyssa. She had been my best friend this entire school year. It just didn't make sense. I needed to see her.

CAN WE MEET UP?
SURE. WHERE?
MAD HATTER, 4:00?
SOUNDS GOOD.

I drove to the Mad Hatter cafe as soon as I sent my last text. I didn't want to be late. I felt as though arriving first gave me the upper hand. I sat at a round two-person table in the corner of the coffee shop. The patrons around me looked relaxed, chatting with their friends over steaming mugs of cappuccinos and lattes. I was anything *but* relaxed.

I rhythmically tapped my foot against the table leg and bit my nails, trying to decide exactly what I would say to Alyssa when she arrived. I looked out the window and saw her red hair shining brightly in the afternoon sun. She had on a short black trench coat, skinny jeans, and large black sunglasses resting on her head. She saw me as soon as she entered the cafe, and I squeezed my mug tighter as she approached me.

"Hey, how are you?" She asked.

"I'm... a little confused, actually."

"What about?"

"About you." I paused. "You're my best friend, and I feel like I don't know you anymore."

Alyssa laughed. "I'm your best friend?"

"Of course you are."

"Oh Tori, are you really that naïve?"

"What are you talking about?"

"Don't you remember when you called me a slut?"

"Alyssa, that was forever ago! I thought we moved past that!"

"Tori, you're so narrow-minded. You saw me as a dumb little slut who only cared about boys, shopping, and partying. Well, guess what? I AM more than that. I was playing an act since the day you called me that god-awful word. You thought we were BFFs? Girl, I feel sorry for you. You had no idea that YOU were the one with the amazing life."

My jaw dropped.

"Alyssa, are you saying you've been playing me this whole time? You were never really my friend?"

"Sweetie, I have two parents who are never around and let me buy whatever I want to make up for it. I wasn't involved in anything in my last school. No clubs, no awards or anything like that. When I met you, I got to hear about all of these cool activities and about your completely normal home life. I mean, that's all I ever wanted. And you took it all for granted. I honestly wanted to be your friend, Tori. But when you called me a slut, everything changed. You only saw what you wanted to see, that's the beauty of it. So how does it feel now?"

Alyssa's smile was simultaneously bitter and triumphant.

"I feel empty." Tears threatened to fill my eyes.

"Did you know that I was a virgin before that Paul guy raped me?" She asked.

"What?! But that's not what you've been saying this whole year..." I was incredulous.

"Oh, that's just what the popular girls wanted to hear. But no, I'd never actually done it. He robbed me of my first time, that dick. You really don't know me at all, do you, Tori?"

"Why are you dating my brother?" I had to know.

"Corey is amazing. I knew it the first day I met him at his soccer game. I want to be with someone who is kind and a gentleman." She said. "Do you want to know what the worst part is?" Alyssa asked. "The worst part is that I really liked you. But you just had to ruin it. And I had to make you pay."

"So, you made me pay by stealing my life?"

"You made it so easy."

All I had ever wanted was to be pretty and popular, but now all I wanted was my old life back. Alyssa had been lying to me this whole time, a true snake.

"I can't believe you did this to me. You made me purge! You turned me into a monster."

"I'm sorry, Tori. But you deserved it. And I've never been happier."

I sat there dumbfounded. "You are a horrible person! I can't believe you were scheming against me, lying to me this entire time…it's sickening."

"It's not all bad," she said, getting up from the table. "At least you lost some weight."

She winked at me and walked out the door.

How had things gotten so screwed up? Alyssa had been plotting to steal my life since the day I called her a slut. Why hadn't I been able to see what she was doing to me? Alienating me from my family and friends, turning me into this person I didn't want to be anymore.

My life had gotten off track and I wasn't going to let it go without a fight. It was time for me to slay the snake.

I told my parents about Alyssa and Corey dating. They went ballistic, as I expected. This wasn't about getting revenge; this was about keeping my brother safe from an evil person.

"How long has this been going on?" Dad asked with worry on his face.

"Not too long, I think. Maybe a month?"

"He's only 14! We let her into our home, allowed her to sleep in Tori's room, and this is how she repays us?"

"I'm sorry I didn't tell you sooner, Dad. I just didn't want you to kick her out."

"I wish you would've told us sooner as well, but I understand, Tori." Dad said.

"So what are you gonna do?" I asked.

"We're going to pay a visit to her parents."

•••

My next step was to tell Eric the truth. I texted him to meet me at the playground.

"Hey," he waved to me, his adorable grin spread across his face.

"Hey, Eric." I motioned for him to sit on the swings with me.

We both sat down, the creaking of the old swing chains the only sound around us.

"So…what's up?" He asked me.

"Eric, I need to tell you something. It's something I should've told you a long time ago."

His cheeks flushed; concern written all over him. He moved back a little, as if guarding himself against the words I would unleash onto him.

"Ever since that party at Joey's house where he kissed me, he's been trying to get with me. He's pulled me into empty rooms and put his hands all over my body. I get away every time, but he keeps doing it. He sends me inappropriate texts and…and he tried to have sex with me while you were away. Thankfully, I got away in time. But I don't know what would've happened had someone not knocked on the door. I'm so sorry, Eric. I don't know why I didn't tell you sooner."He furrowed his brow and punched the ground beneath his swing.

"Is that what happened when you guys went to get milkshakes? Did he put his hands on you then?"

I nodded.

"I have to go." He said, jumping off the swing.

He started walking home, and I tried to catch up with him.

"Eric, wait!" I called out.

His walk turned into a run, and then he disappeared down the road.

I knew I had to tell Eric the truth, but I was angry at the outcome of the conversation. I couldn't lose him; I was in love with him. I didn't know what to do.

For now, I had to turn my pent-up aggression into something productive.

Thankful that Alyssa wasn't in the house, I started packing up her things into boxes. I wanted every piece of her gone. I shoved her clothes into trash bags, emptying out every drawer of hers. As I placed her books into a filing crate, I came across a small stack of yearbooks. Each one was from a different school.

Alyssa did tell me she had moved around a lot. I sat on the floor and paged through the yearbooks, scanning the classmates' faces for Alyssa's. She was easy to pick out with her red hair and beautiful features. I then read the name beside her photo. It said LAUREN HARNER.

That couldn't be right. I looked again, counting the faces and the names in succession on the page. Confusion swept my brain, and I turned to the next yearbook. Once again, the name next to her photo said LAUREN HARNER. My heart began racing as I pulled out the rest of the 4 yearbooks. They all led me to the same conclusion: Alyssa Perdue was not her real name.

"Can you let me in?" Alyssa pounded on my locked bedroom door.

It felt like my heart had stopped. Looking at her yearbooks spread all over my bedroom floor, I yelled "Give me a minute!"

I quickly closed the yearbooks, stacking them into one of the filled boxes of her things. I took a deep breath and opened the door.

"Packing up my stuff?" Alyssa asked, brushing past me to grab her phone charger.

"All done." I told her, wiping my hands together.

"Well, I'm not sure your parents will be okay with you kicking me out of your room like this." She said, crossing her arms in defiance.

"Lyss, they know about you and Corey. It's over. In fact, they are going to meet with your parents and tell them everything."

Alyssa's face reddened in shock and embarrassment.

"Oh, Corey. I have to find him," she said, stepping towards the door.

I moved my body in front of her path.

"Get out of my way, fat ass." She said to me.

"Or what, Lauren Harner?"

The color drained from her face.

"Excuse me?" She said in a poor attempt at ignorance.

"I know who you are."

She fell to the floor and began to sob.

"What's going on in here?" My dad asked as he and mom entered the room.

"I think you both need to take a seat," I told them, motioning for them to sit on my bed.

"Those phone numbers you gave us for your parents are fake numbers." My mom said to Alyssa.

"That's because I don't have parents." Alyssa said in between sobs.

"Everyone has parents, dear." Mom said to her.

"I don't know who my parents are. I'm a foster kid."

The three of us stared at her in silence as she wiped her eyes with her sleeve.

"My real name is Lauren Harner. I've been in foster care my whole life. All I know is my mom didn't want me."

"But then who are your foster parents?" I asked.

"I ran away from the last set, that's how I ended up moving here on my own."

"But you're rich! Right? Where has all the money been coming from?"

"I think you know, Tori."

Then it all made sense to me. The credit cards with other people's names on them. The GoFundMe accounts on her laptop for various charities.

"I think we'd all like to know where the money has been coming from," my Mom said.

Alyssa gave me a pleading look.

"How haven't your foster parents found you by now?" I asked her, trying to change the subject.

"I'm 18. I've aged out of the system. No one's looking for me now."

It sounded sad the way she said that. I thought of her 18th birthday party and how odd she had acted on such a joyous day. Now I understood.

"This is all too overwhelming," my dad said. "I think we need to call the police about this."

"Please don't," Alyssa begged.

"I'm afraid I don't trust you anymore, young lady. You lied to all of us and took advantage of our kindness."

"Dad, it's already after dinnertime. Why don't we take the night to cool off and then talk to the police in the morning?" I suggested.

He looked at mom.

"I think that's a good idea, sweetie." Mom said, dad nodding along.

Alyssa looked relieved.

"I'll bring your things downstairs and you can sleep on the couch tonight." I told her.

"Thanks." She said.

Mom and dad went downstairs, and we could hear them talking to Corey on the phone.

"I want you to sleep over at Ryan's house tonight, okay? We'll come pick you up tomorrow afternoon. I love you."

"Looks like I won't be seeing Corey again." Alyssa said to me.

"No, you won't be."

"Thanks for not ratting me out. After everything I did to you, I was expecting you to," she said. "By the way, how did you figure out my real name?"

"I looked through your yearbooks."

She looked at the ground and smiled.

"I had a good run, though, didn't I?"

"That's not what I would say at all."

"You don't know what it's like to be in the foster system. I've been pushed around and abused. I've never been able to rely on anyone or anything. This was the first year I finally felt stable. I thought I had found my family."

"Except it wasn't your family. It was mine," I said. "I would've gladly shared my family with you, if you had only asked. But instead you stole it from me."

"I'm really sorry, Tori," Alyssa said.

"I don't need your apology. I just hope you are honest with the cops tomorrow."

"You're high if you think I'm talking to the cops tomorrow," she laughed. "I'll be gone before you guys wake up."

"You do what you need to do, but I really hope you make the right choice tomorrow. You can't run forever."

"Watch me."

That night we placed her boxes in our living room and opened the pullout couch for her to sleep on. I made sure she was all tucked in before turning out the lights and heading up to bed.

The next morning, she was gone, just as she had said.

My parents were in an outrage and called the police to look for her. I honestly felt sorry for Alyssa, and I was relieved that she was finally out of my life. I knew the girls at school would be starving for gossip on what happened to her, but I wouldn't expose her secret.

I didn't feel I had the right to, even though she momentarily took everything from me. Just like Kyle had told me earlier, it wasn't my secret to tell. But I knew she would eventually have to face the consequences of her crimes, even if it took a lifetime.

As much as I didn't want to, I knew I had to see Eric. I had no idea what he would say, but I knew it was going to hurt me.

I took the Volvo to his house and knocked on his door.

"Hi, Tori." His mom said to me, smiling as she welcomed me into their cinnamon and clove-scented home.

"Is Eric here?" I asked.

"Eric, Tori is here!" She called up to him.

"Tell her to go away!" He called back.

"I'll just meet him up there," I said, my face reddening.

I slowly ascended the stairs as if walking towards my execution.

"Hey," I said.

Eric was playing a basketball video game, his eyes glued to the screen.

"What do you want?"

"I want your forgiveness."

Silence.

"I want to say I'm sorry and I love you."

He paused the game and turned to face me.

"You're sorry. Sorry for what, Tori?"

I stared at him in embarrassment.

"I'm sorry I lied to you about Joey," I said, tears now stinging my eyes.

He started to cry.

"I love you, Eric. But I swear Joey had some power over me. I know it's no excuse. I'm a horrible person, and I don't deserve you. I am truly sorry."

"I knew from that day in the cafeteria that he had his eye on you," Eric said, "but I never doubted your integrity for a second. I know you were scared, Tori. But it feels like so much was done behind my back. I don't know what to do with this."

"Does this mean you don't want to be with me anymore?" I asked him.

"I need a break, Tori. We need to take a break."

I walked out of his room, closing the door behind me. It felt like someone dug a hole where my heart was and left it completely empty. I was ashamed and angry at myself for losing someone so honest and good. Even worse, I had tainted his ability to completely trust someone.

I went home and cried for hours, taking down every picture I had of the two of us. I couldn't look at his face, a reminder of everything I had lost.

The weekend ended, and I knew the next stop on my apology tour would be with my band director. After several classes of sitting in the back, trying to be invisible, I got up the nerve to walk into Mr. Grayson's office, ready to beg to be let back in.

As soon as I stepped into the familiar coffee and popcorn-scented room with beige walls, I saw Tammi seated by Mr. Grayson's desk. He looked up at me in surprise.

"Tori, hello! What brings you in today?"

"Umm…" I started, staring at Tammi. "I was hoping to talk to you in private."

"Oh, I see." He turned to Tammi. "Okay, Tammi. I think we're done here anyway. Just have that solo ready for me by Tuesday."

Tammi walked out of his office, not making eye contact with me.

"So," Mr. Grayson said, motioning for me to sit down, "What can I do for you?"

I sat down. "I want to rejoin the band."

He gave me a skeptical look.

"I know I've been a flake, but I'm fully dedicated now. I was stupid to leave, but I'm ready to join again."

"Are you going to take it seriously this time around?" He asked me.

"Yes, I promise I will. I let other things get in the way, but this band means everything to me."

Mr. Grayson smiled. "Of course, Tori. You know you've always been an asset to this band. And we can always use more people."

I sighed with relief. "Okay, thank you, Mr. Grayson! I won't let you down."

As I turned to walk away, he stopped me.

"And Tori?"

"Yes?" I asked.

"It's good to have you back."

...

The next day at school was rough; I literally had no friends anymore. Everyone wanted to know where Alyssa was; I simply told them that she moved out of our house and I didn't know where she moved to. Though sad, I did feel empowered as I walked down the hallways alone.

I felt confident in my own skin, which was a first for me. I didn't need any outside validation from anyone. I passed by Joey and Amber, who were apparently a couple again. They glared at me and I smiled at them. How could I not when the whole school knew that I was the reason for Joey's black eye? After seeing me stand up to him, two girls who were sexually assaulted by Joey came forward to the principal. That alone made my actions worth it.

I sat in my bio class, determined to finish the year strong. We were going over sample questions for our upcoming final.

"Who can tell me the answer to number 11?" The teacher asked.

I raised my hand.

April 8th, 2019

It might sound weird, but I don't regret this year at all. I learned how to stand up for myself and speak up, two things I never thought I'd be able to do. I've always been known as the quiet girl, but why is that a bad thing? I don't have to be loud to be heard. I just have to use my voice when it's important. This year has taught me that I don't ever have to stand by and allow someone to treat me badly. We all have at least one snake in our life. It's up to us to slay it. That's when we are truly empowered.

My mom made this journal, and she hopes that it helps me figure out how I feel about things. I feel anger. I feel loss. But I do feel hopeful.

Kyle and Tammi have forgiven me, after finding out the truth about Alyssa. We are hanging out again, and it feels great. I am so thankful for their friendship. And even though what Alyssa did was wrong and manipulative, I do get why she did what she did to me.

I was the one who had the perfect life and I didn't even see it. Why is it so important to be popular? It's all I ever wanted, but I lost everything that I used to love just so more people would like me.

Eric has forgiven me and we are taking things slow right now. I know that I've hurt him, and I want to repair some of the damage that I've done.

I've rejoined band, and I even have a solo for the concert this spring. I'm determined to be a great player.

I've stopped purging for the most part. Mom checks in with me about it every day. I'm seeing a therapist as well. She's made me realize that I was using binging and purging to deal with my anxiety. But I'm done trying to lose weight. I'm happy with my body, and I just want to be healthy.

Basketball has become therapeutic for me. When I feel the need to throw up, I grab a basketball and head to the court. Eric and I play together after school. When we're on the court, there's no need to talk. We can just simply be. It's a good feeling.

I'm not sure what the future holds, but I am hopeful.

I will graduate soon, and I'm planning on getting a part time job before I decide what I want to do with my life. It's such a big decision that I don't feel ready to make yet.

Corey is happy I'm staying home and not leaving him just yet. It was hard for my parents to make him understand why Alyssa dating him was wrong. He's over her now, though, and he has a girlfriend in his grade. Her name is Caitlyn.

Right now, I'm just trying to stay positive. I know that I need to find healthy ways to deal with my anxiety, and basketball has been one of them. I may not be popular anymore, but I know myself better than I did before, and I'm grateful for that.

I'm excited to write in this journal every day and use it as a healthy outlet for my stress. This is the path I choose. It's about time I learned how to stand on my own.